A

HISTORY

OF

NEW-YORK,

FROM THE

BEGINNING OF THE WORLD

TO THE

END OF THE DUTCH DYNASTY.

CONTAINING,

AMONG MANY SURPRISING AND CURIOUS MATTERS,

THE UNUTTERABLE PONDERINGS OF WALTER THE DOUBTER,
THE DISASTROUS PROJECTS OF WILLIAM THE TESTY,
AND THE CHIVALRIC ACHIEVEMENTS OF PETER
THE HEADSTRONG,

THE THREE DUTCH GOVERNORS OF NEW-AMSTERDAM:

Being the only Authentic History of the Times that ever hath been published.

IN TWO VOLUMES.

A NEW EDITION.

BY DIEDRICH KNICKERBOCKER.

VOL. I.

De waarheid die in duister lag,
Die komt met klaarheid aan den dag.

A
FIREBIRD
PRESS
BOOK

Gretna 2001

Manufactured in the United States of America

Published by Pelican Publishing Company, Inc.

1000 Burmaster Street, Gretna, Louisiana 70053

CONTENTS OF VOL. I.

BOOK I.

CONTAINING DIVERS INGENIOUS THEORIES AND PHILOSOPHIC
SPECULATIONS, CONCERNING THE CREATION AND POPULA-
TION OF THE WORLD, AS CONNECTED WITH THE HISTORY
OF NEW-YORK.

BOOK II.

TREATING OF THE FIRST SETTLEMENT OF THE PROVINCE
OF NIEUW-NEDERLANDTS.

BOOK III.

IN WHICH IS RECORDED THE GOLDEN REIGN OF WOUTER VAN TWILLER.

BOOK IV.

CONTAINING THE CHRONICLES OF THE REIGN OF WILLIAM THE TESTY.

A 2

ACCOUNT

OF

THE AUTHOR.

It was some time, if I recollect right, in the early part of the autumn of 1808, that a stranger applied for lodgings at the Independent Columbian Hotel in Mulberry-street, of which I am landlord. He was a small, brisk-looking old gentleman, dressed in a rusty black coat, a pair of olive velvet breeches, and a small cocked hat. He had a few gray hairs plaited and clubbed behind, and his beard seemed to be of some eight-and-forty hours' growth. The only piece of finery which he bore about him, was a bright pair of square silver shoe-buckles, and all his baggage was contained in a pair of saddle-bags, which he carried under his arm. His whole appearance was something out of the common run; and my wife, who is a very shrewd body, at once set him down for some eminent country schoolmaster.

As the Independent Columbian Hotel is a very small house, I was a little puzzled at first where to put him; but my wife, who seemed taken with his looks, would needs put him in her best chamber, which is genteelly set off with the profiles of the whole family, done in black, by those two great

painters, Jarvis and Wood; and commands a very
pleasant view of the new grounds on the Collect, together with the rear of the Poor-House and Bridewell, and a full front of the Hospital; so that it is
the cheerfulest room in the whole house.

During the whole time that he stayed with us, we
found him a very worthy good sort of an old gentleman, though a little queer in his ways. He would
keep in his room for days together, and if any of the
children cried, or made a noise about his door, he
would bounce out in a great passion, with his hands
full of papers, and say something about "deranging
his ideas;" which made my wife believe sometimes
that he was not altogether *compos.* Indeed, there
was more than one reason to make her think so, for
his room was always covered with scraps of paper
and old mouldy books, laying about at sixes and
sevens, which he would never let any body touch;
for he said he had laid them all away in their proper
places, so that he might know where to find them;
though for that matter, he was half his time worrying
about the house in search of some book or writing
which he had carefully put out of the way. I shall
never forget what a pother he once made, because
my wife cleaned out his room when his back was
turned, and put every thing to rights; for he swore
he would never be able to get his papers in order
again in a twelvemonth. Upon this my wife ventured to ask him what he did with so many books
and papers? and he told her that he was "seeking
for immortality;" which made her think more than

ever, that the poor old gentleman's head was a little cracked.

He was a very inquisitive body, and when not in his room was continually poking about town, hearing all the news, and prying into every thing that was going on: this was particularly the case about election time, when he did nothing but bustle about from poll to poll, attending all ward meetings and committee rooms; though I could never find that he took part with either side of the question. On the contrary, he would come home and rail at both parties with great wrath—and plainly proved one day, to the satisfaction of my wife and three old ladies who were drinking tea with her, that the two parties were like two rogues, each tugging at a skirt of the nation; and that in the end they would tear the very coat off its back, and expose its nakedness. Indeed, he was an oracle among the neighbours, who would collect around him to hear him talk of an afternoon, as he smoked his pipe on the bench before the door; and I really believe he would have brought over the whole neighbourhood to his own side of the question, if they could ever have found out what it was.

He was very much given to argue, or, as he called it, *philosophize*, about the most trifling matter; and to do him justice, I never knew any body that was a match for him, except it was a grave-looking old gentleman who called now and then to see him, and often posed him in an argument. But this is nothing surprising, as I have since found out this stranger is the city librarian; and, of course, must be a man of great learning: and I have my doubts, if he had not some hand in the following history.

As our lodger had been a long time with us, and we had never received any pay, my wife began to be somewhat uneasy, and curious to find out who and what he was. She accordingly made bold to put the question to his friend, the librarian, who replied in his dry way that he was one of the *literati*, which she supposed to mean some new party in politics. I scorn to push a lodger for his pay; so I let day after day pass on without dunning the old gentleman for a farthing: but my wife, who always takes these matters on herself, and is, as I said, a shrewd kind of a woman, at last got out of patience, and hinted, that she thought it high time " some people should have a sight of some people's money." To which the old gentleman replied, in a mighty touchy manner, that she need not make herself uneasy, for that he had a treasure there, (pointing to his saddle-bags,) worth her whole house put together. This was the only answer we could ever get from him ; and as my wife, by some of those odd ways in which women find out every thing, learnt that he was of very great connexions, being related to the Knickerbockers of Scaghtikoke, and cousin-german to the Congress-man of that name, she did not like to treat him uncivilly. What is more, she even offered, merely by way of making things easy, to let him live scot-free, if he would teach the children their letters; and to try her best and get her neighbours to send their children also : but the old gentleman took it in such

dudgeon, and seemed so affronted at being taken for
a schoolmaster, that she never dared speak on the
subject again.

About two months ago, he went out of a morning,
with a bundle in his hand—and has never been heard
of since. All kinds of inquiries were made after
him, but in vain. I wrote to his relations at Scaghtikoke, but they sent for answer, that he had not been
there since the year before last, when he had a great
dispute with the Congress-man about politics, and
left the place in a huff, and they had neither heard
nor seen any thing of him from that time to this. I
must own I felt very much worried about the poor
old gentleman, for I thought something bad must have
happened to him, that he should be missing so long,
and never return to pay his bill. I therefore adver-
tised him in the newspapers, and though my melancholy advertisement was published by several humane
printers, yet I have never been able to learn any
thing satisfactory about him.

My wife now said it was high time to take care
of ourselves, and see if he had left any thing behind
in his room, that would pay us for his board and
lodging. We found nothing, however, but some old
books and musty writings, and his saddle-bags;
which, being opened in the presence of the librarian,
contained only a few articles of worn-out clothes,
and a large bundle of blotted paper. On looking
over this, the librarian told us, he had no doubt it
was the treasure which the old gentleman had spoke
about; as it proved to be a most excellent and faith-

ful HISTORY OF NEW-YORK, which he advised us by
all means to publish: assuring us that it would be so
eagerly bought up by a discerning public, that he had
no doubt it would be enough to pay our arrears ten
times over.   Upon this we got a very learned schoolmaster, who teaches our children, to prepare it for
the press, which he accordingly has done; and has,
moreover, added to it a number of valuable notes of
his own.

   This, therefore, is a true statement of my reasons
for having this work printed, without waiting for the
consent of the author: and I here declare, that if he
ever returns, (though I much fear some unhappy accident has befallen him,) I stand ready to account
with him like a true and honest man.   Which is all
at present,

        From the public's humble Serv't.

                        SETH HANDASIDE.

Independent Columbian Hotel, ⎱
        New-York. ⎰

   THE foregoing account of the author was prefixed
to the first edition of this work.   Shortly after its
publication a letter was received from him, by Mr.
Handaside, dated at a small Dutch village on the
banks of the Hudson, whither he had travelled for
the purpose of inspecting certain ancient records.
As this was one of those few and happy villages, into
which newspapers never find their way, it is not a

matter of surprise, that Mr. Knickerbocker should never have seen the numerous advertisements that were made concerning him ; and that he should learn of the publication of his history by mere accident.

He expressed much concern at its premature appearance, as thereby he was prevented from making several important corrections and alterations; as well as from profiting by many curious hints which he had collected during his travels along the shores of the Tappaan Sea, and his sojourn at Haverstraw and Esopus.

Finding that there was no longer any immediate necessity for his return to New-York, he extended his journey up to the residence of his relations at Scaghtikoke. On his way thither, he stopped for some days at Albany, for which city he is known to have entertained a great partiality. He found it, however, considerably altered, and was much concerned at the inroads and improvements which the Yankees were making, and the consequent decline of the good old Dutch manners. Indeed, he was informed that these intruders were making sad innovations in all parts of the State; where they had given great trouble and vexation to the regular Dutch settlers, by the introduction of turnpike gates, and country school-houses. It is said also, that Mr. Knickerbocker shook his head sorrowfully at noticing the gradual decay of the great Vander Heyden palace ; but was highly indignant at finding that the ancient Dutch church, which stood in the middle of the street, had been pulled down, since his last visit.

The fame of Mr. Knickerbocker's history having reached even to Albany, he received much flattering attention from its worthy burghers, some of whom however, pointed out two or three very great errors he had fallen into, particularly that of suspending a lump of sugar over the Albany tea-tables, which, they assur ed him, had been discontinued for some years past. Several families, moreover, were somewhat piqued that their ancestors had not been mentioned in his work, and showed great jealousy of their neighbours who had been thus distinguished; while the latter, it must be confessed, plumed themselves vastly thereupon; considering these recordings in the light of letters-patent of nobility, establishing their claims to ancestry—which, in this republican country, is a matter of no little solicitude and vain glory.

It is also said, that he enjoyed high favour and countenance from the governor, who once asked him to dinner, and was seen two or three times to shake hands with him, when they met in the street; which certainly was going great lengths, considering that they differed in politics. Indeed, certain of the governor's confidential friends, to whom he could venture to speak his mind freely on such matters have assured us, that he privately entertained a con siderable good-will for our author—nay, he even once went so far as to declare, and that openly too, and at his own table, just after dinner, that " Knickerbocker was " a very well-meaning sort of an old gentleman, and no fool." From all which, many have been led to suppose, that had our author been of different politics, and written for the newspapers, instead of wasting his talents on histories, he might have risen to some post of honour and profit; peradventure, to be a notary public, or even a Justice in the Ten Pound Court.

Beside the honours and civilities already mentioned, he was much caressed by the literati of Albany; particularly by Mr. John Cook, who entertained him very hospitably at his circulating library and reading-room, where they used to drink Spa water, and talk about the ancients. He found Mr. Cook a man after his own heart—of great literary research, and a curious collector of books. At parting, the latter, in testimony of friendship, made him a present of the two oldest works in his collection; which were the earliest edition of the Hiedelburgh Catechism, and Adrian Vander Donck's famous account of the New-Netherlands: by the last óf which, Mr. Knicker-bocker profited greatly in this his second edition.

Having passed some time very agreeably at Albany, our author proceeded to Scaghtikoke;—where, it is but justice to say, he was received with open arms, and treated with wonderful loving-kindness. He was much looked up to by the family, being the first historian of the name; and was considered almost as great a man as his cousin the Congress-man—with whom, by-the-bye, he became perfectly reconciled, and contracted a strong friendship.

In spite, however, of the kindness of his relations, and their great attention to his comforts, the old gentleman soon became restless and discontented.

His history being published, he had no longer any
business to occupy his thoughts, or any scheme to ex-
cite his hopes and anticipations. This, to a busy mind
like his, was a truly deplorable situation; and, had
he not been a man of inflexible morals and regular
habits, there would have been great danger of his
taking to politics, or drinking—both which pernicious
vices we daily see men driven to, by mere spleen and
idleness.

It is true, he sometimes employed himself in pre-
paring a second edition of his history, wherein he
endeavoured to correct and improve many passages
with which he was dissatisfied, and to rectify some
mistakes that had crept into it; for he was particularly anxious that his work should be noted for its authenticity; which, indeed, is the very life and soul of
history.—But the glow of composition had departed
—he had to leave many places untouched, which he
would fain have altered; and even where he did
make alterations, he seemed always in doubt whether
they were for the better or the worse.

After a residence of some time at Scaghtikoke, he
began to feel a strong desire to return to New-York,
which he ever regarded with the warmest affection;
not merely because it was his native city, but because
he really considered it the very best city in the
whole world. On his return, he entered into the full
enjoyment of the advantages of a literary reputation
He was continually importuned to write advertisements, petitions, hand-bills, and productions of similar import; and, although he never meddled with the

public papers, yet had he the credit of writing innumerable essays, and smart things, that appeared on all subjects, and all sides of the question; in all which he was clearly detected "by his style."

He contracted, moreover, a considerable debt at the post-office, in consequence of the numerous letters he received from authors and printers soliciting his subscription; and he was applied to by every charitable society for yearly donations, which he gave very cheerfully, considering these applications as so many compliments. He was once invited to a great corporation dinner; and was even twice summoned to attend as a juryman at the court of quarter sessions. Indeed, so renowned did he become, that he could no longer pry about, as formerly, in all holes and corners of the city, according to the bent of his humour, unnoticed and uninterrupted; but several times when he has been sauntering the streets, on his usual rambles of observation, equipped with his cane and cocked hat, the little boys at play have been known to cry, "there goes Diedrich!"—at which the old gentleman seemed not a little pleased, looking upon these salutations in the light of the praises of posterity.

In a word, if we take into consideration all these various honours and distinctions, together with an exuberant eulogium, passed on him in the Port Folio —(with which, we are told, the old gentleman was so much overpowered, that he was sick for two or three days)—it must be confessed, that few authors have ever lived to receive such illustrious rewards,

or have so completely enjoyed in advance their own
immortality.

After his return from Scaghtikoke, Mr. Knickerbocker took up his residence at a little rural retreat,
which the Stuyvesants had granted him on the family
domain, in gratitude for his honourable mention of
their ancestor. It was pleasantly situated on the
borders of one of the salt marshes beyond Corlear's
Hook: subject, indeed, to be occasionally over-
flowed, and much infested, in the summer time, with
musquitoes; but otherwise very agreeable, producing
abundant crops of salt grass and bull-rushes.

Here, we are sorry to say, the good old gentleman
fell dangerously ill of a fever, occasioned by the
neighbouring marshes. When he found his end approaching, he disposed of his worldly affairs, leaving
the bulk of his fortune to the New-York Historical
Society; his Hiedelburgh Catechism, and Vander
Donck's work, to the city library; and his saddle-
bags to Mr. Handaside. He forgave all his enemies,
—that is to say, all who bore any enmity towards
him; for as to himself, he declared he died in good-
will with all the world. And, after dictating several
kind messages to his relations at Scaghtikoke, as well
as to certain of our most substantial Dutch citizens,
he expired in the arms of his friend the librarian.

His remains were interred, according to his own
request, in St. Mark's churchyard, close by the bones
of his favourite hero, Peter Stuyvesant: and it is
rumoured, that the Historical Society have it in mind
to erect a wooden monument to his memory in the
Bowling-Green.

TO THE PUBLIC.

―――――

" To rescue from oblivion the memory of former
incidents, and to render a just tribute of renown to
the many great and wonderful transactions of our
Dutch progenitors, Diedrich Knickerbocker, native
of the city of New-York, produces this historical
essay."* Like the great Father of History, whose
words I have just quoted, I treat of times long past,
over which the twilight of uncertainty had already
thrown its shadows, and the night of forgetfulness
was about to descend for ever. With great solicitude had I long beheld the early history of this venerable and ancient city gradually slipping from our
grasp, trembling on the lips of narrative old age, and
day by day dropping piecemeal into the tomb. In a
little while, thought I, and those reverend Dutch
burghers, who serve as the tottering monuments of
good old times, will be gathered to their fathers ;
their children, engrossed by the empty pleasures or
insignificant transactions of the present age, will
neglect to treasure up the recollections of the past,
and posterity will search in vain for memorials of
the days of the Patriarchs. The origin of our city
will be buried in eternal oblivion, and even the

―――――――――――――――――――――――

* Beloe's Herodotus.

names and achievements of Wouter Van Twiller, William Kieft, and Peter Stuyvesant, be enveloped in doubt and fiction, like those of Romulus and Remus, of Charlemagne, King Arthur, Rinaldo, and Godfrey of Bologne.

Determined, therefore, to avert if possible this threatened misfortune, I industriously set myself to work, to gather together all the fragments of our infant history which still existed, and like my revered prototype, Herodotus, where no written records could be found, I have endeavoured to continue the chain of history by well-authenticated traditions.

In this arduous undertaking, which has been the whole business of a long and solitary life, it is incredible the number of learned authors I have consulted ; and all but to little purpose. Strange as it may seem, though such multitudes of excellent works have been written about this country, there are none extant which give any full and satisfactory account of the early history of New-York, or of its three first Dutch governors. I have, however, gained much valuable and curious matter, from an elaborate manuscript written in exceeding pure and classic Low Dutch, excepting a few errors in orthography, which was found in the archives of the Stuyvesant family. Many legends, letters, and other documents, have I likewise gleaned, in my researches among the family chests and lumber garrets of our respectable Dutch citizens ; and I have gathered a host of well-authenticated traditions from divers excellent old ladies of my acquaintance, who requested that their names might not be mentioned. Nor must I neglect to acknowledge how greatly I have been assisted by that admirable and praiseworthy institution, the NEW-YORK HISTORICAL SOCIETY, to which I here publicly return my sincere acknowledgments.

In the conduct of this inestimable work, I have adopted no individual model; but, on the contrary, have simply contented myself with combining and concentrating the excellencies of the most approved ancient historians. Like Zenophon, I have maintained the utmost impartiality, and the strictest adherence to truth, throughout my history. I have enriched it, after the manner of Sallust, with various characters of ancient worthies, drawn at full length and faithfully coloured. I have seasoned it with profound political speculations like Thucydides, sweetened it with the graces of sentiment like Tacitus, and infused into the whole the dignity, the grandeur, and magnificence of Livy.

I am aware that I shall incur the censure of numerous very learned and judicious critics, for indulging too frequently in the bold excursive manner of my favourite Herodotus. And to be candid, I have found it impossible always to resist the allurements of those pleasing episodes, which, like flowery banks and fragrant bowers, beset the dusty road of the historian, and entice him to turn aside, and refresh himself from his wayfaring. But I trust it will be found that I have always resumed my staff, and addressed myself to my weary journey with renovated spirits, so that both my readers and myself have been benefited by the relaxation.

Indeed, though it has been my constant wish and uniform endeavour to rival Polybius himself, in observing the requisite unity of History, yet the loose and unconnected manner in which many of the facts herein recorded have come to hand, rendered such an attempt extremely difficult. This difficulty was likewise increased, by one of the grand objects contemplated in my work, which was to trace the rise of sundry customs and institutions in this best of cities, and to compare them, when in the germ of infancy, with what they are in the present old age of knowledge and improvement.

But the chief merit on which I value myself, and found my hopes for future regard, is that faithful veracity with which I have compiled this invaluable little work; carefully winnowing away the chaff of hypothesis, and discarding the tares of fable, which are too apt to spring up and choke the seeds of truth and wholesome knowledge.—Had I been anxious to captivate the superficial throng, who skim like swallows over the surface of literature; or had I been anxious to commend my writings to the pampered palates of literary epicures, I might have availed myself of the obscurity that overshadows the infant years of our city, to introduce a thousand pleasing fictions. But I have scrupulously discarded many a pithy tale and marvellous adventure, whereby the drowsy ear of summer indolence might be enthralled; jealously maintaining that fidelity, gravity, and dignity, which should ever distinguish the historian. "For a writer of this class," observes an elegant critic, "must sustain the character of a wise man, writing for the instruction of posterity; one who has studied to inform himself well, who has pondered his subject with care, and addresses himself to our judgment, rather than to our imagination."

Thrice happy, therefore, is this our renowned city, in having incidents worthy of swelling the theme of history; and doubly thrice happy is it in having such a historian as myself to relate them. For after all, gentle reader, cities *of themselves*, and, in fact, empires *of themselves*, are nothing without a historian. It is the patient narrator who records their prosperity as they rise—who blazons forth the splendour of their noontide meridian—who props their feeble memorials as they totter to decay—who gathers together their scattered fragments as they rot—and who piously, at length, collects their ashes into the mausoleum of his work, and rears a monument that will transmit their renown to all succeeding ages.

What has been the fate of many fair cities of antiquity, whose nameless ruins encumber the plains of Europe and Asia, and awaken the fruitless inquiry of the traveller? They have sunk into dust and silence—they have perished from remembrance, for want of a historian! The philanthropist may weep over their desolation—the poet may wander among their mouldering arches and broken columns, and indulge the visionary flights of his fancy—but alas! alas! the modern historian, whose pen, like my own, is doomed to confine itself to dull matter of fact, seeks in vain among their oblivious remains for some memorial that may tell the instructive tale of their glory and their ruin.

"Wars, conflagrations, deluges," says Aristotle, "destroy nations, and with them all their monuments, their discoveries, and their vanities.—The torch of science has more than once been extinguished and rekindled—a few individuals, who have escaped by accident, reunite the thread of generations."

The same sad misfortune which has happened to so many ancient cities, will happen again, and from the same sad cause, to nine-tenths of those which now flourish on the face of the globe. With most of them, the time for recording their early history is gone by; their origin, their foundation, together with the eventful period of their youth, are for ever buried in the rubbish of years; and the same would have been the case with this fair portion of the earth, if I had not snatched it from obscurity in the very nick of time, at the moment that those matters herein recorded were about entering into the wide-spread insatiable maw of oblivion—if I had not dragged them out, as it were, by the very locks, just as the monster's adamantine fangs were closing upon them for ever! And here have I, as before observed, carefully collected, collated, and arranged them, scrip and scrap, "*punt en punt, gat en gat,*" and commenced, in this little work, a history to serve as a foundation, on which other historians may hereafter raise a noble superstructure, swelling in process of time, until *Knickerbocker's New-York* may be equally voluminous with *Gibbon's Rome*, or *Hume and Smollet's England!*

And now indulge me for a moment, while I lay down my pen, skip to some little eminence at the distance of two or three hundred years ahead; and, casting back a birds's-eye glance over the waste of years that is to roll between, discover myself—little I!—at this moment the progenitor, prototype, and precursor of them all, posted at the head of this host of literary worthies, with my book under my arm, and New-York on my back, pressing forward, like a gallant commander, to honour and immortality.

Such are the vain-glorious imaginings that will now and then enter into the brain of the author—that irradiate, as with celestial light, his solitary chamber, cheering his weary spirits, and animating him to persevere in his labours. And I have freely given utterance to these rhapsodies, whenever they have occurred; not, I trust, from an unusual spirit of egotism, but merely that the reader may for once have an idea, how an author thinks and feels while he is writing—a kind of knowledge very rare and curious, and much to be desired.

Vol. I.   C

BOOK I.

CONTAINING DIVERS INGENIOUS THEORIES AND PHILOSOPHIC SPECULATIONS, CONCERNING THE CREATION AND POPULA-TION OF THE WORLD, AS CONNECTED WITH THE HISTORY OF NEW-YORK.

CHAPTER I.

Description of the World.

ACCORDING to the best authorities, the world in which we dwell is a huge, opaque, reflecting, inanimate mass, floating in the vast ethereal ocean of infinite space. It has the form of an orange, being an oblate spheroid, curiously flattened at opposite parts, for the insertion of two imaginary poles, which are supposed to penetrate and unite at the centre; thus forming an axis on which the mighty orange turns with a regular diurnal revolution.

The transitions of light and darkness, whence proceed the alternations of day and night, are produced by this diurnal revolution successively presenting the different parts of the earth to the rays of the sun The latter is, according to the best, that is to say, the latest accounts, a luminous or fiery body, of a prodigious magnitude, from which this world is driven by a centrifugal or repelling power, and to which it is drawn by a centripetal or attractive force, otherwise called the attraction of gravitation; the combination, or rather the counteraction, of these two opposing impulses producing a circular and annual revolution. Hence result the different seasons of the year, viz. spring, summer, autumn, and winter.

This I believe to be the most approved modern theory on the subject—though there be many philosophers who have entertained very different opinions; some, too, of them entitled to much deference from their great antiquity and illustrious characters. Thus it was advanced by some of the ancient sages, that the earth was an extended plain, supported by vast pillars; and by others, that it rested on the head of a snake, or the back of a huge tortoise—but as they did not provide a resting-place for either the pillars or the tortoise, the whole theory fell to the ground, for want of proper foundation.

The Brahmins assert, that the heavens rest upon the earth, and the sun and moon swim therein like fishes in the water, moving from east to west by day, and gliding along the edge of the horizon to their original stations during the night;* while, according to the Pauranicas of India, it is a vast plain, encircled by seven oceans of milk, nectar, and other delicious liquids; that it is studded with seven mountains, and ornamented in the centre by a mountainous rock of burnished gold; and that a great dragon occasionally swallows up the moon, which accounts for the phenomena of lunar eclipses.†

---

* Faria y Souza. Mick. Lus. note b. 7.
† Sir W. Jones, Diss. Antiq. Ind. Zod.

Beside these, and many other equally sage opinions, we have the profound conjectures of ABOUL-HASSAN-ALY, son of Al Khan, son of Aly, son of Abderrahman, son of Abdallah, son of Masoud-el-Had-heli, who is commonly called MASOUDI, and surnamed Cothbeddin, but who takes the humble title of Laheb-ar-rasoul, which means the companion of the ambassador of God. He has written a universal history, entitled " Mouroudge-ed-dharab, or the Golden Meadows, and the Mines of Precious Stones."* In this valuable work he has related the history of the world, from the creation down to the moment of writing; which was under the Caliphate of Mothi Billah, in the month Dgioumadi-el-aoual of the 336th year of the Hegira or flight of the Prophet. He informs us that the earth is a huge bird, Mecca and Medina constituting the head, Persia and India the right wing, the land of Gog the left wing, and Africa the tail. He informs us, moreover, that an earth has existed before the present, (which he considers as a mere chicken of 7000 years) that it has undergone divers deluges, and that, according to the opinion of some well-informed Brahmins of his acquaintance, it will be renovated every seventy-thousandth hazarouam; each hazarouam consisting of 12,000 years.

These are a few of the many contradictory opinions of philosophers concerning the earth, and we find that the learned have had equal perplexity as to the

---

* Mss. Bibliot, Roi. Fr.

C 2

nature of the sun. Some of the ancient philosophers have affirmed that it is a vast wheel of brilliant fire;[*] others, that it is merely a mirror or sphere of transparent crystal;[†] and a third class, at the head of whom stands Anaxagoras, maintained that it was nothing but a huge ignited mass of iron or stone—indeed, he declared the heavens to be merely a vault of stone—and that the stars were stones whirled upward from the earth, and set on fire by the velocity of its revolutions.[‡] But I give little attention to the doctrines of this philosopher, the people of Athens having fully refuted them, by banishing him from their city; a concise mode of answering unwelcome doctrines, much resorted to in former days. Another sect of philosophers do declare, that certain fiery particles exhale constantly from the earth, which concentrating in a single point of the firmament by day, constitute the sun, but being scattered and rambling about in the dark at night, collect in various points, and form stars. These are regularly burnt out and extinguished, not unlike to the lamps in our streets, and require a fresh supply of exhalations for the next occasion.[§]

It is even recorded, that at certain remote and obscure periods, in consequence of a great scarcity

---

[*] Plutarch de Placitis Philosoph. lib. iii. cap. 20.

[†] Achill. Tat. Isag. cap. 19. Ap. Petav. t. iii. p. 81. Stob. Eclog. Phys. lib. i. p. 56. Plut. de Plac. Phi.

[‡] Diogenes Laertius in Anaxag. l. ii. sec. 8. Plat. Apol. t. i. p. 26. Plut. de Plac. Philo. Xenoph. Mem. l. iv. p. 815.

[§] Aristot. Meteor. l. ii. c. 2. Idem. Probl. sec. 15. Stob. Ecl. Phys. l. i. p. 55. Bruck. Hist. Phil. t. i. p. 1154, &c.

of fuel, the sun has been completely burnt out, and
sometimes not rekindled for a month at a time ;—a
most melancholy circumstance, the very idea of
which gave vast concern to Heraclitus, that worthy
weeping philosopher of antiquity. In addition to
these various speculations, it was the opinion of
Herschel, that the sun is a magnificent, habitable
abode; the light it furnishes arising from certain
empyreal, luminous or phosphoric clouds, swimming
in its transparent atmosphere.*

But we will not enter farther at present into the
nature of the sun, that being an inquiry not immediately necessary to the developement of this history ;
neither will we embroil ourselves in any more of the
endless disputes of philosophers touching the form
of this globe, but content ourselves with the theory
advanced in the beginning of this chapter, and will
proceed to illustrate, by experiment, the complexity
of motion therein ascribed to this our rotatory
planet.

Professor Von Poddingcoft (or Puddinghead, as
the name may be rendered into English,) was long
celebrated in the university of Leyden, for profound
gravity of deportment, and a talent of going to sleep
in the midst of examinations, to the infinite relief of
his hopeful students, who thereby worked their way
through college with great ease and little study. In
the course of one of his lectures, the learned pro-

---

* Philos. Trans. 1795 p. 72. Idem. 1801. p. 265. Nich
Philos. Journ. i. p. 13

fessor, seizing a bucket of water, swung it round his head at arm's-length. The impulse with which he threw the vessel from him, being a centrifugal force, the retention of his arm operating as a centripetal power, and the bucket, which was a substitute for the earth, describing a circular orbit round about the globular head and ruby visage of Professor Von Poddingcoft, which formed no bad representation of the sun. All of these particulars were duly explained to the class of gaping students around him. He apprized them, moreover, that the same principle of gravitation, which retained the water in the bucket, restrains the ocean from flying from the earth in its rapid revolutions; and he farther informed them, that should the motion of the earth be suddenly checked, it would incontinently fall into the sun, through the centripetal force of gravitation; a most ruinous event to this planet, and one which would also obscure, though it most probably would not extinguish, the solar luminary. An unlucky stripling, one of those vagrant geniuses who seem sent into the world merely to annoy worthy men of the puddinghead order, desirous of ascertaining the correctness of the experiment, suddenly arrested the arm of the professor, just at the moment that the bucket was in its zenith, which immediately descended with astonishing precision upon the head of the philosopher. A hollow sound, and a red-hot hiss, attended the contact; but the theory was in the amplest manner illustrated, for the unfortunate bucket perished in the conflict; but the blazing countenance of Professor Von Poddingcoft emerged from amidst the waters, glowing fiercer than ever with unutterable indignation, whereby the students were marvellously edified, and departed considerably wiser than before.

It is a mortifying circumstance, which greatly perplexes many a philosopher, that Nature often refuses to second his efforts; so that after having invented one of the most ingenious and natural theories imaginable, she will have the perverseness to act directly in the teeth of it. This is a manifest and unmerited grievance, since it throws the censure of the vulgar and unlearned entirely upon the philosopher; whereas the fault is to be ascribed to dame Nature, who, with the proverbial fickleness of her sex, is continually indulging in coquetries and caprices; and who seems to take pleasure in violating all philosophic rules, and jilting the most learned and indefatigable of her adorers. Thus it happened with respect to the foregoing explanation of the motion of our planet; it appears that the centrifugal force has long since ceased to operate, while its antagonist remains in undiminished potency: the world, therefore, ought in strict propriety to tumble into the sun; philosophers were convinced that it would do so, and awaited in anxious impatience the fulfilment of their prognostics. But the untoward planet pertinaciously continued her course, notwith standing that she had reason, philosophy, and a whole university of learned professors, opposed to her conduct. The philosophers took this in very ill part, and it is thought they would never have pardoned the slight which they conceived put upon them by the world, had not a good-natured professor kindly officiated as a mediator between the parties, and effected a reconciliation.

Finding the world would not accommodate itself to the theory, he wisely accommodated the theory to the world: he informed his brother philosophers, that the circular motion of the earth round the sun was no sooner engendered by the conflicting impulses above described, than it became a regular revolution, independent of the causes which gave it origin. His learned brethren readily joined in the opinion, heartily glad of any explanation that would decently extricate them from their embarrassment— and ever since that era the world has been left to take her own course, and to revolve around the sun in such orbit as she thinks proper.

CHAPTER II.

Cosmogony, or Creation of the World; with a multitude of excellent theories, by which the creation of a world is shown to be no such difficult matter as common folk would imagine.

HAVING thus briefly introduced my reader to the world, and given him some idea of its form and situation, he will naturally be curious to know from whence it came, and how it was created. And, indeed, the clearing up of these points is absolutely essential to my history, inasmuch as if this world had not been formed, it is more than probable, that this renowned island on which is situated the city of New-York, would never have had an existence. The regular course of my history, therefore, requires that I should proceed to notice the cosmogony, or formation of this our globe.

And now I give my readers fair warning, that I am about to plunge, for a chapter or two, into as complete a labyrinth as ever historian was perplexed withal: therefore, I advise them to take fast hold of my skirts, and keep close at my heels, venturing neither to the right hand nor to the left, lest they get bemired in a slough of unintelligible learning, or have their brains knocked out by some of those hard Greek names which will be flying about in all directions. But should any of them be too indolent or chicken-hearted to acccompany me in this perilous undertaking, they had better take a short cut round, and wait for me at the beginning of some smoother chapter.

Of the creation of the world, we have a thousand contradictory accounts; and though a very satisfactory one is furnished us by divine revelation, yet every philosopher feels himself in honour bound to furnish us with a better. As an impartial historian, I consider it my duty to notice their several theories, by which mankind have been so exceedingly edified and instructed.

Thus it was the opinion of certain ancient sages, that the earth and the whole system of the universe was the deity himself;* a doctrine most strenuously maintained by Zenophanes and the whole tribe of Eleatics, as also by Strabo and the sect of peripatetic philosophers. Pythagoras likewise inculcated the famous numerical system of the monad, dyad, and triad, and by means of his sacred quaternary elucidated the formation of the world, the arcana of nature, and the principles both of music and morals.† Other sages adhered to the mathematical system of squares and triangles; the cube, the pyramid, and the sphere; the tetrahedron, the octahedron, the icosahedron, and the dodecahedron.‡ While others advocated the great elementary theory, which refers the construc-

---

* Aristot. ap. Cic. lib. i. cap. 3.

† Aristot. Metaph. lib. i. c. 5. Idem. de Cœlo, l. iii. c. 1 Rousseau mem. sur Musique ancien. p. 39. Plutarch de Plac Philos. lib. i. cap. 3.

‡ Tim. Locr. ap. Plato. t. iii. p. 90.

tion of our globe, and all that it contains, to the combination of four material elements—air, earth, fire, and water; with the assistance of a fifth, an immaterial and vivifying principle.

Nor must I omit to mention the great atomic system, taught by old Moschus, before the siege of Troy; revived by Democritus, of laughing memory; im proved by Epicurus, that king of good fellows, and modernized by the fanciful Descartes.

But I decline inquiring, whether the atoms, of which the earth is said to be composed, are eternal or recent; whether they are animate or inanimate; whether, agreeably to the opinion of the atheists, they were fortuitously aggregated, or, as the theists maintain, were arranged by a supreme intelligence.* Whether, in fact, the earth be an insensate clod, or whether it be animated by a soul;† which opinion was strenuously maintained by a host of philosophers, at the head of whom stands the great Plato, that temperate sage, who threw the cold water of philosophy on the form of sexual intercourse, and inculcated the doctrine of Platonic love—an exquisitely refined intercourse, but much better adapted to the ideal inhabitants of his imaginary island of Atlantis than to the sturdy race, composed of rebellious flesh

---

* Aristot. Nat. Auscult. l. ii. cap. 6. Aristoph. Metaph. lib. i. cap. 3. Cic. de Nat. Deor. lib. i. cap. 10. Justin. Mart. orat. ad gent. p. 20.

† Mosheim in Cudw. lib. i. cap. 4. Tim. de anim. mund. ap. Plat. lib. iii. Mem. de l'Acad. des Belles Lettr. t. xxxii. p. 19. et al.

and blood, which populates the little matter-of-fact island we inhabit.

Beside these systems, we have, moreover, the poetical theogony of old Hesiod, who generated the whole universe in the regular mode of procreation; and the plausible opinion of others, that the earth was hatched from the great egg of night, which floated in chaos, and was cracked by the horns of the celestial bull. To illustrate this last doctrine, Burnet, in his theory of the earth,* has favoured us with an accurate drawing and description, both of the form and texture of this mundane egg; which is found to bear a marvellous resemblance to that of a goose. Such of my readers as take a proper interest in the origin of this our planet, will be pleased to learn, that the most profound sages of antiquity, among the Egyptians, Chaldeans, Persians, Greeks and Latins, have alternately assisted at the hatching of this strange bird, and that their cacklings have been caught, and continued in different tones and inflections, from philosopher to philosopher, unto the present day.

But while briefly noticing long-celebrated systems of ancient sages, let me not pass over with neglec those of other philosophers; which, though less uni versal and renowned, have equal claims to attention, and equal chance for correctness. Thus it is recorded by the Brahmins, in the pages of their inspired Shastah, that the angel Bistnoo, transforming himself

---

* Book i. ch. 5.

into a great boar, plunged into the watery abyss, and brought up the earth on his tusks. Then issued from him a mighty tortoise, and a mighty snake; and Bistnoo placed the snake erect upon the back of the tortoise, and he placed the earth upon the head of the snake.*

The negro philosophers of Congo affirm that the world was made by the hands of angels, excepting their own country, which the Supreme Being constructed himself, that it might be supremely excellent. And he took great pains with the inhabitants, and made them very black, and beautiful; and when he had finished the first man, he was well pleased with him, and smoothed him over the face; and hence his nose, and the nose of all his descendants, became flat.

The Mohawk philosophers tell us, that a pregnant woman fell down from heaven, and that a tortoise took her upon its back, because every place was covered with water; and that the woman, sitting upon the tortoise, paddled with her hands in the water, and raked up the earth, whence it finally happened that the earth became higher than the water.†

But I forbear to quote a number more of these ancient and outlandish philosophers, whose deplorable ignorance, in despite of all their erudition, compelled them to write in languages which but few of my readers can understand; and I shall proceed

* Holwell. Gent. Philosophy.
† Johannes Megapolensis, Jun. Account of Maquaas or Mohawk Indians. 1644.

briefly to notice a few more intelligible and fashionable theories of their modern successors.

And, first, I shall mention the great Buffon, who
conjectures that this globe was originally a globe of
liquid fire, scintillated from the body of the sun, by
the percussion of a comet, as a spark is generated by
the collision of flint and steel. That at first it was
surrounded by gross vapours, which, cooling and
condensing in process of time, constituted, according
to their densities, earth, water, and air; which gradually arranged themselves, according to their respective gravities, round the burning or vitrified mass
that formed their centre.

Hutton, on the contrary, supposes that the waters
at first were universally paramount; and he terrifies
himself with the idea that the earth must be even-
tually washed away by the force of rain, rivers, and
mountain torrents, until it is confounded with the
ocean, or, in other words, absolutely dissolves into
itself.—Sublime idea! far surpassing that of the ten-
der-hearted damsel of antiquity, who wept herself
into a fountain; or the good dame of Narbonne in
France, who, for a volubility of tongue unusual in
her sex, was doomed to peel five hundred thousand
and thirty-nine ropes of onions, and actually run out
at her eyes before half the hideous task was accomplished.

Whiston, the same ingenious philosopher who
rivalled Ditton in his researches after the longitude,
(for which the mischief-loving Swift discharged on
their heads a most savoury stanza,) has distinguished

himself by a very admirable theory respecting the earth. He conjectures that it was originally a *chaotic comet*, which being selected for the abode of man, was removed from its eccentric orbit, and whirled round the sun in its present regular motion; by which change of direction, order succeeded to confusion in the arrangement of its component parts. The philosopher adds, that the deluge was produced by an uncourteous salute from the watery tail of another comet; doubtless through sheer envy of its improved condition: thus furnishing a melancholy proof that jealousy may prevail, even among the heavenly bodies, and discord interrupt that celestial harmony of the spheres, so melodiously sung by the poets.

But I pass over a variety of excellent theories, among which are those of Burnet, and Woodward, and Whitehurst; regretting extremely that my time will not suffer me to give them the notice they deserve—and shall conclude with that of the renowned Dr. Darwin. This learned Theban, who is as much distinguished for rhyme as reason, and for good-natured credulity as serious research, and who has recommended himself wonderfully to the good graces of the ladies, by letting them into all the gallantries, amours, intrigues, and other topics of scandal of the court of Flora, has fallen upon a theory worthy of his combustible imagination. According to his opinion, the huge mass of chaos took a sudden occasion to explode, like a barrel of gunpowder, and in that act exploded the sun—which in its flight, by a

D 2

similar convulsion, exploded the earth—which in like guise exploded the moon—and thus by a concatenation of explosions, the whole solar system was produced, and set most systematically in motion!*

By the great variety of theories here alluded to, every one of which, if thoroughly examined, will be found surprisingly consistent in all its parts; my unlearned readers will perhaps be led to conclude, that the creation of a world is not so difficult a task as they at first imagined. I have shown at least a score of ingenious methods in which a world could be constructed; and I have no doubt that had any of the philosophers above quoted the use of a good manageable comet, and the philosophical warehouse *chaos* at his command, he would engage to manufacture a planet as good, or, if you would take his word for it, better than this we inhabit.

And here I cannot help noticing the kindness of Providence, in creating comets for the great relief of bewildered philosophers. By their assistance, more sudden evolutions and transitions are effected in the system of nature, than are wrought in a pantomimic exhibition, by the wonder-working sword of Harlequin. Should one of our modern sages, in his theoretical flights among the stars, ever find himself lost in the clouds, and in danger of tumbling into the abyss of nonsense and absurdity, he has but to seize a comet by the beard, mount astride of its tail, and away he gallops in triumph, like an enchanter on his

---

* Darw. Bot. Garden. Part. I. Cant. i. l. 105.

hippogriff, or a Connecticut witch on her broom-stick, " to sweep the cobwebs out of the sky."

There is an old and vulgar saying about a " beggar on horseback," which I would not for the world have applied to these reverend philosophers: but I must confess, that some of them, when they are mounted on one of those fiery steeds, are as wild in their curvetings as was Phæton of yore, when he aspired to manage the chariot of Phœbus. One drives his comet at full speed against the sun, and knocks the world out of him with the mighty concussion; another, more moderate, makes his comet a mere beast of burden, carrying the sun a regular supply of food and fagots—a third, of more combustible dispo-sition, threatens to throw his comet, like a bombshell, into the world, and blow it up like a powder-maga-zine; while a fourth, with no great delicacy to this planet and its inhabitants, insinuates that some day or other, his comet—my modest pen blushes while I write it—shall absolutely turn tail upon our world, and deluge it with water!—Surely, as I have already observed, comets were intended by Providence for the benefit of philosophers, to assist them in manu-facturing theories.

And now, having adduced several of the most prominent theories that occur to my recollection, I leave my judicious readers at full liberty to choose among them. They are all serious speculations of learned men—all differ essentially from each other —and all have the same title to belief. It has ever been the task of one race of philosophers to demolish

the works of their predecessors, and elevate more
splendid fantasies in their stead, which in their turn
are demolished and replaced by the air-castles of a
succeeding generation. Thus it would seem that
knowledge and genius, of which we make such great
parade, consist but in detecting the errors and absurdities of those who have gone before, and devising
new errors and absurdities, to be detected by those
who are to come after us. Theories are the mighty
soap-bubbles with which the grown-up children of
science amuse themselves—while the honest vulgar
stand gazing in stupid admiration, and dignify these
learned vagaries with the name of wisdom!—Surely
Socrates was right in his opinion, that philosophers
are but a soberer sort of madmen, busying themselves
in things totally incomprehensible, or which, if they
could be comprehended, would be found not worth
the trouble of discovery.

For my own part, until the learned have come to
an agreement among themselves, I shall content myself with the account handed down to us by Moses;
in which I do but follow the example of our ingenious neighbours of Connecticut; who at their first
settlement proclaimed, that the colony should be
governed by the laws of God—until they had time
to make better.

One thing, however, appears certain—from the
unanimous authority of the before-quoted philosophers, supported by the evidence of our own senses,
(which, though very apt to deceive us, may be cau-
tiously admitted as additional testimony,) it appears,

I say, and I make the assertion deliberately, without fear of contradiction, that this globe really *was created*, and that it is composed of *land and water*. It farther appears that it is curiously divided and parcelled out into continents and islands, among which I boldly declare the renowned ISLAND OF NEW-YORK will be found by any one who seeks for it in its proper place.

CHAPTER III.

*How that famous navigator, Noah, was shamefully
nicknamed; and how he committed an unpardonable oversight in not having four sons. With the
great trouble of philosophers caused thereby, and
the discovery of America.*

NOAH, who is the first sea-faring man we read of,
begat three sons, Shem, Ham, and Japhet. Authors,
it is true, are not wanting, who affirm that the patriarch had a number of other children. Thus Berosus
makes him father of the gigantic Titans. Methodius
gives him a son called Jonithus, or Jonicus, and
others have mentioned a son, named Thuiscon, from
whom descended the Teutons or Teutonic, or in
other words, the Dutch nation.

I regret exceedingly that the nature of my plan
will not permit me to gratify the laudable curiosity
of my readers, by investigating minutely the history
of the great Noah. Indeed, such an undertaking
would be attended with more trouble than many
people would imagine; for the good old patriarch
seems to have been a great traveller in his day, and
to have passed under a different name in every country that he visited. The Chaldeans, for instance, give
us his history, merely altering his name into Xisuthrus
—a trivial alteration, which, to a historian skilled in
etymologies, will appear wholly unimportant. It ap-

pears likewise, that he had exchanged his tarpawling and quadrant among the Chaldeans, for the gorgeous insignia of royalty, and appears as a monarch in their annals. The Egyptians celebrate him under the name of Osiris; the Indians, as Menu; the Greek and Roman writers confound him with Ogyges, and the Theban with Deucalion and Saturn. But the Chinese, who deservedly rank among the most extensive and authentic historians, inasmuch as they have known the world much longer than any one else, declare that Noah was no other than Fohi; and what gives this assertion some air of credibility is, that it is a fact, admitted by the most enlightened literati, that Noah travelled into China, at the time of the building of the tower of Babel, (probably to improve himself in the study of languages,) and the learned Dr. Shuckford gives us the additional information, that the ark rested on a mountain on the frontiers of China.

From this mass of rational conjectures and sage hypotheses, many satisfactory deductions might be drawn; but I shall content myself with the simple fact stated in the Bible, viz. that Noah begat three sons, Shem, Ham, and Japhet. It is astonishing on what remote and obscure contingencies the great affairs of this world depend, and how events the most distant, and to the common observer unconnected, are inevitably consequent the one to the other. It remains for the philosopher to discover these mysterious affinities, and it is the proudest triumph of his skill, to detect and drag forth some latent chain

of causation, which at first sight appears a paradox
to the inexperienced observer. Thus many of my
readers will doubtless wonder what connexion the
family of Noah can possibly have with this history—
and many will stare when informed, that the whole
history of this quarter of the world has taken its character and course from the simple circumstance of
the patriarch's having but three sons—but to explain:

Noah, we are told by sundry very credible historians, becoming sole surviving heir and proprietor of
the earth, in fee simple, after the deluge, like a good
father, portioned out his estate among his children.
To Shem he gave Asia; to Ham, Africa; and to Japhet, Europe. Now it is a thousand times to be lamented that he had but three sons, for had there
been a fourth, he would doubtless have inherited
America; which, of course, would have been dragged forth from its obscurity on the occasion; and
thus many a hard-working historian and philosopher would have been spared a prodigious mass of
weary conjecture respecting the first discovery and
population of this country. Noah, however, having
provided for his three sons, looked in all probability
upon our country as mere wild unsettled land, and
said nothing about it; and to this unpardonable
taciturnity of the patriarch may we ascribe the misfortune, that America did not come into the world
as early as the other quarters of the globe.

It is true, some writers have vindicated him from
this misconduct towards posterity, and asserted that

he really did discover America. Thus it was the opinion of Mark Lescarbot, a French writer, possessed of that ponderosity of thought, and profoundness of reflection, so peculiar to his nation, that the immediate descendants of Noah peopled this quarter of the globe, and that the old patriarch himself, who still retained a passion for the sea-faring life, superintended the transmigration. The pious and enlightened father, Charlevoix, a French Jesuit, remarkable for his aversion to the marvellous, common to all great travellers, is conclusively of the same opinion; nay, he goes still farther, and decides upon the manner in which the discovery was effected, which was by sea, and under the immediate direction of the great Noah. " I have already observed," exclaims the good father, in a tone of becoming indignation, " that it is an arbitrary supposition that the grand-children of Noah were not able to penetrate into the new world, or that they never thought of it. In effect, I can see no reason that can justify such a notion. Who can seriously believe, that Noah and his immediate descendants knew less than we do, and that the builder and pilot of the greatest ship that ever was, a ship which was formed to traverse an unbounded ocean, and had so many shoals and quicksands to guard against, should be ignorant of, or should not have communicated to his descendants, the art of sailing on the ocean?" Therefore, they did sail on the ocean—therefore, they sailed to America—therefore, America was discovered by Noah!

Now all this exquisite chain of reasoning, which is so strikingly characteristic of the good father, being addressed to the faith, rather than the understanding, is flatly opposed by Hans de Laert, who declares it a real and most ridiculous paradox, to suppose that Noah ever entertained the thought of discovering America ; and as Hans is a Dutch writer, I am inclined to believe he must have been much better acquainted with the worthy crew of the ark than his competitors, and of course possessed of more accurate sources of information. It is astonishing how intimate historians do daily become with the patriarchs and other great men of antiquity. As intimacy improves with time, and as the learned are particularly inquisitive and familiar in their acquaintance with the ancients, I should not be surprised if some future writers should gravely give us a picture of men and manners as they existed before the flood, far more copious and accurate than the Bible ; and that, in the course of another century, the log-book of the good Noah should be as current among historians, as the voyages of Captain Cook, or the renowned history of Robinson Crusoe.

I shall not occupy my time by discussing the huge mass of additional suppositions, conjectures and probabilities, respecting the first discovery of this country, with which unhappy historians overload themselves, in their endeavours to satisfy the doubts of an incredulous world. It is painful to see these laborious wights panting, and toiling, and sweating under an enormous burden, at the very outset of their works, which, on being opened, turns out to be nothing but a mighty bundle of straw. As, however, by unwearied assiduity, they seem to have established the fact, to the satisfaction of all the world, that this country *has been discovered*, I shall avail myself of their useful labours to be extremely brief upon this point.

I shall not, therefore, stop to inquire, whether America was first discovered by a wandering vessel of that celebrated Phœnician fleet, which, according to Herodotus, circumnavigated Africa; or by that Carthaginian expedition, which Pliny, the naturalist, informs us, discovered the Canary Islands; or whether it was settled by a temporary colony from Tyre, as hinted by Aristotle and Seneca. I shall neither inquire whether it was first discovered by the Chinese, as Vossius with great shrewdness advances; nor by the Norwegians in 1002, under Biorn; nor by Behem, the German navigator, as Mr. Otto has endeavoured to prove to the scavans of the learned city of Philadelphia.

Nor shall I investigate the more modern claims of the Welsh, founded on the voyage of prince Madoc in the eleventh century, who having never returned, it has since been wisely concluded that he must have gone to America, and that for a plain reason—if he did not go there, where else could he have gone?— a question which most Socratically shuts out all farther dispute.

Laying aside, therefore, all the conjectures above mentioned, with a multitude of others, equally satisfactory, I shall take for granted the vulgar opinion, that America was discovered on the 12th of October, 1492, by Christovallo Colon, a Gcnoese, who has been clumsily nicknamed Columbus, but for what reason I cannot discern. Of the voyages and adventures of this Colon, I shall say nothing, seeing that they are already sufficiently known. Nor shall I undertake to prove that this country should have been called Colonia, after his name, that being notoriously self-evident.

Having thus happily got my readers on this side of the Atlantic, I picture them to myself, all impatience to enter upon the enjoyment of the land of promise, and in full expectation that I will immediately deliver it into their possession. But if I do, may I ever forfeit the reputation of a regular-bred historian! No—no—most curious and thrice learned readers, (for thrice learned ye are, if ye have read all that has gone before, and nine times learned shall ye be, if ye read that which comes after,) we have yet a world of work before us. Think you the first discoverers of this fair quarter of the globe had nothing to do but go on shore and find a country ready laid out and cultivated like a garden, wherein they might revel at their ease? No such thing—they had forests to cut down, underwood to grub up, marshes to drain, and savages to exterminate.

In like manner, I have sundry doubts to clear away, questions to resolve, and paradoxes to explain, before I permit you to range at random; but these difficulties once overcome, we shall be erabled to jog on right merrily through the rest of our history. Thus my work shall, in a manner, echo the nature of the subject, in the same manner as the sound of poetry has been found by certain shrewd critics to echo the sense—this being an improvement in history, which I claim the merit of having invented.

CHAPTER IV.

Showing the great difficulty Philosophers have had in peopling America—and how the Aborigines came to be begotten by accident—to the great relief and satisfaction of the Author.

THE next inquiry at which we arrive in the regular course of our history, is to ascertain, if possible, how this country was originally peopled—a point fruitful of incredible embarrassment; for unless we prove that the aborigines did absolutely come from somewhere, it will be immediately asserted in this age of scepticism that they did not come at all; and if they did not come at all, then was this country never populated—a conclusion perfectly agreeable to the rules of logic, but wholly irreconcileable to every feeling of humanity, inasmuch as it must syllogistically prove fatal to the innumerable aborigines of this populous region.

To avert so dire a sophism, and to rescue from logical annihilation so many millions of fellow-creatures, how many wings of geese have been plundered! what oceans of ink have been benevolently drained! and how many capacious heads of learned historians have been addled, and for ever confounded! I pause with reverential awe, when I contemplate the ponderous tomes, in different languages, with which they have endeavoured to solve this question, so important to the happiness of society, but so involved in clouds of impenetrable obscurity. Historian after historian has engaged in the endless circle of hypothetical argument, and after leading us a weary chase through octavos, quartos, and folios, has let us out at the end of his work just as wise as we were at the beginning. It was doubtless some philosophical wild-goose chase of the kind that made the old poet Macrobius rail in such a passion at curiosity, which he anathematizes most heartily, as " an irksome agonizing care, a superstitious industry about unprofitable things, an itching humour to see what is not to be seen, and to be doing what signifies nothing when it is done." But to proceed :

Of the claims of the children of Noah to the original population of this country, I shall say nothing, as they have already been touched upon in my last chapter. The claimants next in celebrity, are the descendants of Abraham. Thus Christoval Colon (vulgarly called Columbus)' when he first discovered the gold mines of Hispaniola, immediately concluded, with a shrewdness that would have done honour to a philosopher, that he had found the ancient Ophir, from whence Solomon procured the gold for embellishing the temple at Jerusalem ; nay, Colon even imagined that he saw the remains of furnaces of veritable Hebraic construction, employed in refining the precious ore.

So golden a conjecture, tinctured with such fascinating extravagance, was too tempting not to be immediately snapped at by the gudgeons of learning ;

and accordingly, there were divers profound writers, ready to swear to its correctness, and to bring in their usual load of authorities, and wise surmises, wherewithal to prop it up. Vetablus and Robertus Stephens declared nothing could be more clear— Arius Montanus, without the least hesitation, assert that Mexico was the true Ophir, and the Jews the early settlers of the country. While Possevin, Becan, and several other sagacious writers, lug in a *supposed* prophecy of the fourth book of Esdras, which being inserted in the mighty hypothesis, like the key-stone of an arch, gives it, in their opinion, perpetual durability.

Scarce, however, have they completed their goodly superstructure, than in trudges a phalanx of opposite authors, with Hans de Laet, the great Dutchman, at their head, and at one blow tumbles the whole fabric about their ears. Hans, in fact, contradicts outright all the Israelitish claims to the first settlement of this country, attributing all those equivocal symptoms, and traces of Christianity and Judaism, which have been said to be found in divers provinces of the new world, to the *Devil*, who has always affected to counterfeit the worship of the true Deity. " A remark," says the knowing old Padre d'Acosta, " made by all good authors who have spoken of the religion of nations newly discovered, and founded besides on the authority of the *fathers of the church*."

Some writers again, among whom it is with great regret I am compelled to mention Lopez de Gomara, and Juan de Leri, insinuate that the Canaanites, being driven from the land of promise by the Jews, were seized with such a panic that they fled without looking behind them, until, stopping to take breath, they found themselves safe in America. As they brought neither their national language, manners, nor features with them, it is supposed they left them behind in the hurry of their flight—I cannot give my faith to this opinion.

I pass over the supposition of the learned Grotius, who being both an ambassador and a Dutchman to boot, is entitled to great respect; that North America was peopled by a strolling company of Norwegians, and that Peru was founded by a colony from China —Manco or Mango Capac, the first Incas, being himself a Chinese. Nor shall I more than barely mention, that father Kircher ascribes the settlement of America to the Egyptians, Rudbeck to the Scandinavians, Charron to the Gauls, Juffredus Petri to a skaiting party from Friesland, Milius to the Celtæ, Marinocus the Sicilian to the Romans, Le Compte to the Phœnicians, Postel to the Moors, Martyn d'Angleria to the Abyssinians, together with the sage surmise of De Laet, that England, Ireland, and the Orcades, may contend for that honour.

Nor will I bestow any more attention or credit to the idea that America is the fairy region of Zipangri, described by that dreaming traveller, Marco Polo, the Venetian; or that it comprises the visionary island of Atlantis, described by Plato. Neither will I stop to investigate the heathenish assertion of Paracelsus, that each hemisphere of the globe was originally furnished with an Adam and Eve—or the more flattering opinion of Dr. Romayne, supported by many nameless authorities, that Adam was of the Indian race—or the startling conjecture of Buffon, Helvetius, and Darwin, so highly honourable to mankind, that the whole human species is accidentally descended from a remarkable family of monkeys!

This last conjecture, I must own, came upon me very suddenly and very ungraciously. I have often beheld the clown in a pantomime, while gazing in stupid wonder at the extravagant gambols of a harlequin, all at once electrified by a sudden stroke of the wooden sword across his shoulders. Little did I think at such times, that it would ever fall to my lot to be treated with equal discourtesy; and that while I was quietly beholding these grave philosophers, emulating the eccentric transformations of the hero of pantomime, they would on a sudden turn upon me and my readers, and with one hypothetical flourish metamorphose us into beasts! I determined from that moment not to burn my fingers with any more of their theories, but content myself with detailing the different methods by which they transported the descendants of these ancient and respectable mon keys to this great field of theoretical warfare.

This was done either by migrations by land or transmigrations by water. Thus, Padre Joseph D'Acosta enumerates three passages by land—first by the north of Europe, secondly by the north of Asia, and thirdly by regions southward of the straits of Magellan. The learned Grotius marches his Nor-

wegians by a pleasant route across frozen rivers and
arms of the sea, through Iceland, Greenland, Estoti-
land and Naremberga : and various writers, among
whom are Angleria, De Hornn, and Buffon, anxious
for the accommodation of these travellers, have fastened the two continents together by a strong chain
of deductions—by which means they could pass over
dry-shod. But should even this fail, Pinkerton, that
industrious old gentleman, who compiles books, and
manufactures geographies, has constructed a natural
bridge of ice, from continent to continent, at the distance of four or five miles from Behring's straits—for
which he is entitled to the grateful thanks of all the
wandering aborigines who ever did or ever will pass
over it.

It is an evil much to be lamented, that none of the
worthy writers above quoted could ever commence
his work, without immediately declaring hostilities
against every writer who had treated of the same
subject. In this particular, authors may be compared to a certain sagacious bird, which in building
its nest, is sure to pull to pieces the nests of all the
birds in its neighbourhood. This unhappy propensity
tends grievously to impede the progress of sound
knowledge. Theories are at best but brittle productions, and when once committed to the stream, they
should take care that like the notable pots which
were fellow-voyagers, they do not crack each other.

My chief surprise is, that among the many writers
I have noticed, no one has attempted to prove that
this country was peopled from the moon—or that

the first inhabitants floated hither on islands of ice, as white bears cruize about the northern oceans— or that they were conveyed hither by balloons, as modern aeronauts pass from Dover to Calais—or by witchcraft, as Simon Magus posted among the stars —or after the manner of the renowned Scythian Abaris, who, like the New-England witches on full-blooded broomsticks, made most unheard-of journeys on the back of a golden arrow, given him by the Hyperborean Apollo.

But there is still one mode left by which this country could have been peopled, which I have reserved for the last, because I consider it worth all the rest: it is—*by accident!* Speaking of the islands of Solomon, New-Guinea, and New-Holland, the profound father Charlevoix observes, " in fine, all these countries are peopled, and *it is possible* some have been so *by accident.* Now if it could have happened in that manner, why might it not have been at the *same time*, and by the *same means*, with *the other* part of the globe ?" This ingenious mode of deducing certain conclusions from possible premises, is an improvement in syllogistic skill, and proves the good father superior even to Archimedes, for he can turn the world without any thing to rest his lever upon. It is only surpassed by the dexterity with which the sturdy old Jesuit, in another place, cuts the gordian knot—" Nothing," says he, " is more easy. The inhabitants of both hemispheres are certainly the descendants of the same father. The common father of mankind received an express order from Heaven to people the world, and *accordingly it has been peopled.* To bring this about, it was necessary to overcome all difficulties in the way, *and they have also been overcome!*" Pious logician! How does he put all the herd of laborious theorists to the blush, by explaining, in five words, what it has cost them volumes to prove they knew nothing about.

From all the authorities here quoted, and a variety of others which I have consulted, but which are omitted through fear of fatiguing the unlearned reader—I can only draw the following conclusions, which luckily, however, are sufficient for my purpose —First, that this part of the world has actually *been peopled*, (Q. E. D.) to support which we have living proofs in the numerous tribes of Indians that inhabit it. Secondly, that it has been peopled in five hundred different ways, as proved by a cloud of authors, who, from the positiveness of their assertions, seem to have been eye-witnesses to the fact—Thirdly, that the people of this country had a *variety of fathers*, which, as it may not be thought much to their credit by the common run of readers, the less we say on the subject the better. The question, therefore, I trust, is for ever at rest.

CHAPTER V.

*In which the Author puts a mighty question to the rout -
by the assistance of the Man in the Moon—which
not only delivers thousands of people from great
embarrassment, but likewise concludes this intro-
ductory book.*

THE writer of a history may, in some respects, be
likened unto an adventurous knight, who having undertaken a perilous enterprise, by way of establishing
his fame, feels bound in honour and chivalry, to turn
back for no difficulty nor hardship, and never to
shrink or quail, whatever enemy he may encounter.
Under this impression, I resolutely draw my pen, and
fall to, with might and main, at those doughty questions and subtle paradoxes, which, like fiery dragons
and bloody giants, beset the entrance to my history,
and would fain repulse me from the very threshold.
And at this moment a gigantic question has started
up, which I must needs take by the beard and utterly
subdue, before I can advance another step in my
historic undertaking; but I trust this will be the last
adversary I shall have to contend with, and tha
in the next book I shall be enabled to conduct my
readers in triumph into the body of my work.

The question which has thus suddenly arisen, is,
what right had the first discoverers of America to
land and take possession of a country, without first
gaining the consent of its inhabitants, or yielding them

an adequate compensation for their territory ?—a
question which has withstood many fierce assaults,
and has given much distress of mind to multitudes
of kind-hearted folk. And indeed, until it be totally
vanquished, and put to rest, the worthy people of
America can by no means enjoy the soil they inhabit,
with clear right and title, and quiet, unsullied con-
sciences.

The first source of right, by which property is ac
quired in a country, is DISCOVERY. For as all mankind have an equal right to any thing, which has
never before been appropriated, so any nation that
discovers an uninhabited country, and takes possession thereof, is considered as enjoying full property,
and absolute, unquestionable empire therein.*

This proposition being admitted, it follows clearly,
that the Europeans who first visited America, were
the real discoverers of the same ; nothing being
necessary to the establishment of this fact, but simply
to prove that it was totally uninhabited by man.
This would at first appear to be a point of some
difficulty, for it is well known, that this quarter of
the world abounded with certain animals, that walked erect on two feet, had something of the human
countenance, uttered certain unintelligible sounds,
very much like language, in short, had a marvellous
resemblance to human beings. But the zealous and
enlightened fathers, who accompanied the discoverers, for the purpose of promoting the kingdom of

* Grotius Puffendorf, b. v. c. 4. Vattel, b. i. c. 18 &c.

heaven, by establishing fat monasteries and bishoprics
on earth, soon cleared up this point, greatly to the
satisfaction of his holiness the Pope, and of all Christian voyagers and discoverers.

They plainly proved, and as there were no Indian
writers arose on the other side, the fact was considered as fully admitted and established, that the
two-legged race of animals before mentioned were
mere cannibals, detestable monsters, and many of
them giants—which last description of vagrants have,
since the time of Gog, Magog, and Goliath, been
considered as outlaws, and have received no quarter
in either history, chivalry, or song. Indeed, even
the philosophic Bacon declared the Americans to be
people proscribed by the laws of nature, inasmuch as
they had a barbarous custom of sacrificing men, and
feeding upon man's flesh.

Nor are these all the proofs of their utter bar-
barism: among many other writers of discernment,
Ulloa tells us, " their imbecility is so visible, that one
can hardly form an idea of them different from what
one has of the brutes. Nothing disturbs the tranquillity of their souls, equally insensible to disasters
and to prosperity. Though half naked, they are as
contented as a monarch in his most splendid array.
Fear makes no impression on them, and respect as
little." All this is furthermore supported by the authority of M. Bouguer: "It is not easy," says he,
" to describe the degree of their indifference for
wealth and all its advantages. One does not well
know what motives to propose to them, when one

would persuade them to any service. It is vain to
offer them money; they answer that they are not
hungry." And Vanegas confirms the whole, assuring
us that " ambition they have none, and are more
desirous of being thought strong than valiant. The objects of ambition with us—honour, fame, reputation,
riches, posts, and distinctions, are unknown among
them. So that this powerful spring of action, the
cause of so much *seeming* good and *real* evil in the
world, has no power over them. In a word, these
unhappy mortals may be compared to children, in
whom the developement of reason is not completed."

Now all these peculiarities, although in the unenlightened states of Greece they would have entitled
their possessors to immortal honour, as having reduced to practice those rigid and abstemious maxims,
the mere talking about which acquired certain old
Greeks the reputation of sages and philosophers ;—
yet, were they clearly proved in the present instance
to betoken a most abject and brutified nature, totally
beneath the human character. But the benevolent
fathers, who had undertaken to turn these unhappy
savages into dumb beasts, by dint of argument, advanced still stronger proofs ; for as certain divines of
the sixteenth century, and among the rest, Lullus,
affirm—the Americans go naked, and have no beards!
—" They have nothing," says Lullus, " of the reasonable animal, except the mask."—And even that
mask was allowed to avail them but little, for it was
soon found that they were of a hideous copper complexion—and being of a copper complexion, it was

all the same as if they were negroes—and negroes
are black, " and black," said the pious fathers, devoutly crossing themselves, " is the colour of the
Devil!" Therefore, so far from being able to own
property, they had no right even to personal freedom
—for liberty is too radiant a deity to inhabit such
gloomy temples. All which circumstance plainly
convinced the righteous followers of Cortes and
Pizarro, that these miscreants had no title to the soil
that they infested—that they were a perverse, illite-
rate, dumb, beardless, black-seed—mere wild beasts
of the forests, and like them should either be subdued
or exterminated.

From the foregoing arguments, therefore, and a
variety of others equally conclusive, which I forbear
to enumerate, it is clearly evident that this fair
quarter of the globe when first visited by Europeans,
was a howling wilderness, inhabited by nothing but
wild beasts; and that the transatlantic visiters acquired an incontrovertible property therein, by the
right of discovery.

This right being fully established, we now come
to the next, which is the right acquired by *cultivation.*
" The cultivation of the soil," we are told, " is an
obligation imposed by nature on mankind. The
whole world is appointed for the nourishment of its
inhabitants : but it would be incapable of doing it,
was it uncultivated. Every nation is then obliged
by the law of nature to cultivate the ground that has
fallen to its share. Those people, like the ancient
Germans and modern Tartars, who, having fertile

countries, disdain to cultivate the earth, and choose
to live by rapine, are wanting to themselves, and *deserve to be exterminated as savage and pernicious
beasts.**

Now it is notorious, that the savages knew nothing
of agriculture, when first discovered by the Europeans, but lived a most vagabond, disorderly, un-
righteous life,—rambling from place to place, and
prodigally rioting upon the spontaneous luxuries of
nature, without tasking her generosity to yield them
any thing more; whereas it has been most unquestionably shown, that Heaven intended the earth
should be ploughed and sown, and manured, and
laid out into cities, and towns, and farms, and coun-
try-seats, and pleasure grounds, and public gardens,
all which the Indians knew nothing about—therefore,
they did not improve the talents Providence had
bestowed on them—therefore, they were careless
stewards—therefore, they had no right to the soil—
therefore, they deserved to be exterminated.

It is true, the savages might plead that they drew
all the benefits from the land which their simple
wants required—they found plenty of game to hunt,
which, together with the roots and uncultivated fruits
of the earth, furnished a sufficient variety for their
frugal repasts ;—and that as Heaven merely designed
the earth to form the abode, and satisfy the wants of
man ; so long as those purposes were answered, the
will of Heaven was accomplished.—But this only

* Vattel, b. i. ch. 17.

proves how undeserving they were of the blessings around them—they were so much the more savages, for not having more wants ; for knowledge is in some degree an increase of desires, and it is this superiority both in the number and magnitude of his desires, that distinguishes the man from the beast. Therefore, the Indians, in not having more wants, were very unreasonable animals ; and it was but just that they should make way for the Europeans, who had a thousand wants to their one, and, therefore, would turn the earth to more acccount, and by cultivating it, more truly fulfil the will of Heaven. Besides—Grotius and Lauterbach, and Puffendorff, and Titus, and many wise men beside, who have considered the matter properly, have determined, that the property of a country cannot be acquired by hunting, cutting wood, or drawing water in it—nothing but precise demarcation of limits, and the intention of cultivation, can establish the possession. Now, as the savages (probably from never having read the authors above quoted) had never complied with any of these necessary forms, it plainly followed that they had no right to the soil, but that it was completely at the disposal of the first comers, who had more knowledge, more wants, and more elegant, that is to say, artificial desires than themselves.

In entering upon a newly-discovered, uncultivated country, therefore, the new comers were but taking possession of what, according to the aforesaid doctrine, was their own property—therefore, in opposing them, the savages were invading their just rights, in-

fringing the immutable laws of Nature, and counter-
acting the will of Heaven—therefore, they were
guilty of impiety, burglary, and trespass on the case,
—therefore, they were hardened offenders against
God and man—therefore, they ought to be exterminated.

But a more irresistible right than either that I
have mentioned, and one which which will be the
most readily admitted by my reader, provided he be
blessed with bowels of charity and philanthropy, is
the right acquired by civilization. All the world
knows the lamentable state in which these poor
savages were found—not only deficient in the comforts of life, but what is still worse, most piteously
and unfortunately blind to the miseries of their situation. But no sooner did the benevolent inhabitants
of Europe behold their sad condition, than they immediately went to work to meliorate and improve it.
They introduced among them rum, gin, brandy, and
the other comforts of life—and it is astonishing to
read how soon the poor savages learned to estimate
these blessings—they likewise made known to them
a thousand remedies, by which the most inveterate
diseases are alleviated and healed; and that they
might comprehend the benefits and enjoy the comforts of these medicines, they previously introduced
among them the diseases which they were calculated
to cure. By these, and a variety of other methods
was the condition of these poor savages wonderfully
improved; they acquired a thousand wants, of which
they had before been ignorant; and as he has most

sources of happiness who has most wants to be grat-
ified, they were doubtlessly rendered a much happier
race of beings.

But the most important branch of civilization, and
which has most strenuously been extolled by the
zealous and pious fathers of the Romish Church, is
the introduction of the Christian faith. It was truly a
sight that might well inspire horror, to behold these
savages stumbling among the dark mountains of pa-
ganism, and guilty of the most horrible ignorance of
religion. It is true, they neither stole nor defrauded;
they were sober, frugal, continent, and faithful to their
word ; but though they acted right habitually, it was
all in vain, unless they acted so from precept. The
new comers, therefore, used every method to induce
them to embrace and practise the true religion—except indeed that of setting them the example.

But notwithstanding all these complicated labours
for their good, such was the unparalleled obstinacy
of these stubborn wretches, that they ungratefully refused to acknowledge the strangers as their benefactors, and persisted in disbelieving the doctrines they
endeavoured to inculcate ; most insolently alleging,
that from their conduct, the advocates of Christianity
did not seem to believe in it themselves. Was not
this too much for human patience?—would not one
suppose that the ·benign visitants from Europe, pro-
voked at their incredulity, and discouraged by their
stiff-necked obstinacy, would for ever have abandoned their shores, and consigned them to their original
ignorance and misery?—But no—so zealous were

they to effect the temporal comfort and eternal salvation of these pagan infidels, that they even proceeded from the milder means of persuasion, to the more painful and troublesome one of persecution, let loose among them whole troops of fiery monks and furious bloodhounds—purified them by fire and sword, by stake and fagot; in consequence of which indefatigable measures, the cause of Christian love and charity was so rapidly advanced, that in a very few years not one-fifth of the number of unbelievers existed in South America that were found there at the time of its discovery.

What stronger right need the European settlers advance to the country, than this? Have not whole nations of uninformed savages been made acquainted with a thousand imperious wants and indispensable comforts, of which they were before wholly ignorant? —Have they not been literally hunted and smoked out of the dens and lurking-places of ignorance and infidelity, and absolutely scourged into the right path? Have not the temporal things, the vain baubles and filthy lucre of this world, which were too apt to engage their worldly and selfish thoughts, been benevolently taken from them? and have they not, instead thereof, been taught to set their affections on things above?—And finally, to use the words of a reverend Spanish father, in a letter to his superior in Spain— "Can any one have the presumption to say, that these savage pagans have yielded any thing mor than an inconsiderable recompense to their benefactors, in surrendering to them a little pitiful tract of this dirty sublunary planet, in exchange for a glorious inheritance in the kingdom of heaven!"

Here then are three complete and undeniable sources of right established, any one of which was more than ample to establish a property in the newly-discovered regions of America. Now, so it has happened in certain parts of this delightful quarter of the globe, that the right of discovery has been so strenuously asserted—the influence of cultivation so industriously extended, and the progress of salvation and civilization so zealously prosecuted, that, what with their attendant wars, persecutions, oppressions, diseases, and other partial evils that often hang on the skirts of great benefits—the savage aborigines have, somehow or another, been utterly annihilated—and this all at once brings me to a fourth right, which is worth all the others put together—For the original claimants to the soil being all dead and buried, and no one remaining to inherit or dispute the soil, the Spaniards, as the next immediate occupants, entered upon the possession as clearly as the hangman succeeds to the clothes of the malefactor—and as they have Blackstone,* and all the learned expounders of the law on their side, they may set all actions of ejectment at defiance—and this last right may be entitled the RIGHT BY EXTERMINATION, or in other words, the RIGHT BY GUNPOWDER.

But lest any scruples of conscience should remain on this head, and to settle the question of right for

---

* Bl. Com. b. ii. c. 1.

ever, his holiness Pope Alexander VI. issued a bull,
by which he generously granted the newly-discover·
ed quarter of the globe to the Spaniards and Portu·
guese; who, thus having law and gospel on their
side, and being inflamed with great spiritual zeal,
showed the pagan savages neither favour nor affection, but prosecuted the work of discovery, coloni-
zation, civilization, and extermination, with ten times
more fury than ever.

Thus were the European worthies who first discovered America, clearly entitled to the soil; and
not only entitled to the soil, but likewise to the
eternal thanks of these infidel savages, for having
come so far, endured so many perils by sea and land,
and taken such unwearied pains, for no other purpose
but to improve their forlorn, uncivilized, and heathenish condition—for having made them acquainted
with the comforts of life; for having introduced
among them the light of religion, and finally—for
having hurried them. out of the world, to enjoy its
reward!

But as argument is never so well understood by us
selfish mortals as when it comes home to ourselves,
and as I am particularly anxious that this question
should be put to rest for ever, I will suppose a
parallel case, by way of arousing the candid attention
of my readers.

Let us suppose, then, that the inhabitants of the
moon, by astonishing advancement in science, and
by profound insight into that lunar philosophy, the
mere flickerings of which have of late years dazzled

the feeble optics, and addled the shallow brains of the good people of our globe—let us suppose, I say, that the inhabitants of the moon, by these means, had arrived at such a command of their *energies*, such an enviable state of *perfectibility*, as to control the elements, and navigate the boundless regions of space. Let us suppose a roving crew of these soaring philosophers, in the course of an aerial voyage of discovery among the stars, should chance to alight upon this outlandish planet.

And here I beg my readers will not have the uncharitableness to smile, as is too frequently the fault of volatile readers, when perusing the grave speculations of philosophers. I am far from indulging in any sportive vein at present; nor is the supposition I have been making so wild as many may deem it. It has long been a very serious and anxious question with me, and many a time and oft, in the course of my overwhelming cares and contrivances for the welfare and protection of this my native planet, have I lain awake whole nights debating in my mind, whether it were most probable we should first discover and civilize the moon, or the moon discover and civilize our globe. Neither would the prodigy of sailing in the air and cruizing among the stars be a whit more astonishing and incomprehensible to us, than was the European mystery of navigating floating castles, through the world of waters, to the simple savages. We have already discovered the art of coasting along the aerial shores of our planet, by means of balloons, as the savages had of venturing

along their sea-coasts in canoes; and the disparity between the former, and the aerial vehicles of the
philosophers from the moon, might not be greater
than that between the bark canoes of the savages,
and the mighty ships of their discoverers. I might
here pursue an endless chain of similar speculations;
but as they would be unimportant to my subject, I
abandon them to my reader, particularly if he be a
philosopher, as matters well worthy of his attentive
consideration.

To return then to my supposition—let us suppose
that the aerial visitants I have mentioned, possessed
of vastly superior knowledge to ourselves; that is to
say, possessed of superior knowledge in the art of extermination—riding on hippogriffs—defended with
impenetrable armour—armed with concentrated sun-
beams, and provided with vast engines, to hurl enormous moon-stones: in short, let us suppose them, if
our vanity will permit the supposition, as superior to
us in knowledge, and consequently in power, as the
Europeans were to the Indians, when they first discovered them. All this is very possible; it is only
our self-sufficiency that makes us think otherwise;
and I warrant the poor savages, before they had any
knowledge of the white men, armed in all the terrors
of glittering steel and tremendous gunpowder, were
as perfectly convinced that they themselves were the
wisest, the most virtuous, powerful, and perfect of
created beings, as are at this present moment, the
lordly inhabitants of Old England, the volatile popu-

lace of France, or even the self-satisfied citizens of
this most enlightened republic.

Let us suppose, moreover, that the aerial voyagers,
finding this planet to be nothing but a howling wilderness, inhabited by us, poor savages and wild beasts,
shall take formal possession of it in the name of his
most gracious and philosophic excellency, the man
in the moon. Finding, however, that their numbers
are incompetent to hold it in complete subjection, on
account of the ferocious barbarity of its inhabitants;
they shall take our worthy President, the King of
England, the Emperor of Hayti, the mighty Bona-
parte, and the great King of Bantam, and returning
to their native planet, shall carry them to court, as
were the Indian chiefs led about as spectacles in the
courts of Europe.

Then making such obeisance as the etiquette of
the court requires, they shall address the puissant
man in the moon, in, as near as I can conjecture, the
following terms:

"Most serene and mighty Potentate, whose do-
minions extend as far as eye can reach, who rideth
on the Great Bear, useth the sun as a looking-glass,
and maintaineth unrivalled control over tides, madmen, and sea-crabs: We, thy liege subjects, have just
returned from a voyage of discovery, in the course
of which we have landed and taken possession of
that obscure little dirty planet which thou beholdest
rolling at a distance. The five uncouth monsters,
which we have brought into this august presence,

were once very important chiefs among their fellow-savages, who are a race of beings totally destitute of the common attributes of humanity; and differing in every thing from the inhabitants of the moon, inasmuch as they carry their heads upon their shoulders, instead of under their arms—have two eyes instead of one—are utterly destitute of tails, and of a variety of unseemly complexions, particularly of a horrible whiteness—instead of pea-green.

" We have moreover found these miserable savages sunk into a state of the utmost ignorance and depravity, every man shamelessly living with his own wife, and rearing his own children, instead of indulging in that community of wives enjoined by the law of nature, as expounded by the philosophers of the moon. In a word, they have scarcely a gleam of true philosophy among them, but are, in fact, utter heretics, ignoramuses, and barbarians. Taking compassion, therefore, on the sad condition of these sublunary wretches, we have endeavoured, while we remained on their planet, to introduce among them the light of reason—and the comforts of the moon. We have treated them to mouthfuls of moonshine, and draughts of nitrous oxyde, which they swallowed with incredible voracity, particularly the females; and we have likewise endeavoured to instil into them the precepts of lunar philosophy. We have insisted upon their renouncing the contemptible shackles of religion and common sense, and adoring the profound, omnipotent, and all-perfect energy, and the ecstatic, immutable, immoveable perfection. But such was the unparalleled obstinacy of these wretched savages, that they persisted in cleaving to their wives. and adhering to their religion, and absolutely set at nought the sublime doctrines of the moon—nay, among other abominable heresies, they even went so far as blasphemously to declare, that this ineffable planet was made of nothing more nor less than green cheese !"

At these words, the great man in the moon (being a very profound philosopher) shall fall into a terrible passion, and possessing equal authority over things that do not belong to him, as did whilome his holiness the Pope, shall forthwith issue a formidable bull, specifying, " That, whereas a certain crew of Lunatics have lately discovered, and taken possession of, a newly discovered planet called *the earth*—and that whereas it is inhabited by none but a race of two-legged animals, that carry their heads on their shoulders instead of under their arms ; cannot talk the lunatic language ; have two eyes instead of one ; are destitute of tails, and of a horrible whiteness, instead of pea-green—therefore, and for a variety of other excellent reasons, they are considered incapable of possessing any property in the planet they infest, and the right and title to it are confirmed to its original discoverers.—And furthermore, the colonists who are now about to depart to the aforesaid planet are authorized and commanded to use every means to convert these infidel savages from the darkness of Christianity, and make them thorough and absolute Lunatics."

In consequence of this benevolent bull, our philosophic benefactors go to work with hearty zeal. They seize upon our fertile territories, scourge us from our rightful possessions, relieve us from our wives, and when we are unreasonable enough to complain, they will turn upon us and say, Miserable barbarians! ungrateful wretches! have we not come thousands of miles to improve your worthless planet? have we not fed you with moonshine? have we not intoxicated you with nitrous oxyde? does not our moon give you light every night, and have you the baseness to murmur, when we claim a pitiful return for all these benefits? But finding that we not only persist in absolute contempt of their reasoning and disbelief in their philosophy, but even go so far as daringly to defend our property, their patience shall be exhausted, and they shall resort to their superior powers of argument; hunt us with hippogriffs, transfix us with concentrated sun-beams, demolish our cities with moon-stones; until having, by main force, converted us to the true faith, they shall graciously permit us to exist in the torrid deserts of Arabia, or the frozen regions of Lapland, there to enjoy the blessings of civilization and the charms of lunar philosophy, in much the same manner as the reformed and enlightened savages of this country are kindly suffered to inhabit the inhospitable forests of the north, or the impenetrable wilderness of South America.

Thus, I hope, I have clearly proved, and strikingly illustrated, the right of the early colonists to the pos-

session of this country; and thus is this gigantic
question completely vanquished : so having manfully
surmounted all obstacles, and subdued all opposition,
what remains but that I should forthwith conduct my
readers into the city which we have been so long in
a manner besieging? But hold—before I proceed
another step, I must pause to take breath, and recover
from the excessive fatigue I have undergone, in pre-
paring to begin this most accurate of histories. And
in this I do but imitate the example of a renowned
Dutch tumbler of antiquity, who took a start of three
miles for the purpose of jumping over a hill, but having run himself out of breath by the time he reached
the foot, sat himself quietly down for a few moments
to blow, and then walked over it at his leisure.

BOOK II.

CHAPTER I.

*In which are contained divers reasons why a man
should not write in a hurry. Also, of Master Hendrick Hudson, his discovery of a strange country—
and how he was magnificently rewarded by the
munificence of their High Mightinesses.*

My great-grandfather, by the mother's side, Her-
manus Van Clattercop, when employed to build the
large stone church at Rotterdam, which stands about
three hundred yards to your left after you turn off
from the Boomkeys, and which is so conveniently
constructed, that all the zealous Christians of Rotterdam prefer sleeping through a sermon there to any
other church in the city—my great-grandfather, I say,
when employed to build that famous church, did, in
the first place, send to Delft for a box of long pipes;
then having purchased a new spitting-box and a hundred weight of the best Virginia, he sat himself down,
and did nothing for the space of three months but
smoke most laboriously. Then did he spend full
three months more in trudging on foot, and voyaging
in trekschuit, from Rotterdam to Amsterdam—to
Delft—to Haerlem—to Leyden—to the Hague,

knocking his head and breaking his pipe against every church in his road. Then did he advance gradually nearer and nearer to Rotterdam, until he came in full sight of the identical spot whereon the church was to be built. Then did he spend three months longer in walking round it and round it, contemplating it, first from one point of view, and then from another—now would he be paddled by it on the canal—now would he peep at it through a telescope, from the other side of the Meuse, and now would he take a bird's-eye glance at it, from the top of one of those gigantic windmills which protect the gates of the city. The good folks of the place were on the tiptoe of expectation and impatience—notwithstanding all the turmoil of my great-grandfather, not a symptom of the church was yet to be seen; they even began to fear it would never be brought into the world, but that its great projector would lie down and die in labour of the mighty plan he had conceived. At length, having occupied twelve good months in puffing and paddling, and talking and walking—having travelled over all Holland, and even taken a peep into France and Germany—having smoked five hundred and ninety-nine pipes, and three hundred weight of the best Virginia tobacco— my great-grandfather gathered together all that knowing and industrious class of citizens who prefer attending to any body's business sooner than their own, and having pulled off his coat and five pair of breeches, he advanced sturdily up, and laid the corner-stone of the church, in the presence of the whole multitude—just at the commencement of the thirteenth month.

In a similar manner, and with the example of my worthy ancestor full before my eyes, have I proceeded in writing this most authentic history. The honest Rotterdamers no doubt thought my great-grandfather was doing nothing at all to the purpose, while he was making such a world of prefatory bustle, about the building of his church—and many of the ingenious inhabitants of this fair city will unquestionably suppose that all the preliminary chapters, with the discovery, population, and final settlement of America, were totally irrevalent and superfluous—and that the main business, the history of New-York, is not a jot more advanced, than if I had never taken up my pen. Never were wise people more mistaken in their conjectures; in consequence of going to work slowly and deliberately, the church came out of my grandfather's hands one of the most sumptuous, goodly, and glorious edifices in the known world— excepting that, like our magnificent capitol, at Washington, it was begun on so grand a scale that the good folks could not afford to finish more than the wing of it. So, likewise, I trust, if ever I am able to finish this work on the plan I have commenced, (of which, in simple truth, I sometimes have my doubts,) it will be found that I have pursued the latest rules of my art, as exemplified in the writings of all the great American historians, and wrought a very large history out of a small subject—which now-a-days is considered one of the great triumphs of historic skill. To proceed, then, with the thread of my story.

In the ever-memorable year of our Lord, 1609, on a Saturday morning, the five-and-twentieth day of March, old style, did that " worthy and irrecoverable discoverer, (as he has justly been called,) Master Henry Hudson," set sail from Holland in a stout vessel called the Half Moon, being employed by the Dutch East India Company, to seek a north-west passage to China.

Henry (or, as the Dutch historians call him, Hendrick) Hudson, was a sea-faring man of renown, who had learned to smoke tobacco under Sir Walter Raleigh, and is said to have been the first to introduce it into Holland, which gained him much popularity in that country, and caused him to find great favour in the eyes of their High Mightinesses, the Lords States General, and also of the honourable West India Company. He was a short, square, brawny old gentleman, with a double chin, a mastiff mouth, and a broad copper nose, which was supposed in those days to have acquired its fiery hue from the constant neighbourhood of his tobacco-pipe.

He wore a true Andrea Ferrara, tucked in a leathern belt, and a commodore's cocked hat on one side of his head. He was remarkable for always jerking up his breeches when he gave out his orders; and his voice sounded not unlike the brattling of a tin trumpet—owing to the number of hard north-westers which he had swallowed in the course of his sea-faring.

Such was Hendrick Hudson, of whom we have heard so much, and know so little : and I have been thus particular in his description, for the benefit of modern painters and statuaries, that they may represent him as he was ; and not, according to their common custom with modern heroes, make him look like Cæsar, or Marcus Aurelius, or the Apollo of Belvidere.

As chief mate and favourite companion, the commodore chose master Robert Juet, of Limehouse, in England. By some his name has been spelled *Chewit*, and ascribed to the circumstance of his having been the first man that ever chewed tobacco ; but this I believe to be a mere flippancy ; more especially as certain of his progeny are living at this day, who write their name Juet. He was an old comrade and early schoolmate of the great Hudson, with whom he had often played truant and sailed chip boats in a neighbouring pond, when they were little boys— from whence it is said the commodore first derived his bias towards a sea-faring life. Certain it is, that the old people about Limehouse declared Robert Juet to be an unlucky urchin, prone to mischief, that would one day or other come to the gallows.

He grew up as boys of that kind often grow up, a rambling, heedless varlet, tossed about in all quarters of the world—meeting with more perils and wonders than did Sinbad the Sailor, without growing a whit more wise, prudent, or ill-natured. Under every misfortune, he comforted himself with a quid of tobacco, and the truly philosophic maxim, that " it

will be all the same thing a hundred years hence.'
He was skilled in the art of carving anchors and true
lovers' knots on the bulk-heads and quarter-railings,
and was considered a great wit on board ship, in
consequence of his playing pranks on every body
around, and now and then even making a wry face
at old Hendrick, when his back was turned.

To this universal genius are we indebted for many
particulars concerning this voyage; of which he
wrote a history, at the request of the commodore,
who had an unconquerable aversion to writing himself, from having received so many floggings about it
when at school. To supply the deficiencies of master Juet's journal, which is written with true log-
book brevity, I have availed myself of divers family
traditions, handed down from my great-great-grandfather, who accompanied the expedition in the ca-
pacity of cabin-boy.

From all that I can learn, few incidents worthy of
remark happened in the voyage; and it mortifies me
exceedingly that I have to admit so noted an expedi-
dition into my work, without making any more of it.

Suffice it to say, the voyage was prosperous and
tranquil—the crew, being a patient people, much
given to slumber and vacuity, and but little troubled
with the disease of thinking—a malady of the mind,
which is the sure breeder of discontent. Hudson had
laid in abundance of gin and sour-crout, and every
man was allowed to sleep quietly at his post unless
the wind blew. True it is, some slight dissatisfaction

was shown on two or three occasions, at certain unreasonable conduct of Commodore Hudson.   Thus,
for instance, he forbore to shorten sail when the wind
was light, and the weather serene, which was considered among the most experienced Dutch seamen,
as certain *weather-breeders*, or prognostics, that the
weather would change for the worse.   He acted,
moreover, in direct contradiction to that ancient and
sage rule of the Dutch navigators, who always took
in sail at night—put the helm a-port, and turned in
—by which precaution they had a good night's rest
—were sure of knowing where they were the next
morning, and stood but little chance of running down
a continent in the dark.   He likewise prohibited the
seamen from wearing more than five jackets and six
pair of breeches, under pretence of rendering them
more alert; and no man was permitted to go aloft,
and hand in sails with a pipe in his mouth, as is the
invariable Dutch custom at the present day.   All
these grievances, though they might ruffle for a moment the constitutional tranquillity of the honest
Dutch tars, made but transient impression ; they eat
hugely, drank profusely, and slept immeasurably, and
being under the especial guidance of Providence, the
ship was safely conducted to the coast of America ;
where, after sundry unimportant touchings and standing off and on, she at length, on the fourth day of
September, entered that majestic bay, which at this
day expands its ample bosom before the city of New-

York, and which had never before been visited by
any European.*

It has been traditionary in our family, that when
the great navigator was first blessed with a view of
this enchanting island, he was observed, for the first

---

* True it is—and I am not ignorant of the fact, that in a certain aprocryphal book of voyages, compiled by one Hakluyt, is
to be found a letter written to Francis the First, by one Gio-
vanne, or John Verazzani, on which some writers are inclined
to found a belief that this delightful bay had been visited nearly
a century previous to the voyage of the enterprising Hudson.
Now this (albeit it has met with the countenance of certain
very judicious and learned men) I hold in utter disbelief, and
that for various good and substantial reasons: *First*, Because
on strict examination it will be found, that the description given
by this Verazzani applies about as well to the bay of New-York
as it does to my night-cap. *Secondly*, Because that this John
Verazzani, for whom I already begin to feel a most bitter enmity, is a native of Florence; and every body knows the crafty
wiles of these losel Florentines, by which they filched away the
laurels from the brows of the immortal Colon, (vulgarly called
Columbus,) and bestowed them on their officious townsman,
Amerigo Vespucci; and I make no doubt they are equally
ready to rob the illustrious Hudson of the credit of discovering
this beautiful island, adorned by the city of New-York, and
placing it beside their usurped discovery of South America.
And, *thirdly*, I award my decision in favour of the pretensions
of Hendrick Hudson, inasmuch as his expedition sailed from
Holland, being truly and absolutely a Dutch enterprise—and
though all the proofs in the world were introduced on the other
side, I would set them at nought, as undeserving my attention.
If these three reasons be not sufficient to satisfy every burgher
of this ancient city—all I can say is, they are degenerate descendants from their venerable Dutch ancestors, and totally
unworthy the trouble of convincing. Thus, therefore, the title
of Hendrick Hudson to his renowned discovery is fully vindicated.

and only time in his life, to exhibit strong symptoms
of astonishment and admiration. He is said to have
turned to master Juet, and uttered these remarkable
words, while he pointed towards this paradise of the
new world—" See ! there !"—and thereupon, as was
always his way when he was uncommonly pleased,
he did puff out such clouds of dense tobacco-smoke,
that in one minute the vessel was out of sight of
land, and master Juet was fain to wait until the
winds dispersed this impenetrable fog.

It was indeed—as my great-great-grandfather used
to say—though in truth I never heard him, for he died,
as might be expected, before I was born—" it was
indeed a spot on which the eye might have revelled
for ever, in ever-new and never-ending beauties."
The island of Mannahata spread wide before them,
like some sweet vision of fancy, or some fair creation
of industrious magic. Its hills of smiling green
swelled gently one above another, crowned with
lofty trees of luxuriant growth ; some pointing their
tapering foliage towards the clouds, which were glo-
riously transparent ; and others loaded with a verdant
burthen of clambering vines, bowing their branches
to the earth, that was covered with flowers. On the
gentle declivities of the hills were scattered in gay
profusion, the dog-wood, the sumach, and the wild
brier, whose scarlet berries and white blossoms
glowed brightly among the deep green of the surrounding foliage ; and here and there a curling column of smoke rising from the little glens that opened
along the shore, seemed to promise the weary voy-

H 2

agers a welcome at the hands of their fellow-creatures. As they stood gazing with entranced attention
on the scene before them, a red man, crowned with
feathers, issued from one of these glens, and after
contemplating in silent wonder the gallant ship, as
she sat like a stately swan swimming on a silver lake,
sounded the war-whoop, and bounded into the woods
like a wild deer, to the utter astonishment of the
phlegmatic Dutchmen, who had never heard such a
noise, or witnessed such a caper, in their whole
lives.

Of the transactions of our adventurers with the
savages, and how the latter smoked copper pipes, and
ate dried currants; how they brought great store of
tobacco and oysters; how they shot one of the ship's
crew, and how he was buried, I shall say nothing;
being that I consider them unimportant to my history.
After tarrying a few days in the bay, in order to refresh themselves after their sea-faring, our voyagers
weighed anchor, to explore a mighty river which
emptied into the bay. This river, it is said, was
known among the savages by the name of the *Shate-
muck;* though we are assured, in an excellent little
history published in 1674, by John Josselyn, Gent.
that it was called the *Mohegan,** and master Richard
Bloome, who wrote some time afterwards, asserts
the same—so that I very much incline in favour of
the opinion of these two honest gentlemen.   Be this

---

* This river is likewise laid down in Ogilvy's map as Man-
nattan—Noordt—Montaigne and Mauritius river.

as it may, up this river did the adventurous Hendrick proceed, little doubting but it would turn out to be the much-looked-for passage to China!

The journal goes on to make mention of divers interviews between the crew and the natives, in the voyage up the river; but as they would be impertinent to my history, I shall pass over them in silence, except the following dry joke, played off by the old commodore and his school-fellow, Robert Juet, which does such vast credit to their experimental philosophy, that I cannot refrain from inserting it. "Our master and his mate determined to try some of the chiefe men of the countrey, whether they had any treacherie in them. So they tooke them downe into the cabin and gave them so much wine and aqua vitæ, that they were all merrie; and one of them had his wife with him, which sate so modestly, as any of our countrey women would do in a strange place. In the end, one of them was drunke, which had been aboarde of our ship all the time that we had been there, and that was strange to them, for they could not tell how to take it."*

Having satisfied himself by this ingenious experiment, that the natives were an honest, social race of jolly roysters, who had no objection to a drinking bout, and were very merry in their cups, the old commodore chuckled hugely to himself, and thrusting a double quid of tobacco in his cheek, directed master Juet to have it carefully recorded, for the satis-

* Juet's Journ. Purch. Pil.

faction of all the natural philosophers of the university of Leyden—which done, he proceeded on his voyage, with great self-complacency. After sailing, however, above a hundred miles up the river, he found the watery world around him began to grow more shallow and confined, the current more rapid, and perfectly fresh—-phenomena not uncommon in the ascent of rivers, but which puzzled the honest Dutchmen prodigiously. A consultation was therefore called, and having deliberated full six hours, they were brought to a determination, by the ship's running aground—whereupon they unanimously concluded, that there was but little chance of getting to China in this direction. A boat, however, was despatched to explore higher up the river, which, on its return, confirmed the opinion—upon this the ship was warped off and put about, with great difficulty, being like most of her sex, exceedingly hard to govern ; and the adventurous Hudson, according to the account of my great-great-grandfather, returned down the river—with a prodigious flea in his ear !

Being satisfied that there was little likelihood of getting to China, unless, like the blind man, he returned from whence he sat out, and took a fresh start, he forthwith recrossed the sea to Holland, where he was received with great welcome by the honourable East India Company, who were very much rejoiced to see him come back safe—with their ship; and at a large and respectable meeting of the first merchants and burgomasters of Amsterdam, it was unanimously determined, that as a munificent reward for the eminent services he had performed, and the important discovery he had made, the great river Mohegan should be called after his name!—and it continues to be called Hudson river unto this very day.

CHAPTER II.

*Containing an account of a mighty Ark, which float
ed, under the protection of St. Nicholas, from Holland to Gibbet Island—the descent of the strange
Animals therefrom—a great victory, and a description of the ancient village of Communipaw.*

THE delectable accounts given by the great Hudson, and master Juet, of the country they had discovered, excited not a little talk and speculation
among the good people of Holland. Letters-patent
were granted by government to an association of
merchants, called the West India Company, for the
exclusive trade on Hudson river, on which they
erected a trading house called Fort Aurania, or
Orange, from whence did spring the great city of Albany. But I forbear to dwell on the various com-
mercial and colonizing enterprises, which took place;
among which was that of Mynheer Adrian Block,
who discovered and gave a name to Block Island
since famous for its cheese—and shall barely confine
myself to that which gave birth to this renowned
city.

It was some three or four years after the return of
the immortal Hendrick, that a crew of honest, Low
Dutch colonists set sail from the city of Amsterdam,
for the shores of America. It is an irreparable loss
to history, and a great proof of the darkness of the
age, and the lamentable neglect of the noble art of

book-making, since so industriously cultivated by knowing sea-captains, and learned supercargoes, that an expedition so interesting and important in its results, should be passed over in utter silence. To my great-great-grandfather am I again indebted for the few facts I am enabled to give concerning it—he having once more embarked for this country, with a full determination, as he said, of ending his days here —and of begetting a race of Knickerbockers, that should rise to be great men in the land.

The ship in which these illustrious adventurers set sail was called the *Goede Vrouw*, or good woman, in compliment to the wife of the President of the West India Company, who was allowed by every body (except her husband) to be a sweet tempered lady—when not in liquor. It was in truth a most gallant vessel, of the most approved Dutch construction, and made by the ablest ship-carpenters of Amsterdam, who, it is well known, always model their ships after the fair forms of their countrywomen. Accordingly, it had one hundred feet in the beam, one hundred feet in the keel, and one hundred feet from the bottom of the stern-post to the tafferel. Like the beauteous model, who was declared to be the greatest belle in Amsterdam, it was full in the bows, with a pair of enormous cat-heads, a copper bottom, and withal, a most prodigious poop !

The architect, who was somewhat of a religious man, far from decorating the ship with pagan idols such as Jupiter, Neptune, or Hercules, (which heathenish abominations, I have no doubt, occasion the

misfortunes and shipwreck of many a noble vessel,)
he, I say, on the contrary, did laudably erect for a
head, a goodly image of St. Nicholas, equipped with
a low, broad-brimmed hat, a huge pair of Flemish
trunk hose, and a pipe that reached to the end of the
bowsprit. Thus gallantly furnished, the staunch ship
floated sideways, like a majestic goose, out of the
harbour of the great city of Amsterdam, and all the
bells, that were not otherwise engaged, rang a triple
bobmajor on the joyful occasion.

My great-great-grandfather remarks, that the voyage was uncommonly prosperous, for, being under
the especial care of the ever-revered St. Nicholas,
the Goede Vrouw seemed to be endowed with qualities unknown to common vessels. Thus she made
as much lee-way as head-way, could get along very
nearly as fast with the wind a-head, as when it was
a-poop—and was particularly great in a calm; in
consequence of which singular advantages, she made
out to accomplish her voyage in a very few months,
and came to anchor at the mouth of the Hudson, a
little to the east of Gibbet Island.

Here lifting up their eyes, they beheld, on what is
at present called the Jersey shore, a small Indian village, pleasantly embowered in a grove of spreading
elms, and the natives all collected on the beach,
gazing in stupid admiration at the Goede Vrouw. A
boat was immediately despatched to enter into a
treaty with them, and approaching the shore, hailed
them through a trumpet, in the most friendly terms;
but so horribly confounded were these poor savages

at the tremendous and uncouth sound of the Low Dutch language, that they one and all took to their heels, and scampered over the Bergen hills; nor did they stop until they had buried themselves, head and ears, in the marshes on the other side, where they all miserably perished to a man—and their bones being collected and decently covered by the Tammany Society of that day, formed that singular mound called RATTLESNAKE HILL, which rises out of the centre of the salt marshes, a little to the east of the Newark Causeway.

Animated by this unlooked-for victory, our valiant heroes sprang ashore in triumph, took possession of the soil as conquerors in the name of their High Mightinesses the Lords States General; and marching fearlessly forward, carried the village of COMMUNIPAW by storm, notwithstanding that it was vigorously defended by some half-a-score of old squaws and poppooses. On looking about them, they were so transported with the excellencies of the place, that they had very little doubt the blessed St. Nicholas had guided them thither, as the very spot whereon to settle their colony. The softness of the soil was wonderfully adapted to the driving of piles; the swamps and marshes around them afforded ample opportunities for the constructing of dikes and dams; the shallowness of the shore was peculiarly favourable to the building of docks—in a word, this spot abounded with all the requisites for the foundation of a great Dutch city. On making a faithful report, therefore, to the crew of the Goede Vrouw, they one

and all determined that this was the destined end of
their voyage. Accordingly they descended from the
Goede Vrouw, men, women, and children, in goodly
groups, as did the animals of yore from the ark, and
formed themselves into a thriving settlement, which
they called by the Indian name COMMUNIPAW.

As all the world is doubtless perfectly acquainted
with Communipaw, it may seem somewhat superfluous to treat of it in the present work; but my
readers will please to recollect, that notwithstanding
it is my chief desire to satisfy the present age, yet I
write likewise for posterity, and have to consult the
understanding and curiosity of some half a score of
centuries yet to come; by which time, perhaps, were
it not for this invaluable history, the great Communipaw, like Babylon, Carthage, Nineveh, and other
great cities, might be perfectly extinct—sunk and
forgotten in its own mud—its inhabitants turned into
oysters,* and even its situation a fertile subject of
learned controversy and hard-headed investigation
among indefatigable historians. Let me then piously
rescue from oblivion the humble relics of a place,
which was the egg from whence was hatched the
mighty city of New-York!

Communipaw is at present but a small village
pleasantly situated, among rural scenery, on that
beauteous part of the Jersey shore which was known
in ancient legends by the name of Pavonia,† and

---

* Men by inaction degenerate into oysters.—*Kaimes.*

† Pavonia, in the ancient maps, is given to a tract of country
extending from about Hoboken to Amboy.

commands a grand prospect of the superb bay of New-York. It is within but half an hour's sail of the latter place, provided you have a fair wind, and may be distinctly seen from the city. Nay, it is a well-known fact, which I can testify from my own experience, that on a clear still summer evening, you may hear, from the Battery of New-York, the ob-streperous peals of broad-mouthed laughter of the Dutch negroes at Communipaw, who, like most other negroes, are famous for their risible powers. This is peculiarly the case on Sunday evenings, when, it is remarked by an ingenious and observant philos-opher, who has made great discoveries in the neigh-bourhood of this city, that they always laugh loudest —which he attributes to the circumstance of their having their holiday clothes on.

These negroes, in fact, like the monks in the dark ages, engross all the knowledge of the place, and be-ing infinitely more adventurous and more knowing than their masters, carry on all the foreign trade; making frequent voyages to town in canoes loaded with oysters, buttermilk, and cabbages. They are great astrologers, predicting the different changes of weather almost as accurately as an almanac—they are moreover exquisite performers on three-stringed fiddles: in whistling, they almost boast the far-famed powers of Orpheus's lyre, for not a horse or an ox in the place, when at the plough or before the wagon, will budge a foot until he hears the well-known whistle of his black driver and companion.—And from their amazing skill at casting up accounts upon

their fingers, they are regarded with as much venera-
tion as were the disciples of Pythagoras of yore,
when initiated into the sacred quaternary of numbers.

As to the honest burghers of Communipaw, like
wise men and sound philosophers, they never look
beyond their pipes, nor trouble their heads about any
affairs out of their immediate neighbourhood ; so that
they live in profound and enviable ignorance of all
the troubles, anxieties, and revolutions, of this distracted planet. I am even told that many among
them do verily believe that Holland, of which they
have heard so much from tradition, is situated somewhere on Long Island—that *Spiking-devil* and *the
Narrows* are the two ends of the world—that the
country is still under the dominion of their High
Mightinesses, and that the city of New-York still goes
by the name of Nieuw Amsterdam. They meet every
Saturday afternoon at the only tavern in the place,
which bears as a sign, a square-headed likeness of
the Prince of Orange, where they smoke a silent
pipe, by way of promoting social conviviality, and
invariably drink a mug of cider to the success of
Admiral Van Tromp, who they imagine is still
sweeping the British channel, with a broom at his
mast-head.

Communipaw, in short, is one of the numerous
little villages in the vicinity of this most beautiful of
cities, which are so many strong-holds and fastnesses,
whither the primitive manners of our Dutch forefathers have retreated, and where they are cherished

with devout and scrupulous strictness. The dress of the original settlers is handed down inviolate, from father to son—the identical broad-brimmed hat, broad-skirted coat, and broad-bottomed breeches continue from generation to generation; and several gigantic knee-buckles of massy silver, are still in wear, that made gallant display in the days of the patriarchs of Communipaw. The language likewise continues unadulterated by barbarous innovations; and so critically correct is the village schoolmaster in his dialect, that his reading of a Low Dutch psalm has much the same effect on the nerves as the filing of a handsaw.

I 2

CHAPTER III.

In which is set forth the true art of making a bargain —together with the miraculous escape of a great Metropolis in a fog—and the biography of certain Heroes of Communipaw.

HAVING, in the trifling digression which concluded the last chapter, discharged the filial duty which the city of New-York owed to Communipaw, as being the mother settlement; and having given a faithful picture of it as it stands at present, I return with a soothing sentiment of self-approbation, to dwell upon its early history. The crew of the Goede Vrouw being soon reinforced by fresh importations from Holland, the settlement went jollily on, increasing in magnitude and prosperity. The neighbouring Indians in a short time became accustomed to the uncouth sound of the Dutch language, and an intercourse gradually took place between them and the new comers. The Indians were much given to long talks, and the Dutch to long silence—in this particular, therefore, they accommodated each other completely. The chiefs would make long speeches about the big bull, the wabash, and the great spirit, to which the others would listen very attentively, smoke their pipes, and grunt *yah myn-her*—whereat the poor savages were wondrously delighted. They instructed the new settlers in the best art of curing and smoking tobacco, while the latter, in return, made them drunk with true Hollands—and then learned them the art of making bargains.

A brisk trade for furs was soon opened : the Dutch traders were scrupulously honest in their dealings, and purchased by weight, establishing it as an invariable table of avoirdupois, that the hand of a Dutchman weighed one pound, and his foot two pounds. It is true, the simple Indians were often puzzled by the great disproportion between bulk and weight, for let them place a bundle of furs, never so large, in one scale, and a Dutchman put his hand or foot in the other, the bundle was sure to kick the beam—never was a package of furs known to weigh more than two pounds in the market of Communipaw!

This is a singular fact— but I have it direct from my great-great-grandfather, who had risen to considerable importance in the colony, being promoted to the office of weighmaster, on account of the uncommon heaviness of his foot.

The Dutch possessions in this part of the globe began now to assume a very thriving appearance, and were comprehended under the general title of Nieuw Nederlandts, on account, as the sage Vander Donck observes, of their great resemblance to the Dutch Netherlands—which indeed was truly remarkable, excepting that the former were rugged and mountainous, and the latter level and marshy. About this time the tranquillity of the Dutch colonists was doomed to suffer a temporary interruption. In 1614, Captain Sir Samuel Argal, sailing under a commission from Dale, governor of Virginia, visited the Dutch settlements on Hudson River, and demanded their submission to the English crown and Virginian dominion.—To this arrogant demand, as they were in no condition to resist it, they submitted for the time like discreet and reasonable men.

It does not appear that the valiant Argal molested the settlement of Communipaw; on the contrary, I am told that when his vessel first hove in sight, the worthy burghers were seized with such a panic, that they fell to smoking their pipes with astonishing vehemence; insomuch that they quickly raised a cloud, which, combining with the surrounding woods and marshes, completely enveloped and concealed their beloved village, and overhung the fair regions of Pavonia;—so that the terrible Captain Argal passed on, totally unsuspicious that a sturdy little Dutch settlement lay snugly couched in the mud, under cover of all this pestilent vapour In commemoration of this fortunate escape, the worthy inhabitants have continued to smoke, almost without intermission, unto this very day; which is said to be the cause of the remarkable fog that often hangs over Communipaw of a clear afternoon.

Upon the departure of the enemy, our magnanimous ancestors took full six months to recover their wind, having been exceedingly discomposed by the consternation and hurry of affairs. They then called a council of safety to smoke over the state of the province. After six months more of mature deliberation, during which nearly five hundred words were spoken, and almost as much tobacco was smoked as would have served a certain modern general through a whole winter's campaign of hard drinking, it was determined to fit out an armament of canoes, and despatch them on a voyage of discovery; to search if, peradventure, some more sure and formidable position might not be found, where the colony would be less subject to vexatious visitations.

This perilous enterprise was intrusted to the superintendence of Mynheers Oloffe Van Kortlandt, Abraham Hardenbroeck, Jacobus Van Zandt, and Winant Ten Broeck—four indubitably great men, but of whose history, although I have made diligent inquiry, I can learn but little, previous to their leaving Holland. Nor need this occasion much surprise; for adventurers, like prophets, though they make great noise abroad, have seldom much celebrity in their own countries; but this much is certain, that the overflowings and offscourings of a country are invariably composed of the richest parts of the soil. And here I cannot help remarking how convenient it would be to many of our great men and great families of doubtful origin, could they have the privilege of the heroes of yore, who, whenever their origin was involved in obscurity, modestly announced themselves descended from a god—and who never visited a foreign country but what they told some cock-and-bull stories about their being kings and princes at home. This venal trespass on the truth, though it has occasionally been played off by some pseudo marquis, baronet, and other illustrious foreigner, in our land of good-natured credulity, has been completely discountenanced in this sceptical matter-of-fact age—and I even question whether any tender virgin, who was accidentally and unaccountably enriched with a bantling, would save her character at parlour firesides and evening tea-parties by ascribing the phenomenon to a swan, a shower of gold, or a river-god.

Thus being denied the benefit of mythology and classic fable, I should have been completely at a loss as to the early biography of my heroes, had not a gleam of light been thrown upon their origin from their names.

By this simple means, have I been enabled to gather some particulars concerning the adventurers in question. Van Kortlandt, for instance, was one of those peripatetic philosophers who tax Providence for a livelihood, and, like Diogenes, enjoy a free and unencumbered estate in sunshine. He was usually arrayed in garments suitable to his fortune, being curiously fringed and fangled by the hand of time; and was helmeted with an old fragment of a hat, which had acquired the shape of a sugar-loaf; and so far did he carry his contempt for the adventitious distinction of dress, that it is said the remnant of a shirt, which covered his back, and dangled like a pocket handkerchief out of a hole in his breeches, was never washed, except by the bountiful showers of heaven. In this garb was he usually to be seen, sunning himself at noon-day, with a herd of philosophers of the same sect, on the side of the great canal of Amsterdam. Like your nobility of Europe, he took his name of *Kortlandt* (or *lackland*) from his landed estate, which lay somewhere in terra incog nita.

Of the next of our worthies, might I have had the benefit of mythological assistance, the want of which I have just lamented, I should have made honourable mention, as boasting equally illustrious pedigree with the proudest hero of antiquity. His name of *Van Zandt*, which being freely translated, signifies, *from the dirt*, meaning, beyond a doubt, that like Triptolemus, Themis, the Cyclops and the Titans, he sprang from dame Terra, or the earth! This supposition is strongly corroborated by his size, for it is well known that all the progeny of mother earth were of a gigantic stature; and Van Zandt, we are told, was a tall raw-boned man, above six feet high—with an astonishing hard head. Nor is this origin of the illustrious Van Zandt a whit more improbable or repugnant to belief than what is related and universally admitted of certain of our greatest, or rather richest men; who, we are told with the utmost gravity, did originally spring from a dunghill!

Of the third hero, but a faint description has reached to this time, which mentions that he was a sturdy, obstinate, burly, bustling little man; and from being usually equipped with an old pair of buckskins, was familiarly dubbed Harden Broeck, or *Tough Breeches*.

Ten Broeck completed this junto of adventurers. It is a singular, but ludicrous fact, which, were I not scrupulous in recording the whole truth, I should

almost be tempted to pass over in silence, as incom‧
patible with the gravity and dignity of history, that
this worthy gentleman should likewise have been
nicknamed from the most whimsical part of his dress.
In fact, the small-clothes seems to have been a very
important garment in the eyes of our venerated ancestors, owing in all probability to its really being
the largest article of raiment among them. The
name of Ten Broeck, or Tin Broeck, is indifferently
translated into Ten Breeches and Tin Breeches—
the High Dutch commentators incline to the former
opinion; and ascribe it to his being the first who introduced into the settlement the ancient Dutch fashion
of wearing ten pair of breeches. But the most elegant and ingenious writers on the subject declare in
favour of Tin, or rather *Thin* Breeches; from whence
they infer, that he was a poor, but merry rogue,
whose galligaskins were none of the soundest, and
who was the identical author of that truly philosophical stanza :

> " Then why should we quarrel for riches,
>   Or any such glittering toys?
> A light heart and *thin pair of breeches*,
>   Will go through the world, my brave boys !"

Such was the gallant junto chosen to conduct this
voyage into unknown realms; and the whole was
put under the superintending care and direction of
Oloffe Van Kortlandt, who was held in great reverence among the sages of Communipaw, for the
variety and darkness of his knowledge. Having, as

I before observed, passed a great part of his life in the open air, among the peripatetic philosophers of Amsterdam, he had become amazingly well acquainted with the aspect of the heavens, and could as accurately determine when a storm was brewing, or a squall rising, as a dutiful husband can foresee, from the brow of his spouse, when a tempest is gathering about his ears. He was moreover a great seer of ghosts and goblins, and a firm believer in omens; but what especially recommended him to public confidence was his marvellous talent at dreaming, for there never was any thing of consequence happened at Communipaw but what he declared he had previously dreamt it; being one of those infallible prophets who always predict events after they have come to pass.

This supernatural gift was as highly valued among the burghers of Pavonia, as it was among the enlightened nations of antiquity. The wise Ulysses was more indebted to his sleeping than his waking moments for all his subtle achievements, and seldom undertook any great exploit without first soundly sleeping upon it; and the same may be truly said of the good Van Kortlandt, who was thence aptly denominated, Oloffe the Dreamer.

This cautious commander, having chosen the crews that should accompany him in the proposed expedition, exhorted them to repair to their homes, take a good night's rest, settle all family affairs, and make their wills, before departing on this voyage into unknown realms. And indeed this last was a precaution always taken by our forefathers, even in after times, when they became more adventurous, and voyaged to Haverstraw, or Kaatskill, or Groodt Esopus, or any other far country that lay beyond the great waters of the Tappaan Zee.

CHAPTER IV.

How the Heroes of Communipaw voyaged to Hell-
Gate, and how they were received there.

AND now the rosy blush of morn began to mantle
in the east, and soon the rising sun, emerging from
amidst golden and purple clouds, shed his blithesome
rays on the tin weathercocks of Communipaw. It
was that delicious season of the year, when nature,
breaking from the chilling thraldom of old winter,
like a blooming damsel from the tyranny of a sordid
old father, threw herself, blushing with ten thousand
charms, into the arms of youthful spring. Every
tufted copse and blooming grove resounded with the
notes of hymeneal love. The very insects, as they
sipped the dew that gemmed the tender grass of the
meadows, joined in the joyous epithalamium—the
virgin bud timidly put forth its blushes, " the voice
of the turtle was heard in the land," and the heart
of man dissolved away in tenderness. Oh! sweet
Theocritus! had I thine oaten reed, wherewith thou
erst didst charm the gay Sicilian plains—Or, oh!
gentle Bion! thy pastoral pipe, wherein the happy
swains of the Lesbian isle so much delighted, then
might I attempt to sing, in soft Bucolic or negligent
Idyllium, the rural beauties of the scene—but having
nothing, save this jaded goose-quill, wherewith to
wing my flight, I must fain resign all poetic disport-
ings of the fancy, and pursue my narrative in humble

prose; comforting myself with the hope, that though it may not steal so sweetly upon the imagination of my reader, yet may it commend itself, with virgin modesty, to his better judgment, clothed in the chaste and simple garb of truth.

No sooner did the first rays of cheerful Phœbus dart into the windows of Communipaw, than the little settlement was all in motion. Forth issued from his castle the sage Van Kortlandt, and seizing a conch-shell, blew a far-resounding blast, that soon summoned all his lusty followers. Then did they trudge resolutely down to the water-side, escorted by a multitude of relatives and friends, who all went down, as the common phrase expresses it, " to see them off." And this shows the antiquity of those long family processions, often seen in our city, composed of all ages, sizes, and sexes, laden with bundles and bandboxes, escorting some bevy of country cousins, about to depart for home in a market-boat.

The good Oloffe bestowed his forces in a squadron of three canoes, and hoisted his flag on board a little round Dutch boat, shaped not unlike a tub, which had formerly been the jolly-boat of the Goede Vrouw. And now all being embarked, they bade farewell to the gazing throng upon the beach, who continued shouting after them, even when out of hearing, wishing them a happy voyage, advising them to take good care of themselves, and not to get drowned—with an abundance other of those sage and invaluable cautions, generally given by landsmen to such as go down to the sea in ships, and adventure upon the deep waters. In the meanwhile, the voyagers cheerily urged their course across the crystal bosom of the bay, and soon left behind them the green shores of ancient Pavonia.

And first they touched at two small islands which ie nearly opposite Communipaw, and which are said to have been brought into existence about the time of the great irruption of the Hudson, when it broke through the Highlands, and made its way to the ocean.* For in this tremendous uproar of the waters, we are told that many huge fragments of rock and land were rent from the mountains and swept down by this runaway river, for sixty or seventy miles; where some of them ran aground on the shoals just opposite Communipaw, and formed the identical islands in question, while others drifted out to sea, and were never heard of more! A sufficient proof of the fact is, that the rock which forms the bases of these islands is exactly similar to that of the Highlands, and moreover one of our philosophers,

---

* It is a matter long since established by certain of our philosophers, that is to say, having been often advanced, and never contradicted, it has grown to be pretty nigh equal to a settled fact, that the Hudson was originally a lake, dammed up by the mountains of the Highlands. In process of time, however, becoming very mighty and obstreperous, and the mountains waxing pursy, dropsical, and weak in the back, by reason of their extreme old age, it suddenly rose upon them, and after a violent struggle effected its escape. This is said to have come to pass in very remote time, probably before that rivers had lost the art of running up hill. The foregoing is a theory in which I do not pretend to be skilled, notwithstanding that I do fully give it my belief.

K 2

who has diligently compared the agreement of their respective surfaces, has even gone so far as to assure me, in confidence, that Gibbet Island was originally nothing more nor less than a wart on Anthony's Nose.*

Leaving these wonderful little isles, they next coasted by Governor's Island, since terrible from its frowning fortress and grinning batteries. They would by no means, however, land upon this island, since they doubted much it might be the abode of demons and spirits which in those days did greatly abound throughout this savage and pagan country.

Just at this time a shoal of jolly porpoises came rolling and tumbling by, turning up their sleek sides to the sun, and spouting up the briny element in sparkling showers. No sooner did the sage Oloffe mark this, than he was greatly rejoiced. "This," exclaimed he, "if I mistake not, augurs well—the porpoise is a fat well-conditioned fish—a burgomaster among fishes—his looks betoken ease, plenty, and prosperity—I greatly admire this round, fat fish, and doubt not but this is a happy omen of the success of our undertaking." So saying, he directed his squadron to steer in the track of these alderman fishes.

Turning, therefore, directly to the left, they swept up the strait vulgarly called the East River. And here the rapid tide which courses through this strait, seizing on the gallant tub in which Commodore Van Kortlandt had embarked, hurried it forward with a

---

* A promontory in the Highlands.

velocity unparalleled in a Dutch boat, navigated by Dutchmen ; insomuch that the good commodore, who had all his life long been accustomed only to the drowsy navigation of canals, was more than ever convinced that they were in the hands of some supernatural power, and that the jolly porpoises were towing them to some fair haven that was to fulfil all their wishes and expectations.

Thus borne away by the resistless current, they doubled that boisterous point of land since called Corlear's Hook,* and leaving to the right the rich winding cove of the Wallabout, they drifted into a magnificent expanse of water, surrounded by pleasant shores, whose verdure was exceedingly refreshing to the eye. While the voyagers were looking around them, on what they conceived to be a serene and sunny lake, they beheld at a distance a crew of painted savages, busily employed in fishing, who seemed more like the genii of this romantic region—their slender canoe lightly balanced like a feather on the undulating surface of the bay.

At sight of these, the hearts of the heroes of Communipaw were not a little troubled. But as good fortune would have it, at the bow of the commodore's boat was stationed a very valiant man, named Hendrick Kip, (which being interpreted, means *chicken*, a name given him in token of his courage.) No sooner did he behold these varlet heathens than he trembled with excessive valour, and although a good

---

* Properly spelt *hoeck*, (i. e. a point of land.)

half mile distant, he seized a musquetoon that lay at hand, and turning away his head, fired it most intrepidly in the face of the blessed sun. The blundering weapon recoiled and gave the valiant Kip an ignominious kick, that laid him prostrate with uplifted heels in the bottom of the boat. But such was the effect of this tremendous fire, that the wild men of the woods, struck with consternation, seized hastily upon their paddles, and shot away into one of the deep inlets of the Long Island shore.

This signal victory gave new spirits to the hardy voyagers, and in honour of the achievement they gave the name of the valiant Kip to the surrounding bay, and it has continued to be called KIP'S BAY from that time to the present. The heart of the good Van Kortlandt—who, having no land of his own, was a great admirer of other people's—expanded at the sumptuous prospect of rich unsettled country around him, and falling into a delicious reverie, he straightway began to riot in the possession of vast meadows of salt marsh and interminable patches of cabbages. From this delectable vision he was all at once awakened by the sudden turning of the tide, which would soon have hurried him from this land of promise, had not the discreet navigator given signal to steer for shore; where they accordingly landed hard by the rocky heights of Bellevue—that happy retreat, where our jolly aldermen eat for the good of the city, and fatten the turtle that are sacrificed on civic solemnities.

Here, seated on the greensward, by the side of a

small stream that ran sparkling among the grass, they refreshed themselves after the toils of the seas, by feasting lustily on the ample stores which they had provided for this perilous voyage. Thus having well fortified their deliberative powers, they fell into an earnest consultation, what was farther to be done. This was the first council dinner ever eaten at Belle-vue by·Christian burghers, and here, as tradition relates, did originate the great family feud between the Hardenbroecks and the Tenbroecks, which afterwards had a singular influence on the building of the city. The sturdy Hardenbroeck, whose eyes had been wonderously delighted with the salt marshes that spread their reeking bosoms along the coast, at the bottom of Kip's Bay, counselled by all means to return thither, and found the intended city. This was strenuously opposed by the unbending Ten Broeck, and many testy arguments passed between them. The particulars of the controversy have not reached us, which is ever to be lamented ; this much is certain, that the sage Oloffe put an end to the dispute, by determining to explore still farther in the route which the mysterious porpoises had so clearly pointed out—whereupon the sturdy Tough Breeches abandoned the expedition, took possession of a neighbouring hill, and in a fit of great wrath peopled all that tract of country, which has continued to be inhabited by the Hardenbroecks unto this very day.

By this time the jolly Phœbus, like some wanton urchin sporting on the side of a green hill, began to roll down the declivity of the heavens ; and now, the

tide having once more turned in their favour, the resolute Pavonians again committed themselves to its
discretion, and coasting along the western shores,
were borne towards the straits of Blackwell's Island.

And here the capricious wanderings of the current
occasioned not a little marvel and perplexity to these
illustrious mariners.   Now would they be caught by
the wanton eddies, and, sweeping round a jutting
point, would wind deep into some romantic little
cove, that indented the fair island of Manna-hata;
now were they hurried narrowly by the very basis
of impending rocks, mantled with the flaunting grape-
vine, and crowned with groves that threw a broad
shade on the waves beneath; and anon they were
borne away into the mid-channel, and wafted along
with a rapidity that very much discomposed the sage
Van Kortlandt, who, as he saw the land swiftly
receding on either side, began exceedingly to doubt
that terra firma was giving them the slip.

Wherever the voyagers turned their eyes, a new
creation seemed to bloom around.   No signs of
human thrift appeared to check the delicious wildness
of nature, who here revelled in all her luxuriant variety.   Those hills, now bristled, like the fretful por-
cupine, with rows of poplars, (vain upstart plants!
minions of wealth and fashion!) were then adorned
with the vigorous natives of the soil; the lordly oak,
the generous chesnut, the graceful elm—while here
and there the tulip-tree reared his majestic head, the
giant of the forest.—Where now are seen the gay
retreats of luxury—villas half buried in twilight

bowers, whence the amorous flute oft breathes the sighings of some city swain—there the fish-hawk built his solitary nest, on some dry trees that over-looked his watery domain. The timid deer fed un-disturbed along those shores now hallowed by the lover's moonlight walk, and printed by the slender foot of beauty; and a savage solitude extended over those happy regions, where now are reared the state-ly towers of the Jones's, the Schermerhornes, and the Rhinelanders.

Thus gliding in silent wonder through these new and unknown scenes, the gallant squadron of Pavonia swept by the foot of a promontory, that strutted forth boldly into the waves, and seemed to frown upon them as they brawled against its base. This is the bluff well known to modern mariners by the name of Gracie's point, from the fair castle which, like an elephant, it carries upon its back. And here broke upon their view a wild and varied prospect, where land and water were beauteously intermingled, as though they had combined to heighten and set off each other's charms. To their right lay the sedgy point of Blackwell's Island, drest in the fresh garni-ture of living green—beyond it stretched the pleasant coast of Sundswick, and the small harbour well known by the name of Hallet's Cove—a place infa-mous in latter days, by reason of its being the haunt of pirates who infest these seas, robbing orchards and watermelon patches, and insulting gentlemen navigators, when voyaging in their pleasure-boats. To the left a deep bay, or rather creek, gracefully receded between shores fringed with forests, and forming a kind of vista, through which were beheld the sylvan regions of Haerlem, Morrisania, and East Chester. Here the eye reposed with delight on a richly wooded country, diversified by tufted knolls, shadowy intervals, and waving lines of upland, swelling above each other; while over the whole, the purple mists of spring diffused a hue of soft voluptuousness.

Just before them, the grand course of the stream, making a sudden bend, wound among embowered promontories, and shores of emerald verdure, that seemed to melt into the wave. A character of gentleness and mild fertility prevailed around. The sun had just descended, and the thin haze of twilight, like a transparent veil drawn over the bosom of virgin beauty, heightened the charms which it half concealed.

Ah! witching scenes of foul delusion! Ah! hapless voyagers, gazing with simple wonder on these Circean shores! Such, alas! are they, poor easy souls, who listen to the seductions of a wicked world—treacherous are its smiles! fatal its caresses! He who yields to its enticements launches upon a whelming tide, and trusts his feeble bark among the dimpling eddies of a whirlpool! And thus it fared with the worthies of Pavonia, who little mistrusting the guileful scene before them, drifted quietly on, until they were aroused by an uncommon tossing and agitation of their vessels. For now the late dimpling current began to brawl around them, and the waves

to boil and foam with horrific fury. Awakened as
if from a dream, the astonished Oloffe bawled aloud
to put about, but his words were lost amid the roaring of the waters. And now ensued a scene of direful consternation—at one time they were borne with
dreadful velocity among tumultuous breakers, at another, hurried down boisterous rapids. Now they
were nearly dashed upon the Hen and Chickens;
(infamous rocks!—more voracious than Scylla and
her whelps;) and anon they seemed sinking into
yawning gulfs, that threatened to entomb them beneath the waves. All the elements combined to produce a hideous confusion. The waters raged—the
winds howled—and as they were hurried along,
several of the astonished mariners beheld the rocks
and trees of the neighbouring shores driving through
the air!

At length the mighty tub of Commodore Van
Kortlandt was drawn into the vortex of that tremendous whirlpool called the Pot, where it was whirled
about in giddy mazes, until the senses of the good
commander and his crew were overpowered by the
horror of the scene, and the strangeness of the revolution.

How the gallant squadron of Pavonia was snatched
from the jaws of this modern Charybdis, has never
been truly made known, for so many survived to tell
the tale, and, what is still more wonderful, told it in
so many different ways, that there has ever prevailed
a great variety of opinions on the subject.

As to the commodore and his crew, when they

came to their senses they found themselves stranded on the Long Island shore. The worthy commodore, indeed, used to relate many and wonderful stories of his adventures in this time of peril; how that he saw spectres flying in the air, and heard the yelling of hobgoblins, and put his hand into the pot when they were whirled around, and found the water scalding hot, and beheld several uncouth-looking beings seated on rocks and skimming it with huge ladles—but particularly he declared with great exultation, that he saw the losel porpoises, which had betrayed them into this peril, some broiling on the Gridiron and others hissing in the Frying-pan!

These, however, were considered by many as mere phantasies of the commodore's imagination, while he lay in a trance; especially as he was known to be given to dreaming; and the truth of them has never been clearly ascertained. It is certain, however, that to the accounts of Oloffe and his followers may be traced the various traditions handed down of this marvellous strait—as how the devil has been seen there, sitting astride of the Hog's Back and playing on the fiddle—how he broils fish there before a storm; and many other stories, in which we mus be cautious of putting too much faith. In conse quence of all these terrific circumstances, the Pavonian commander gave this pass the name of *Helle-gat*, or as it has been interpreted, *Hell-gate;** which it continues to bear at the present day.

---

* This is a narrow strait in the Sound, at the distance of six miles above New-York. It is dangerous to shipping, unless

under the care of skilful pilots, by reason of numerous rocks, shelves, and whirlpools. These have received sundry appellations, such as the Gridiron, Frying-pan, Hog's Back, Pot, &c. and are very violent and turbulent at certain times of the tide. Certain wise men, who instruct these modern days, have softened the above characteristic name into *Hurl-gate*, which means nothing. I leave them to give their own etymology. The name as given by our author is supported by the map in Vander Donck's history, published in 1656—by Ogilvie's history of America, 1671—as also by a journal still extant, written in the 16th century, and to be found in Hazard's State Papers. And an old MS. written in French, speaking of various alterations in names about this city, observes, " De *Helle-gat* trou d'Enfer, ils ont fait *Hell-gate.* Porte d'Enfer."

CHAPTER V.

How the Heroes of Communipaw returned somewhat wiser than they went—and how the sage Oloffe dreamed a dream—and the dream that he dreamed.

THE darkness of night had closed upon this disastrous day, and a doleful night was it to the shipwrecked Pavonians, whose ears were incessantly assailed with the raging of the elements, and the howling of the hobgoblins that infested this perfidious strait. But when the morning dawned, the horrors of the preceding evening had passed away ; rapids, breakers, and whirlpools, had disappeared, the stream again ran smooth and dimpling, and having changed its tide, rolled gently back, towards the quarter where lay their much-regretted home.

The woe-begone heroes of Communipaw eyed each other with rueful countenances ; their squadron had been totally dispersed by the late disaster. Some were cast upon the western shore, where, headed by one Ruleff Hopper, they took possession of all the country laying about the six-mile stone ; which is held by the Hoppers at this present writing.

The Waldrons were driven by stress of weather to a distant coast, were, having with them a jug of genuine Hollands, they were enabled to conciliate the savages, setting up a kind of tavern ; from whence, it is said, did spring the fair town of Haerlem, in which their descendants have ever since continued

to be reputable publicans.   As to the Suydams, they
were thrown upon the Long Island coast, and may
still be found in those parts.   But the most singular
luck attended the great Ten Broeck, who, falling
overboard, was miraculously preserved from sinking
by the multitude of his nether garments.   Thus
buoyed up, he floated on the waves, like a merman,
or like the cork float of an angler, until he landed
safely on a rock, where he was found the next morning, busily drying his many breeches in the sunshine.

I forbear to treat of the long consultation of our
adventurers—how they determined that it would not
do to found a city in this diabolical neighbourhood—
and how at length, with fear and trembling, they ventured once more upon the briny element, and steered
their course back for Communipaw.   Suffice it, in
simple brevity, to say, that after toiling back through
the scenes of their yesterday's voyage, they at length
opened the southern point of Manna-hata, and gained
a distant view of their beloved Communipaw.

And here they were opposed by an obstinate eddy,
that resisted all the efforts of the exhausted mariners.
Weary and dispirited, they could no longer make
head against the power of the tide, or rather, as some
will have it, of old Neptune, who, anxious to guide
them to a spot, whereon should be founded his strong-
hold in this western world, sent half a score of potent
billows, that rolled the tub of Commodore Van
Kortlandt high and dry on the shores of Manna-
hata.

Having thus in a manner been guided by supernatural power to this delightful island, their first care was to light a fire at the foot of a large tree, that stood upon the point at present called the Battery. Then gathering together great store of oysters which abounded on the shore, and emptying the contents of their wallets, they prepared and made a sumptuous council repast. The worthy Van Kortlandt was observed to be particularly zealous in his devotions to the trencher; for having the cares of the expedition especially committed to his care, he deemed it incumbent on him to eat profoundly for the public good. In proportion as he filled himself to the very brim with the dainty viands before him, did the heart of this excellent burgher rise up towards his throat, until he seemed crammed and almost choked with good eating and good nature. And at such times it is, when a man's heart is in his throat, that he may more truly be said to speak from it, and his speeches abound with kindness and good-fellowship. Thus the worthy Oloffe having swallowed the last possible morsel, and washed it down with a fervent potation, felt his heart yearning, and his whole frame in a manner dilating with unbounded benevolence. Every thing around him seemed excellent and delightful; and, laying his hands on each side of his capacious periphery, and rolling his half-closed eyes around on the beautiful diversity of land and water before him, he exclaimed, in a fat half-smothered voice, " what a charming prospect!" The words died away in his throat—he seemed to ponder on the fair scene for a moment—his eye-lids heavily closed over their orbs

—his head drooped upon his bosom—he slowly sunk upon the green turf, and a deep sleep stole gradually upon him.

And the sage Oloffe dreamed a dream—and lo, the good St. Nicholas came riding over the tops of the trees, in that self-same wagon wherein he brings his yearly presents to children, and he came and descended hard by where the heroes of Communipaw had made their late repast. And the shrewd Van Kortlandt knew him by his broad hat, his long pipe, and the resemblance which he bore to the figure on the bow of the Goede Vrouw. And he lit his pipe by the fire, and sat himself down and smoked; and as he smoked, the smoke from his pipe ascended into the air, and spread like a cloud over head. And Oloffe bethought him, and he hastened and climbed up to the top of one of the tallest trees, and saw that the smoke spread over a great extent of country— and as he considered it more attentively, he fancied that the great volume of smoke assumed a variety of marvellous forms, where in dim obscurity he saw shadowed out palaces and domes and lofty spires, all of which lasted but a moment, and then faded away, until the whole rolled off, and nothing but the green woods were left. And when St. Nicholas had smoked his pipe, he twisted it in his hat-band, and laying his finger beside his nose, gave the astonished Van Kortlandt a very significant wink, then mounting his wagon, he returned over the tree-tops and disappeared.

And Van Kortlandt awoke from his sleep greatly

instructed, and he aroused his companions, and related to them his dream, and interpreted it, that it
was the will of St. Nicholas that they should settle
down and build the city here. And that the smoke
of the pipe was a type how vast should be the exten
of the city; inasmuch as the volumes of its smok
should spread over a wide extent of country. And
they all with one voice assented to this interpretation
excepting Mynheer Ten Broeck, who declared the
meaning to be that it should be a city wherein a little
fire should occasion a great smoke, or in other words,
a very vapouring little city—both which interpreta-
tions have strangely come to pass!

The great object of their perilous expedition,
therefore, being thus happily accomplished, the
voyagers returned merrily to Communipaw, where
they were received with great rejoicings. And here
calling a general meeting of all the wise men and
the dignitaries of Pavonia, they related the whole
history of their voyage, and of the dream of Oloffe
Van Kortlandt. And the people lifted up their
voices and blessed the good St. Nicholas, and from
that time forth the sage Van Kortlandt was held
more in honour than ever, for his great talent at
dreaming, and was pronounced a most useful citizen
and a right good man—when he was asleep.

CHAPTER VI.

Containing an attempt at etymology—and of the founding of the great city of New-Amsterdam.

· THE original name of the island wherein the squadron of Communipaw was thus propitiously thrown, is a matter of some dispute, and has already undergone considerable vitiation—a melancholy proof of the instability of all sublunary things, and the vanity of all our hopes of lasting fame! for who can expect his name will live to posterity, when even the names of mighty islands are thus soon lost in contradiction and uncertainty?

The name most current at the present day, and which is likewise countenanced by the great historian Vander Donck, is MANHATTAN; which is said to have originated in a custom among the squaws, in the early settlement, of wearing men's hats, as is still done among many tribes. " Hence," as we are told by an old governor who was somewhat of a wag, and flourished almost a century since, and had paid a visit to the wits of Philadelphia, " hence arose the appellation of man-hat-on, first given to the Indians, and afterwards to the island"—a stupid joke! ·—but well enough for a governor.

Among the more venerable sources of information on this subject, is that valuable history of the American possessions, written by Master Richard Blome in 1687, wherein it is called Manhadaes and Manahanent; nor must I forget the excellent little book, full of precious matter, of that authentic historian, John Josselyn, Gent. who expressly calls it Manadaes.

Another etymology still more ancient, and sanctioned by the countenance of our ever-to-be-lamented Dutch ancestors, is that found in certain letters still extant;* which passed between the early governors and their neighbouring powers, wherein it is called indifferently Monhattoes—Munhatos, and Manhattoes, which are evidently unimportant variations of the same name; for our wise forefathers set little store by those niceties either in orthography or orthoepy, which form the sole study and ambition of many learned men and women of this hypercritical age. This last name is said to be derived from the great Indian spirit Manetho; who was supposed to make this island his favourite abode, on account of its uncommon delights. For the Indian traditions affirm that the bay was once a translucid lake, filled with silver and golden fish, in the midst of which lay this beautiful island, covered with every variety of fruits and flowers; but that the sudden irruption of the Hudson laid waste these blissful scenes, and Manetho took his flight beyond the great waters of Ontario.

These, however, are fabulous legends to which very cautious credence must be given; and although I am willing to admit the last quoted orthography

---

* Vide Hazard's Col. State Papers.

of the name, as very suitable for prose, yet is there
another one founded on still more ancient and indis-
putable authority, which I particularly delight in,
seeing that it is at once poetical, melodious, and significant—and this is recorded in the before-mention-
ed voyage of the great Hudson, written by master
Juet; who clearly and correctly calls it MANNA-HATA
—that is to say, the island of Manna, or in other
words—" a land flowing with milk and honey !"

It having been solemnly resolved that the seat of
empire should be transferred from the green shores
of Pavonia to this delectable island, a vast multitude
embarked, and migrated across the mouth of the
Hudson, under the guidance of Oloffe the Dreamer,
who was appointed protector or patron to the new
settlement.

And here let me bear testimony to the matchless
honesty and magnanimity of our worthy forefathers,
who purchased the soil of the native Indians before
erecting a single roof—a circumstance singular and
almost incredible in the annals of discovery and col-
onization.

The first settlement was made on the south-west
point of the island, on the very spot where the good
St. Nicholas had appeared in the dream. Here they
built a mighty and impregnable fort and trading house,
called FORT AMSTERDAM, which stood on that eminence at present occupied by the custom-house, with
the open space now called the Bowling-Green in
front.

Around this potent fortress was soon seen a numerous progeny of little Dutch houses, with tiled roofs, all which seemed most lovingly to nestle under its walls, like a brood of half-fledged chickens sheltered under the wings of the mother hen. The whole was surrounded by an inclosure of strong palisadoes, to guard against any sudden irruption of the savages, who wandered in hordes about the swamps and forests that extended over those tracts of country at present called Broadway, Wall-street, William-street, and Pearl-street.

No sooner was the colony once planted, than it took root and throve amazingly; for it would seem that this thrice-favoured island is like a munificent dunghill, where every foreign weed finds kindly nourishment, and soon shoots up and expands to greatness.

And now the infant settlement having advanced in age and stature, it was thought high time it should receive an honest Christian name, and it was accordingly called NEW-AMSTERDAM. It is true, there were some advocates for the original Indian name, and many of the best writers of the province did long continue to call it by the title of " Manhattoes;" but this was discountenanced by the authorities, a being heathenish and savage. Besides, it was considered an excellent and praiseworthy measure to name it after a great city of the old world; as by that means it was induced to emulate the greatness and renown of its namesake—in the manner that little snivelling urchins are called after great statesmen, saints, and worthies and renowned generals of yore, upon which they all industriously copy their examples, and come to be very mighty men in their day and generation.

The thriving state of the settlement, and the rapid increase of houses, gradually awakened the good Oloffe from a deep lethargy, into which he had fallen after the building of the fort. He now began to think it was time some plan should be devised, on which the increasing town should be built. Summoning, therefore, his counsellors and coadjutors together, they took pipe in mouth, and forthwith sunk into a very sound deliberation on the subject.

At the very outset of the business an unexpected difference of opinion arose, and I mention it with much sorrowing, as being the first altercation on record in the councils of New-Amsterdam. It was a breaking forth of the grudge and heartburning that had existed between those two eminent burghers, Mynhers Tenbroeck and Hardenbroeck, ever since their unhappy altercation on the coast of Bellevue. The great Hardenbroeck had waxed very wealthy and powerful, from his domains, which embraced the whole chain of Apulean mountains that stretched along the gulf of Kip's Bay, and from part of which his descendants have been expelled in latter ages by the powerful clans of the Jones's and the Schermerhornes.

An ingenious plan for the city was offered by Mynher Tenbroeck, who proposed that it should be cut up and intersected by canals, after the manner of the most admired cities in Holland. To this Mynher

Hardenbroeck was diametrically opposed, suggesting in place thereof, that they should run out docks and wharves, by means of piles driven into the bottom of the river, on which the town should be built. By these means, said he triumphantly, shall we rescue a considerable space of territory from these immense rivers, and build a city that shall rival Amsterdam, Venice, or any amphibious city in Europe. To this proposition, Ten Broeck (or Ten Breeches) replied, with a look of as much scorn as he could possibly assume. He cast the utmost censure upon the plan of his antagonist, as being preposterous, and against the very order of things, as he would leave to every true Hollander. "For what," said he "is a town without canals?—it is a body without veins and arteries, and must perish for want of a free circulation of the vital fluid."—Tough Breeches, on the contrary, retorted with a sarcasm upon his antagonist, who was somewhat of an arid, dry-boned habit; he remarked, that as to the circulation of the blood being necessary to existence, Mynher Ten Breeches was a living contradiction to his own assertion; for every body knew there had not a drop of blood circulated through his wind-dried carcass for good ten years, and yet there was not a greater busy-body in the whole colony. Personalities have seldom much effect in making converts in argument—nor have I ever seen a man convinced of error by being convicted of deformity. At least such was not the case at present. Ten Breeches was very acrimonious in reply, and Tough Breeches, who was a sturdy little

man, and never gave up the last word, rejoined with
increasing spirit—Ten Breeches had the advantage
of the greatest volubility, but Tough Breeches had
that invaluable coat of mail in argument called obstinacy—Ten Breeches had, therefore, the most
mettle, but Tough Breeches the best bottom—so
that though Ten Breeches made a dreadful clatter-
ing about his ears, and battered and belaboured him
with hard words and sound arguments, yet Tough
Breeches hung on most resolutely to the last. They
parted, therefore, as is usual in all arguments where
both parties are in the right, without coming to any
conclusion—but they hated each other most heartily
for ever after, and a similar breach with that between
the houses of Capulet and Montague did ensue between the families of Ten Breeches and Tough
Breeches.

I would not fatigue my reader with these dull matters of fact, but that my duty, as a faithful historian,
requires that I should be particular—and in truth,
as I am now treating of the critical period, when
our city, like a young twig, first received the twists
and turns that have since contributed to give it the
present picturesque irregularity for which it is celebrated, I cannot be too minute in detailing their first
causes.

After the unhappy altercation I have just mentioned, I do not find that any thing farther was said on
the subject worthy of being recorded. The council,
consisting of the largest and oldest heads in the community, met regularly once a week, to ponder on this

momentous subject. But either they were deterred by the war of words they had witnessed, or they were naturally averse to the exercise of the tongue, and the consequent exercise of the brains—certain it is, the most profound silence was maintained—the question as usual lay on the table—the members quietly smoked their pipes, making but few laws, without ever enforcing any, and in the mean time the affairs of the settlement went on—as it pleased God.

As most of the council were but little skilled in the mystery of combining pot-hooks and hangers, they determined most judiciously not to puzzle either themselves or posterity with voluminous records. The secretary, however, kept the minutes of the council with tolerable precision, in a large vellum folio, fastened with massy brass clasps; the journal of each meeting consisted but of two lines, stating in Dutch, that, "the council sat this day, and smoked twelve pipes, on the affairs of the colony."—By which it appears that the first settlers did not regulate their time by hours, but pipes, in the same manner as they measure distances in Holland at this very time; an admirably exact measurement, as a pipe in the mouth of a true-born Dutchman is never liable to those accidents and irregularities that are continually putting our clocks out of order. It is said, moreover, that a regular smoker was appointed as council clock, whose duty was to sit at the elbow of the president and smoke incessantly: every puff marked a division of time as exactly as a second-

hand, and the knocking out of the ashes of his pipe
was equivalent to striking the hour.

In this manner did the profound council of NEW-
AMSTERDAM smoke, and doze, and ponder, from week
to week, month to month, and year to year, in what
manner they should construct their infant settlement
—meanwhile, the town took care of itself, and like
a sturdy brat which is suffered to run about wild, un-
shackled by clouts and bandages, and other abominations by which your notable nurses and sage old
women cripple and disfigure the children of men,
increased so rapidly in strength and magnitude, that
before the honest burgomasters had determined
upon a plan, it was too late to put it in execution
—whereupon they wisely abandoned the subject altogether.

M 2

CHAPTER VII.

How the city of New-Amsterdam waxed great, under the protection of Oloffe the Dreamer.

THERE is something exceedingly delusive in thus looking back, through the long vista of departed years, and catching a glimpse of the fairy realms of antiquity that lie beyond. Like some goodly landscape melting into distance, they receive a thousand charms from their very obscurity, and the fancy delights to fill up their outlines with graces and excellencies of its own creation. Thus beam on my imagination those happier days of our city, when as yet New-Amsterdam was a mere pastoral town, shrouded in groves of sycamore and willows, and surrounded by trackless forests and wide-spreading waters, that seemed to shut out all the cares and vanities of a wicked world.

In those days did this embryo city present the rare and noble spectacle of a community governed without laws; and thus being left to its own course, and the fostering care of Providence, increased as rapidly as though it had been burthened with a dozen panniers-full of those sage laws that are usually heaped on the backs of young cities—in order to make them grow. And in this particular I greatly admire the wisdom and sound knowledge of human nature, displayed by the sage Oloffe the Dreamer, and his fellow-legislators. For my part, I have not so bad an opinion of mankind as many of my brother philosophers. I do not think poor human nature so sorry a piece of workmanship as they would make it out to be; and as far as I have observed, I am fully satisfied that man, if left to himself, would about as readily go right as wrong. It is only this eternally sounding in his ears that it is his duty to go right, that makes him go the very reverse. The noble independence of his nature revolts at this intolerable tyranny of law, and the perpetual interference of officious morality, which is ever besetting his path with finger-posts and directions to " keep to the right, as the law directs;" and like a spirited urchin, he turns directly contrary, and gallops through mud and mire, over hedges and ditches, merely to show that he is a lad of spirit, and out of his leading-strings. And these opinions are amply substantiated by what I have above said of our worthy ancestors; who never being be-preached and be-lectured, and guided and governed by statutes and laws and by-laws, as are their more enlightened descendants, did one and all demean themselves honestly and peaceably, out of pure ignorance, or in other words—because they knew no better.

Nor must I omit to record one of the earliest measures of this infant settlement, inasmuch as it shows the piety of our forefathers, and that, like good Christians, they were always ready to serve God, after they had first served themselves. Thus, having quietly settled themselves down, and provided for their own comfort, they bethought themselves of testifying their gratitude to the great and good St.

Nicholas, for his protecting care, in guiding them to this delectable abode. To this end they built a fair and goodly chapel within the fort, which they consecrated to his name; whereupon he immediately took the town of New-Amsterdam under his peculiar patronage, and he has ever since been, and I devoutly hope will ever be, the tutelar saint of this excellent city.

I am moreover told that there is a little legendary book, somewhere extant, written in Low Dutch, which says, that the image of this renowned saint, which whilome graced the bowsprit of the Goede Vrouw, was elevated in front of this chapel, in the very centre of what, in modern days, is called the Bowling-Green. And the legend further treats of divers miracles wrought by the mighty pipe, which the saint held in his mouth; a whiff of which was a sovereign cure for an indigestion—an invaluable relic in this colony of brave trenchermen. As, however, in spite of the most diligent search, I cannot lay my hands upon this little book, I must confess that I entertain considerable doubt on the subject.

Thus benignly fostered by the good St. Nicholas, the burghers of New-Amsterdam beheld their settlement increase in magnitude and population, and soon become the metropolis of divers settlements, and an extensive territory. Already had the disastrous pride of colonies and dependencies, those banes of a sound-hearted empire, entered into their imaginations; and Fort Aurania on the Hudson, Fort Nassau on the Delaware, and Fort Goede Hoep on the Connecticut river, seemed to be the darling offspring of the venerable council.* Thus prosperously, to all appearance, did the province of New-Netherlands advance in power; and the early history of its metropolis presents a fair page, unsullied by crime or calamity.

Hordes of painted savages still lurked about the tangled forests and rich bottoms of the unsettled part of the island—the hunter pitched his rude bower of skins and bark beside the rills that ran through the cool and shady glens; while here and there might be seen on some sunny knoll, a group of Indian wigwams, whose smoke rose above the neighbouring trees, and floated in the transparent atmosphere.. By degrees, a mutual good-will had grown up between these wandering beings and the burghers of New-Amsterdam. Our benevolent forefathers endeavoured as much as possible to meliorate their situation, by giving them gin, rum, and glass beads, in exchange for their peltries; for it seems the kind-hearted Dutchmen had conceived a great friendship for their savage

---

* The province, about this time, extended on the north to Fort Aurania, or Orange (now the city of Albany,) situated about 160 miles up the Hudson river. Indeed, the province claimed quite to the river St. Lawrence; but this claim was not much insisted on at the time, as the country beyond Fort Aurania was a perfect wilderness. On the south, the province reached to Fort Nassau, on the South river, since called the Delaware; and on the east, it extended to the Varshe (or fresh) river, now the Connecticut. On this last frontier was likewise erected a fort or trading house, much about the spot where at present is situated the pleasant town of Hartford. This was called Fort Goede Hoep, (or Good Hope) and was intended as well for the purposes of trade, as of defence.

neighbours, on account of their being pleasant men
to trade with, and little skilled in the art of making
a bargain.

Now and then a crew of these half-human sons of
the forest would make their appearance in the streets
of New-Amsterdam, fantastically painted and decorated with beads and flaunting feathers, sauntering
about with an air of listless indifference—sometimes
in the market-place, instructing the little Dutch boys
in the use of the bow and arrow—at other times,
inflamed with liquor, swaggering and whooping and
yelling about the town like so many fiends, to the
great dismay of all the good wives, who would hurry
their children into the house, fasten the doors, and
throw water upon the enemy from the garret-win-
dows. It is worthy of mention here, that our forefathers were very particular in holding up these wild
men as excellent domestic examples—and for reasons
that may be gathered from the history of master
Ogilby, who tells us, that "for the least offence the
bridegroom soundly beats his wife and turns her out
of doors, and marries another, insomuch that some
of them have every year a new wife." Whether this
awful example had any influence or not, history does
not mention; but it is certain that our grandmothers
were miracles of fidelity and obedience.

True it is, that the good understanding between
our ancestors and their savage neighbours, was liable
to occasional interruptions; and I have heard my
grandmother, who was a very wise old woman, and
well versed in the history of these parts, tell a long

story, of a winter's evening, about a battle between the New-Amsterdammers and the Indians, which was known by the name of the *Peach War*, and which took place near a peach orchard, in a dark glen, which for a long while went by the name of the Murderer's Valley.

The legend of this sylvan war was long curren among the nurses, old wives, and other ancient chroniclers of the place; but time and improvement have almost obliterated both the tradition and the scene of battle; for what was once the blood-stained valley is now in the centre of this populous city, and known by the name of *Dey-street*.

The accumulating wealth and consequence of New-Amsterdam and its dependencies at length awakened the tender solicitude of the mother country; who, finding it a thriving and opulent colony, and that it promised to yield great profit, and no trouble, all at once became wonderfully anxious about its safety, and began to load it with tokens of regard, in the same manner that your knowing people are sure to overwhelm rich relations with their affection and loving kindness.

The usual marks of protection shown by mother countries to wealthy colonies were forthwith manifested—the first care always being to send rulers to the new settlement, with orders to squeeze as much revenue from it as it will yield. Accordingly, in the year of our Lord, 1629, Mynher WOUTER VAN TWILLER was appointed governor of the province of Nieuw-Nederlandts, under the commission and control of their High Mightinesses, the Lords States General of the United Netherlands, and the privileged West India Company.

This renowned old gentleman arrived at New-Amsterdam in the merry month of June, the sweetest month in all the year; when Dan Apollo seems to dance up the transparent firmament—when the robin, the thrush, and a thousand other wanton songsters, make the woods to resound with amorous ditties, and the luxurious little boblincon revels among the clover blossoms of the meadows—all which happy coincidence persuaded the old dames of New-Amsterdam, who were skilled in the art of foretelling events, that this was to be a happy and prosperous administration.

But as it would be derogatory to the consequence of the first Dutch governor of the great province of Nieuw-Nederlandts, to be thus scurvily introduced at the end of the chapter, I will put an end to this second book of my history, that I may usher him in with more dignity in the beginning of my next.

BOOK III.

IN WHICH IS RECORDED THE GOLDEN REIGN OF WOUTER
VAN TWILLER.

CHAPTER I.

*Of the renowned Walter Van Twiller—his unparallel-
ed virtues—and likewise his unutterable wisdom in
the law case of Wandle Schoonhoven and Barent
Bleecher—and the great admiration of the public
thereat.*

GRIEVOUS and very much to be commiserated is
the task of the feeling historian, who writes the history of his native land.   If it fall to his lot to be the
sad recorder of calamity or crime, the mournful page
is watered with his tears—nor can he recall the most
prosperous and blissful era, without a melancholy
sigh at the reflection, that it has passed away for
ever! I know not whether it be owing to an im-
moderate love for the simplicity of former times, or
to that certain tenderness of heart incident to all sentimental historians ; but I candidly confess that I cannot look back on the happier days of our city, which
I now describe, without a sad dejection of the spirits.
With a faltering hand do I withdraw the curtain of
oblivion, that veils the modest merit of our venerable
ancestors, and as their figures rise to my mental vision, humble myself before the mighty shades.

Such are my feelings when I revisit the family mansion of the Knickerbockers, and spend a lonely hour in the chamber where hang the portraits of my forefathers, shrouded in dust, like the forms they represent. With pious reverence do I gaze on the countenances of those renowned burghers, who have preceded me in the steady march of existence—whose sober and temperate blood now meanders through my veins, flowing slower and slower in its feeble conduits, until its current shall soon be stopped for ever!

These, say I to myself, are but frail memorials of the mighty men who flourished in the days of the patriarchs; but who, alas, have long since mouldered in that tomb, towards which my steps are insensibly and irresistibly hastening! As I pace the darkened chamber, and lose myself in melancholy musings, the shadowy images around me almost seem to steal once more into existence—their countenances to assume the animation of life—their eyes to pursue me in every movement! Carried away by the delusions of fancy, I almost imagine myself surrounded by the shades of the departed, and holding sweet converse with the worthies of antiquity! Ah, hapless Died rich! born in a degenerate age, abandoned to the buffetings of fortune—a stranger and a weary pilgrim in thy native land—blest with no weeping wife, nor family of helpless children; but doomed to wander neglected through those crowded streets, and elbowed by foreign upstarts from those fair abodes where once thine ancestors held sovereign empire!

Let me not, however, lose the historian in the man, nor suffer the dating recollections of age to overcome me, while dwelling with fond garrulity on the virtuous days of the patriarchs—on those sweet days of simplicity and ease, which never more will dawn on the lovely island of Manna-hata!

The renowned Wouter (or Walter) Van Twiller, was descended from a long line of Dutch burgomasters, who had successively dozed away their lives, and grown fat upon the bench of magistracy in Rotterdam; and who had comported themselves with such singular wisdom and propriety, that they were never either heard or talked of—which, next to being universally applauded, should be the object of ambition of all sage magistrates and rulers.

His surname of Twiller, is said to be a corruption of the original *Twijfler*, which in English means *doubter;* a name admirably descriptive of his deliberative habits. For, though he was a man shut up within himself like an oyster, and of such a profoundly reflective turn, that he scarcely ever spoke except in monosyllables, yet did he never make up his mind on any doubtful point. This was clearly accounted for by his adherents, who affirmed that he always conceived every object on so comprehensive a scale, that he had not room in his head to turn it over and examine both sides of it, so that he always remained in doubt, merely in consequence of the astonishing magnitude of his ideas!

There are two opposite ways by which some men get into notice—one by talking a vast deal and thinking a little, and the other by holding their tongues and not thinking at all. By the first, many a vapouring superficial pretender acquires the reputation of a man of quick parts—by the other, many a vacant dunderpate, like the owl, the stupidest of birds, comes to be complimented by a discerning world with all the attributes of wisdom. This, by the way, is a mere casual remark, which I would not for the universe have it thought I apply to Governor Van Twiller. On the contrary, he was a very wise Dutchman, for he never said a foolish thing—and of such invincible gravity, that he was never known to laugh, or even to smile, through the course of a long and prosperous life. Certain, however, it is, there never was a matter proposed, however simple, and on which your common narrow-minded mortals would rashly determine at the first glance, but what the renowned Wouter put on a mighty mysterious, vacant kind of look, shook his capacious head, and having smoked for five minutes with redoubled earnestness, sagely observed, that "he had his doubts about the matter"—which in process of time gained him the character of a man slow in belief, and not easily imposed on.

The person of this illustrious old gentleman was as regularly formed, and nobly proportioned, as though it had been moulded by the hands of some cunning Dutch statuary, as a model of majesty and lordly grandeur. He was exactly five feet six inches in height, and six feet five inches in circumference. His head was a perfect sphere, and of such stupendous dimensions, that dame Nature, with all her sex's ingenuity, would have been puzzled to construct a neck capable of supporting it; wherefore she wisely declined the attempt, and settled it firmly on the top of his back-bone, just between the shoulders. His body was of an oblong form, particularly capacious at bottom; which was wisely ordered.by Providence, seeing that he was a man of sedentary habits, and very averse to the idle labour of walking. His legs, though exceeding short, were sturdy in proportion to the weight they had to sustain; so that when erect he had not a little the appearance of a robustious beer-barrel, standing on skids. His face, that infallible index of the mind, presented a vast expanse, perfectly unfurrowed or deformed by any of those lines and angles which disfigure the human countenance with what is termed expression. Two small gray eyes twinkled feebly in the midst, like two stars of lesser magnitude in the hazy firmament; and his full-fed cheeks, which seemed to have taken toll of every thing that went into his mouth, were curiously mottled and streaked with dusky red, like a Spitzenberg apple.

His habits were as regular as his person. He daily took his four stated meals, appropriating exactly an hour to each; he smoked and doubted eight hours, and he slept the remaining twelve of the four-and-twenty. Such was the renowned Wouter Van Twiller—a true philosopher, for his mind was either elevated above, or tranquilly settled below, the cares and perplexities of this world. He had lived in it for years, without feeling the least curiosity to know whether the sun revolved round it, or it round the sun ; and he had watched, for at least half a century, the smoke curling from his pipe to the ceiling, without once troubling his head with any of those numerous theories, by which a philosopher would have perplexed his brain, in accounting for its rising above the surrounding atmosphere.

In his council he presided with great state and solemnity. He sat in a huge chair of solid oak, hewn in the celebrated forest of the Hague, fabricated by an experienced timmerman of Amsterdam, and curiously carved about the arms and feet, into exact imitations of gigantic eagle's claws. Instead of a sceptre, he swayed a long Turkish pipe, wrought with jasmin and amber, which had been presented to a Stadtholder of Holland, at the conclusion of a treaty with one of the petty Barbary powers. In this stately chair would he sit, and this magnificent pipe would he smoke, shaking his right knee with a constant motion, and fixing his eye for hours together upon a little print of Amsterdam, which hung in a black frame against the opposite wall of the council chamber. Nay, it has even been said, that when any deliberation of extraordinary length and intricacy was on the carpet, the renowned Wouter would absolutely shut his eyes for full two hours at a time, that he might not be disturbed by external objects—and at such times the internal commotion of his mind was evinced by certain regular guttural sounds, which

his admirers declared were merely the noise of conflict, made by his contending doubts and opinions.

It is with infinite difficulty I have been enabled to
collect these biographical anecdotes of the great man
under consideration. The facts respecting him were
so scattered and vague, and divers of them so ques-
tionable in point of authenticity, that I have had to
give up the search after many, and decline the admission of still more, which would have tended to
heighten the colouring of his portrait.

I have been the more anxious to delineate fully
the person and habits of the renowned Van Twiller,
from the consideration that he was not only the first,
but also the best governor that ever presided over
this ancient and respectable province ; and so tranquil
and benevolent was his reign, that I do not find
throughout the whole of it, a single instance of any
offender being brought to punishment—a most indu-
bitable sign of a merciful governor, and a case unparalleled, excepting in the reign of the illustrious
King Log, from whom, it is hinted, the renowned
Van Twiller was a lineal descendant.

The very outset of the career of this excellent
magistrate was distinguished by an example of legal
acumen, that gave flattering presage of a wise and
equitable administration. The morning after he had
been solemnly installed in office, and at the moment
that he was making his breakfast, from a prodigious
earthen dish, filled with milk and Indian pudding, he
was suddenly interrupted by the appearance of one
Wandle Schoonhoven, a very important old burgher

of New-Amsterdam, who complained bitterly of one
Barent Bleecker, inasmuch as he fraudulently refused
to come to a settlement of accounts, seeing that there
was a heavy balance in favour of the said Wandle.
Governor Van Twiller, as I have already observed,
was a man of few words; he was likewise a mortal
enemy to multiplying writings—or being disturbed
at his breakfast. Having listened attentively to the
statement of Wandle Schoonhoven, giving an occasional grunt, as he shovelled a spoonful of Indian
pudding into his mouth—either as a sign that he rel-
ished the dish, or comprehended the story—he called
unto him his constable, and pulling out of his breeches
pocket a huge jack-knife, despatched it after the de-
fendant as a summons, accompanied by his tobacco-
box as a warrant.

This summary process was as effectual in those
simple days as was the seal-ring of the great Haroun
Alraschid among the true believers. The two parties being confronted before him, each produced a
book of accounts, written in a language and character
that would have puzzled any but a High Dutch com-
mentator, or a learned decipherer of Egyptian obe-
lisks, to understand. The sage Wouter took them
one after the other, and having poised them in his
hands, and attentively counted over the number of
leaves, fell straightway into a very great doubt, and
smoked for half an hour without saying a word; at
length, laying his finger beside his nose, and shutting
his eyes for a moment, with the air of a man who has
just caught a subtle idea by the tail, he slowly took

his pipe from his mouth, puffed forth a column of tobacco-smoke, and with marvellous gravity and solemnity pronounced—that having carefully counted over the leaves and weighed the books, it was found, that one was just as thick and as heavy as the other —therefore it was the final opinion of the court that the accounts were equally balanced—therefore Wandle should give Barent a receipt, and Barent should give Wandle a receipt—and the constable should pay the costs.

This decision being straightway made known, diffused general joy throughout New-Amsterdam, for the people immediately perceived, that they had a very wise and equitable magistrate to rule over them. But its happiest effect was, that not another law-suit took place throughout the whole of his administration —and the office of constable fell into such decay, that there was not one of those losel scouts known in the province for many years. I am the more particular in dwelling on this transaction, not only because I deem it one of the most sage and righteous judgments on record, and well worthy the attention of modern magistrates, but because it was a miraculous event in the history of the renowned Wouter— being the only time he was ever known to come to a decision in the whole course of his life.

CHAPTER II.

Containing some account of the grand council of New-Amsterdam, as also divers especial good philosophical reasons why an alderman should be fat— with other particulars touching the state of the province.

IN treating of the early governors of the province, I must caution my readers against confounding them, in point of dignity and power, with those worthy gentlemen, who are whimsically denominated governors in this enlightened republic—a set of unhappy victims of popularity, who are in fact the most dependent, henpecked beings in the community : doomed to bear the secret goadings and corrections of their own party, and the sneers and revilings of the whole world beside ;—set up, like geese at Christmas holydays, to be pelted and shot at by every whipster and vagabond in the land.   On the contrary, the Dutch governors enjoyed that uncontrolled authority, vested in all commanders of distant colonies or territories. They were in a manner absolute despots in their little domains, lording it, if so disposed, over both law and gospel, and accountable to none but the mother country; which it is well known is astonishingly deaf to all complaints against its governors, provided they discharge the main duty of their station— squeezing out a good revenue.   This hint will be of importance, to prevent my readers from being seized with doubt and incredulity, whenever, in the course of this authentic history, they encounter the uncommon circumstance of a governor acting with independence, and in opposition to the opinions of the multitude.

To assist the doubtful Wouter in the arduous business of legislation, a board of magistrates was appointed, which presided immediately over the police. This potent body consisted of a schout or bailiff, with powers between those of the present mayor and sheriff—five burgermeesters, who were equivalent to aldermen, and five schepens, who officiated as scrubs, subdevils, or bottle-holders to the burgermeesters, in the same manner as do assistant aldermen to their principals at the present day; it being their duty to fill the pipes of the lordly burgermeesters—hunt the markets for delicacies for corporation dinners, and to discharge such other little offices of kindness as were occasionally required. It was, moreover, tacitly understood, though not specifically enjoined, that they should consider themselves as butts for the blunt wits of the burgermeesters, and should laugh most heartily at all their jokes; but this last was a duty as rarely called in action in those days as it is at present, and was shortly remitted, in consequence of the tragical death of a fat little schepen—who actually died of suffocation, in an unsuccessful effort to force a laugh at one of the burgermeester Van Zandt's best jokes.

In return for these humble services, they were permitted to say *yes* and no at the council board, and to have that enviable privilege, the run of the public kitchen—being graciously permitted to eat, and drink, and smoke, at all those snug junketings and public gormandizings, for which the ancient magistrates were equally famous with their modern successors. The post of schepen, therefore, like that of assistant alderman, was eagerly coveted by all your burghers of a certain description, who have a huge relish for good feeding, and an humble ambition to be great men in a small way—who thirst after a little brief authority, that shall render them the terror of the alms-house and the bridewell—that shall enable them to lord it over obsequious poverty, vagrant vice, outcast prostitution, and hunger-driven dishonesty—that shall give to their beck a hound-like pack of catch-poles and bum-bailiffs—tenfold greater rogues than the culprits they hunt down!—My readers will excuse this sudden warmth, which I confess is unbecoming of a grave historian—but I have a mortal antipathy to catch-poles, bum-bailiffs, and little great men.

The ancient magistrates of this city corresponded with those of the present time no less in form, magnitude, and intellect, than in prerogative and privilege. The burgomasters, like our aldermen, were generally chosen by weight—and not only the weight of the body, but likewise the weight of the head. It is a maxim practically observed in all honest, plain-thinking regular cities, that an alderman should be fat—and the wisdom of this can be proved to a certainty. That the body is in some measure an image of the mind, or rather that the mind is moulded to the body, like melted lead to the clay in which it is cast, has been insisted on by many philosophers, who have made human nature their peculiar study—for as a learned gentleman of our own city observes, "there is a constant relation between the moral character of all intelligent creatures, and their physical constitution—between their habits and the structure of their bodies." Thus we see, that a lean, spare, diminutive body, is generally accompanied by a petulant, restless, meddling mind—either the mind wears down the body, by its continual motion; or else the body, not affording the mind sufficient house-room, keeps it continually in a state of fretfulness, tossing and worrying about from the uneasiness of its situation. Whereas your round, sleek, fat, un-wieldly periphery is ever attended by a mind like itself, tranquil, torpid, and at ease; and we may always observe, that your well-fed robustious burghers are in general very tenacious of their ease and comfort; being great enemies to noise, discord, and disturbance—and surely none are more likely to study the public tranquillity than those who are so careful of their own. Who ever hears of fat men heading a riot, or herding together in turbulent mobs?—no—no—it is your lean, hungry men, who are continually worrying society, and setting the whole community by the ears.

The divine Plato, whose doctrines are not sufficiently attended to by philosophers of the present age, allows to every man three souls—one immortal and rational, seated in the brain, that it may overlook and regulate the body—a second consisting of the surly and irascible passions, which, like belligerent powers, lie encamped around the heart—a third mortal and sensual, destitute of reason, gross and brutal in its propensities, and enchained in the belly, that it may not disturb the divine soul, by its ravenous howlings. Now, according to this excellent theory, what can be more clear, than that your fat alderman is most likely to have the most regular and well-conditioned mind. His head is like a huge, spherical chamber, containing a prodigious mass of soft brains, whereon the rational soul lies softly and snugly couched, as on a feather bed; and the eyes, which are the windows of the bed-chamber, are usually half closed, that its slumberings may not be disturbed by external objects. A mind thus comfortably lodged, and protected from disturbance, is manifestly most likely to perform its functions with regularity and ease. By dint of good feeding, moreover, the mortal and malignant soul, which is confined in the belly, and which, by its raging and roaring, puts the irritable soul in the neighbourhood of the heart in an intolerable passion, and thus renders men crusty and quarrelsome when hungry, is completely pacified silenced, and put to rest—whereupon a host of honest good fellow qualities and kind-hearted affections, which had lain perdue, slyly peeping out of the loopholes of the heart, finding this Cerberus asleep, do pluck up their spirits, turn out one and all in their holyday suits, and gambol up and down the diaphragm—disposing their possessor to laughter, good humour, and a thousand friendly offices towards his fellow-mortals.

As a board of magistrates, formed on this model, think but very little, they are the less likely to differ and wrangle about favourite opinions—and as they generally transact business upon a hearty dinner, they are naturally disposed to be lenient and indulgent in the administration of their duties. Charlemagne was conscious of this, and therefore (a pitiful measure, for which I can never forgive him) ordered in his cartularies, that no judge should hold a court of justice, except in the morning, on an empty stomach— a rule, which, I warrant, bore hard upon all the poor culprits in his kingdom. The more enlightened and humane generation of the present day have taken an opposite course, and have so managed, that the aldermen are the best-fed men in the community; feasting lustily on the fat things of the land, and gorging so heartily oysters and turtles, that in process of time they acquire the activity of the one, and the form, the waddle, and the green fat of the other. The consequence is, as I have just said, these luxurious feastings do produce such a dulcet equanimity and repose of the soul, rational and irrational, that their transactions are proverbial for unvarying monotony—and the profound laws which they enact in their dozing moments, amid the labours of digestion, are quietly suffered to remain as dead letters, and never enforced, when awake. In a word, your fair round-bellied burgomaster, like a full-fed mastiff, dozes quietly at the house-door, always at home, and always at hand to watch over its safety—but as to electing a lean, meddling candidate to the office, as has now and then been done, I would as lief put a grayhound to watch the house, or a race-horse to drag an ox wagon.

The burgomasters then, as I have already mention ed, were wisely chosen by weight, and the schephens, or assistant aldermen, were appointed to attend upon them, and help them eat; but the latter, in the course of time, when they had been fed and fattened into sufficient bulk of body and drowsiness of brain, became very eligible candidates for the burgomasters' chairs, having fairly eaten themselves into office, as a mouse eats his way into a comfortable lodgement in a goodly, blue-nosed, skimmed-milk, New-England cheese.

Nothing could equal the profound deliberations that took place between the renowned Wouter, and these his worthy compeers, unless it be the sage divans of some of our modern corporations. They would sit for hours smoking and dozing over public affairs, without speaking a word to interrupt that perfect stillness, so necessary to deep reflection. Under the sober sway of Wouter Van Twiller, and these his worthy coadjutors, the infant settlement waxed vigorous apace, gradually emerging from the swamps and forests, and exhibiting that mingled appearance of town and country, customary in new cities, and which at this day may be witnessed in the city of Washington—that immense metropolis, which makes so glorious an appearance on paper.

It was a pleasing sight, in those times, to behold the honest burgher, like a patriarch of yore, seated on the bench at the door of his whitewashed house, under the shade of some gigantic sycamore or over-hanging willow. Here would he smoke his pipe of a sultry afternoon, enjoying the soft southern breeze, and listening with silent gratulation to the clucking of his hens, the cackling of his geese, and the sonorous grunting of his swine; that combination of farm-yard melody, which may truly be said to have a silver sound, inasmuch as it conveys a certain assurance of profitable marketing.

The modern spectator, who wanders through the streets of this populous city, can scarcely form an idea of the different appearance they presented in the primitive days of the Doubter. The busy hum of multitudes, the shouts of revelry, the rumbling equipages of fashion, the rattling of accursed carts, and all the spirit-grieving sounds of brawling commerce, were unknown in the settlement of New-Amsterdam. The grass grew quietly in the highways—the bleating sheep and frolicsome calves sported about the verdant ridge, where now the Broadway loungers take their morning stroll—the cunning fox or ravenous wolf skulked in the woods, where now are to be seen the dens of Gomez and his righteous fraternity of money-brokers—and flocks of vociferous geese cackled about the fields, where now the great Tammany wigwam and the patriotic tavern of Mart-ling echo with the wranglings of the mob.

In these good times did a true and enviable equality

of rank and property prevail, equally removed from the arrogance of wealth, and the servility and heart-burnings of repining poverty—and what in my mind is still more conducive to tranquillity and harmony among friends, a happy equality of intellect was likewise to be seen. The minds of the good burghers of New-Amsterdam seemed all to have been cast in one mould, and to be those honest, blunt minds, which, like certain manufactures, are made by the gross, and considered as exceedingly good for common use.

Thus it happens that your true dull minds are generally preferred for public employ, and especially promoted to city honours; your keen intellects, like razors, being considered too sharp for common service. I know that it is common to rail at the unequal distribution of riches, as the great source of jealousies, broils, and heart-breakings; whereas, for my part, I verily believe it is the sad inequality of intellect that prevails, that embroils communities more than any thing else; and I have remarked that your knowing people, who are so much wiser than any body else, are eternally keeping society in a ferment. Happily for New-Amsterdam, nothing of the kind was known within its walls—the very words of learning, education, taste, and talents, were unheard of—a bright genius was an animal unknown, and a blue-stocking lady would have been regarded with as much wonder as a horned frog or a fiery dragon. No man in fact seemed to know more than his neighbour, nor any man to know more than an honest man ought to know, who has nobody's business to mind but his own; the parson and the council clerk were the only men that could read in the community, and the sage Van Twiller always signed his name with a cross.

Thrice happy and ever to be envied little burgh! existing in all the security of harmless insignificance —unnoticed and unenvied by the world, without ambition, without vain glory, without riches, without learning, and all their train of carking cares—and as of yore, in the better days of man, the deities were wont to visit him on earth and bless his rural habitations, so we are told, in the sylvan days of New-Amsterdam, the good St. Nicholas would often make his appearance in his beloved city, of a holyday afternoon, riding jollily among the tree-tops, or over the roofs of the houses, now and then drawing forth magnificent presents from his breeches pockets, and dropping them down the chimneys of his favourites. Whereas in these degenerate days of iron and brass, he never shows us the light of his countenance, nor ever visits us, save one night in the year; when he rattles down the chimneys of the descendants of the patriarchs, confining his presents merely to the children, in token of the degeneracy of the parents.

Such are the comfortable and thriving effects of a fat government. The province of the New-Netherlands, destitute of wealth, possessed a sweet tranquillity that wealth could never purchase. There were neither public commotions, nor private quarrels; neither parties, nor sects, nor schisms; neither persecutions, nor trials, nor punishments; nor were there counsellors, attorneys, catch-poles, or hangmen.

Every man attended to what little business he was lucky enough to have, or neglected it if he pleased, without asking the opinion of his neighbour. In those days, nobody meddled with concerns above his comprehension, nor thrust his nose into other people' affairs; nor neglected to correct his own conduct and reform his own character, in his zeal to pull to pieces the characters of others—but in a word, every respectable citizen eat when he was not hungry, drank when he was not thirsty, and went regularly to bed when the sun set, and the fowls went to roost, whether he were sleepy or not; all which tended so remarkably to the population of the settlement, that I am told every dutiful wife throughout New-Amsterdam made a point of enriching her husband with at least one child a year, and very often a brace—this superabundance of good things clearly constituting the true luxury of life, according to the favourite Dutch maxim, that " more than enough constitutes a feast." Every thing, therefore, went on exactly as it should do; and in the usual words employed by historians to express the welfare of a country, " the profoundest *tranquillity* and *repose* reigned throughout the province."

CHAPTER III.

How the town of New-Amsterdam arose out of mud,
and came to be marvellously polished and polite—
together with a picture of the manners of our
great-great-grandfathers.

MANIFOLD are the tastes and dispositions of the enlightened literati, who turn over the pages of history. Some there be, whose hearts are brimful of the yest of courage, and whose bosoms do work, and swell, and foam, with untried valour, like a barrel of new cider, or a train-band captain, fresh from under the hands of his tailor. This doughty class of readers can be satisfied with nothing but bloody battles, and horrible encounters; they must be continually storming forts, sacking cities, springing mines, marching up to the muzzles of cannon, charging bayonet through every page, and revelling in gunpowder and carnage. Others, who are of a less martial, but equally ardent imagination, and who, withal, are a little given to the marvellous, will dwell with wonderous satisfaction on descriptions of prodigies, unheard-of events, hairbreadth escapes, hardy adventures, and all those astonishing narrations that just amble along the boundary line of possibility. A third class, who, not to speak slightly of them, are of a lighter turn, and skim over the records of past times, as they do over the edifying pages of a novel, merely for relaxation and innocent amusement, do singularly delight in treasons, executions, Sabine rapes, Tarquin outrages, conflagrations, murders, and all the other catalogue of hideous crimes, that, like cayenne in cookery, do give a pungency and flavour to the dull detail of history—while a fourth class, of more philosophic habits, do diligently pore over the musty chronicles of time, to investigate the operations of the human kind, and watch the gradual changes in men and manners, effected by the progress of knowledge, the vicissitudes of events, or the influence of situation.

If the three first classes find but little wherewithal to solace themselves in the tranquil reign of Wouter Van Twiller, I entreat them to exert their patience for a while, and bear with the tedious picture of happiness, prosperity, and peace, which my duty as a faithful historian obliges me to draw; and I promise them that as soon as I can possibly light upon any thing horrible, uncommon, or impossible, it shall go hard but I will make it afford them entertainment. This being premised, I turn with great complacency to the fourth class of my readers, who are men, or, if possible, women, after my own heart; grave, philosophical, and investigating; fond of analyzing characters, of taking a start from first causes, and so hunting a nation down, through all the mazes of innovation and improvement. Such will naturally be anxious to witness the first developement of the newly-hatched colony, and the primitive manners and customs prevalent among its inhabitants, during the halcyon reign of Van Twiller, or the Doubter.

I will not grieve their patience, however, by de-

scribing minutely the increase and improvement of
New-Amsterdam. Their own imaginations will doubtless present to them the good burghers, like so many
pains-taking and persevering beavers, slowly and
surely pursuing their labours—they will behold the
prosperous tranformation from the rude log hut to
the stately Dutch mansion, with brick front, glazed
windows, and tiled roof—from the tangled thicket to
the luxuriant cabbage garden; and from the skulking
Indian to the ponderous burgomaster. In a word,
they will picture to themselves the steady, silent, and
undeviating march to prosperity, incident to a city
destitute of pride or ambition, cherished by a fat
government, and whose citizens do nothing in a
hurry.

The sage council, as has been mentioned in a preceding chapter, not being able to determine upon any
plan for the building of their city—the cows, in a
laudable fit of patriotism, took it under their peculiar charge, and as they went to and from pasture,
established paths through the bushes, on each side
of which the good folks built their houses; which is
one cause of the rambling and picturesque turns and
labyrinths, which distinguish certain streets of New-
York at this very day.

The houses of the higher class were generally constructed of wood, excepting the gable end, which was
of small black and yellow Dutch bricks, and always
faced on the street, as our ancestors, like their descendants, were very much given to outward show,
and were noted for putting the best leg foremost.

The house was always furnished with abundance of large doors and small windows on every floor; the date of its erection was curiously designated by iron figures on the front; and on the top of the roof was perched a fierce little weathercock, to let the family into the important secret, which way the wind blew These, like the weathercocks on the tops of our steeples, pointed so many different ways, that every man could have a wind to his mind;—the most staunch and loyal citizens, however, always went according to the weathercock on the top of the governor's house, which was certainly the most correct, as he had a trusty servant employed every morning to climb up and set it to the right quarter.

In those good days of simplicity and sunshine, a passion for cleanliness was the leading principle in domestic economy, and the universal test of an able housewife—a character which formed the utmost ambition of our unenlightened grandmothers. The front door was never opened except on marriages, funerals, new-years' days, the festival of St. Nicholas, or some such great occasion. It was ornamented with a gorgeous brass knocker, curiously wrought, sometimes in the device of a dog, and sometimes of a lion's head, and was daily burnished with such religious zeal, that it was oft-times worn out by the very precautions taken for its preservation. The whole house was constantly in a state of inundation, under the discipline of mops and brooms and scrubbing-brushes; and the good housewives of those days were a kind of amphibious animal, delighting exceed-

ingly to be dabbling in water—insomuch that a historian of the day gravely tells us, that many of his
townswomen grew to have webbed fingers like unto
a duck ; and some of them, he had little doubt, could
the matter be examined into, would be found to have
the tails of mermaids—but this I look upon to be a
mere sport of fancy, or what is worse, a wilful mis
representation.

The grand parlour was the sanctum sanctorum,
where the passion for cleaning was indulged without
control. In this sacred apartment no one was permitted to enter, excepting the mistress and her confidential maid, who visited it once a week, for the
purpose of giving it a thorough cleaning, and putting
things to rights—always taking the precaution of
leaving their shoes at the door, and entering devoutly
on their stocking-feet. After scrubbing the floor,
sprinkling it with fine white sand, which was curiously stroked into angles, and curves, and rhom-
boids, with a broom—after washing the windows,
rubbing and polishing the furniture, and putting a
new bunch of evergreens in the fire-place—the
window-shutters were again closed to keep out the
flies, and the room carefully locked up until the revolution of time brought round the weekly cleaning day.

As to the family, they always entered in at the
gate, and most generally lived in the kitchen. To
have seen a numerous household assembled around
the fire, one would have imagined that he was transported back to those happy days of primeval simplicity, which float before our imaginations like golden

VOL. I.   P

visions. The fire-places were of a truly patriarchal magnitude, where the whole family, old and young, master and servant, black and white, nay, even the very cat and dog, enjoyed a community of privilege, and had each a right to a corner. Here the old burgher would sit in perfect silence, puffing his pipe looking in the fire with half-shut eyes, and thinking of nothing for hours together; the goede vrouw on the opposite side would employ herself diligently in spinning yarn, or knitting stockings. The young folks would crowd around the hearth, listening with breathless attention to some old crone of a negro, who was the oracle of the family, and who, perched like a raven in a corner of the chimney, would croak forth for a long winter afternoon a string of incredible stories about New-England witches—grisly ghosts, horses without heads—and hairbreadth escapes and bloody encounters among the Indians.

In those happy days a well-regulated family always rose with the dawn, dined at eleven, and went to bed at sun-down. Dinner was invariably a private meal, and the fat old burghers showed incontestible symptoms of disapprobation and uneasiness at being surprised by a visit from a neighbour on such occasions But though our worthy ancestors were thus singu larly averse to giving dinners, yet they kept up the social bands of intimacy by occasional banquetings, called tea-parties. ▲

These fashionable parties were generally confined to the higher classes, or noblesse, that is to say, such as kept their own cows, and drove their own wagons.

The company commonly assembled at three o'clock, and went away about six, unless it was in winter time, when the fashionable hours were a little earlier, that the ladies might get home before dark. The tea-table was crowned with a huge earthen dish, well stored with slices of fat pork, fried brown, cut up into morsels, and swimming in gravy. The company being seated around the genial board, and each furnished with a fork, evinced their dexterity in lanching at the fattest pieces in this mighty dish—in much the same manner as sailors harpoon porpoises at sea, or our Indians spear salmon in the lakes. Sometimes the table was graced with immense apple pies, or saucers full of preserved peaches and pears; but it was always sure to boast an enormous dish of balls of sweetened dough, fried in hog's fat, and called doughnuts, or olykoeks—a delicious kind of cake, at present scarce known in this city, excepting in genuine Dutch families.

The tea was served out of a majestic delft teapot, ornamented with paintings of fat little Dutch shepherds and shepherdesses tending pigs—with boats sailing in the air, and houses built in the clouds, and sundry other ingenious Dutch fantasies. The beaux distinguished themselves by their adroitness in replenishing this pot from a huge copper tea-kettle, which would have made the pigmy macaronies of these degenerate days sweat merely to look at it. To sweeten the beverage, a lump of sugar was laid beside each cup—and the company alternately nibbled and sipped with great decorum, until an improvement was introduced by a shrewd and economic old lady, which was to suspend a large lump directly over the tea-table, by a string from the ceiling, so that it could be swung from mouth to mouth—an ingenious expedient which is still kept up by some families in Albany; but which prevails without exception in Communipaw, Bérgen, Flatbush, and all our uncontaminated Dutch villages.

At these primitive tea-parties the utmost propriety and dignity of deportment prevailed. No flirting nor coqueting—no gambling of old ladies, nor hoyden chattering and romping of young ones—no self-satisfied struttings of wealthy gentlemen, with their brains in their pockets—nor amusing conceits, and monkey divertisements, of smart young gentlemen with no brains at all. On the contrary, the young ladies seated themselves demurely in their rush-bottomed chairs, and knit their own woollen stockings; nor ever opened their lips, excepting to say, *yaw Mynher*, or *yah yah Vrouw*, to any question that was asked them; behaving, in all things, like decent, well-educated damsels. As to the gentlemen, each of them tranquilly smoked his pipe, and seemed lost in contemplation of the blue and white tiles with which the fire-places were decorated; wherein sundry passages of scripture were piously portrayed—Tobit and his dog figured to great advantage; Haman swung conspicuously on his gibbet; and Jonah appeared most manfully bouncing out of the whale, like Harlequin through a barrel of fire.

The parties broke up without noise and without

confusion. They were carried home by their own carriages, that is to say, by the vehicles Nature had provided them, excepting such of the wealthy as could afford to keep a wagon. The gentlemen gallantly attended their fair ones to their respective abodes, and took leave of them with a hearty smack at the door; which, as it was an established piece of etiquette, done in perfect simplicity and honesty of heart, occasioned no scandal at that time, nor should it at the present—if our great-grandfathers approved of the custom, it would argue a great want of reverence in their descendants to say a word against it.

CHAPTER IV.

Containing further particulars of the Golden Age, and what constituted a fine Lady and Gentleman in the days of Walter the Doubter.

In this dulcet period of my history, when the beauteous island of Manna-hata presented a scene, the very counterpart of those glowing pictures drawn of the golden reign of Saturn, there was, as I have before observed, a happy ignorance, an honest simplicity, prevalent among its inhabitants, which, were I even able to depict, would be but little understood by the degenerate age for which I am doomed to write. Even the female sex, those arch innovators upon the tranquillity, the honesty, and gray-beard customs of society, seemed for a while to conduct themselves with incredible sobriety and comeliness.

Their hair, untortured by the abominations of art, was scrupulously pomatumed back from their foreheads with a candle, and covered with a little cap of quilted calico, which fitted exactly to their heads. Their petticoats of linsey-woolsey were striped with a variety of gorgeous dyes—though I must confess these gallant garments were rather short, scarce reaching below the knee; but then they made up in the number, which generally equalled that of the gentlemen's small-clothes; and what is still more praiseworthy, they were all of their own manu-

facture—of which circumstance, as may well be supposed, they were not a little vain.

These were the honest days, in which every woman staid at home, read the Bible, and wore pockets
—ay, and that too of a goodly size, fashioned with
patchwork into many curious devices, and ostenta-
tiously worn on the outside. These, in fact, were
convenient receptacles, where all good housewives
carefully stored away such things as they wished to
have at hand; by which means they often came to
be incredibly crammed—and I remember there was
a story current when I was a boy, that the lady of
Wouter Van Twiller once had occasion to empty her
right pocket in search of a wooden ladle, and the
utensil was discovered lying among some rubbish in
one corner—but we must not give too much faith to
all these stories; the anecdotes of those remote periods being very subject to exaggeration.

Besides these notable pockets, they likewise wore
scissors and pincushions suspended from their girdles
by red ribands, or, among the more opulent and
showy classes, by brass, and even silver chains, in-
dubitable tokens of thrifty housewives and industrious
spinsters. I cannot say much in vindication of the
shortness of the petticoats; it doubtless was introduced for the purpose of giving the stockings a chance
to be seen, which were generally of blue worsted,
with magnificent red clocks—or perhaps to display
a well-turned ankle, and a neat, though serviceable,
foot, set off by a high-heeled leathern shoe, with a
large and splendid silver buckle. Thus we find that

the gentle sex in all ages have shown the same disposition to infringe a little upon the laws of decorum,
in order to betray a lurking beauty, or gratify an innocent love of finery.

From the sketch here given, it will be seen that
our good grandmothers differed considerably in their
ideas of a fine figure from their scantily-dressed descendants of the present day. A fine lady, in those
times, waddled under more clothes, even on a fair
summer's day, than would have clad the whole bevy
of a modern ball-room. Nor were they the less admired by the gentlemen in consequence thereof. On
the contrary, the greatness of a lover's passion seemed to increase in proportion to the magnitude of its
object—and a voluminous damsel, arrayed in a dozen
of petticoats, was declared by a Low Dutch sonnet-
teer of the province to be radiant as a sunflower,
and luxuriant as a full-blown cabbage. Certain it is,
that in those days, the heart of a lover could not contain more than one lady at a time ; whereas the heart
of a modern gallant has often room enough to accommodate half-a-dozen. The reason of which I conclude to be, that either the hearts of the gentlemen
have grown larger, or the persons of the ladies small-
er—this, however, is a question for physiologists to
determine.

But there was a secret charm in these petticoats,
which no doubt entered into the consideration of the
prudent gallants. The wardrobe of a lady was in
those days her only fortune ; and she who had a good
stock of petticoats and stockings, was as absolutely

an heiress as is a Kamtschatka damsel with a store of bear-skins, or a Lapland belle with a plenty of reindeer. The ladies, therefore, were very anxious to display these powerful attractions to the greatest advantage; and the best rooms in the house, instead of being adorned with caricatures of dame Nature, in water colours and needle-work, were always hung round with abundance of homespun garments, the manufacture and the property of the females—a piece of laudable ostentation that still prevails among the heiresses of our Dutch villages.

The gentlemen, in fact, who figured in the circles of the gay world in these ancient times, corresponded, in most particulars, with the beauteous damsels whose smiles they were ambitious to deserve. True it is, their merits would make but a very inconsiderable impression upon the heart of a modern fair; they neither drove their curricles nor sported their tandems, for as yet those gaudy vehicles were not even dreamt of—neither did they distinguish themselves by their brilliancy at the table and their consequent rencontres with watchmen, for our forefathers were of too pacific a disposition to need those guardians of the night, every soul throughout the town being sound asleep before nine o'clock. Neither did they establish their claims to gentility at the expense of their tailors—for as yet those offenders against the pockets of society, and the tranquillity of all aspiring young gentlemen, were unknown in New-Amsterdam; every good housewife made the clothes of her husband and family, and even the goede vrouw of Van Twiller himself thought it no disparagement to cut out her husband's linsey-woolsey galligaskins.

Not but what there were some two or three youngsters, who manifested the first dawnings of what is called fire and spirit—who held all labour in contempt; skulked about docks and market-places; loitered in the sunshine; squandered what little money they could procure at hustle-cap and chuck-farthing, swore, boxed, fought cocks, and raced their neighbour's horses—in short, who promised to be the wonder, the talk, and abomination of the town, had not their stylish career been unfortunately cut short by an affair of honour with a whipping-post.

Far other, however, was the truly fashionable gentleman of those days—his dress, which served for both morning and evening, street and drawing-room, was a linsey-woolsey coat, made, perhaps, by the fair hands of the mistress of his affections, and gallantly bedecked with abundance of large brass buttons— half a score of breeches heightened the proportions of his figure—his shoes were decorated by enormous copper buckles—a low-crowned broad-brimmed hat overshadowed his burly visage, and his hair dangled down his back in a prodigious queue of eel-skin.

Thus equipped, he would manfully sally forth with pipe in mouth, to besiege some fair damsel's obdurate heart—not such a pipe, good reader, as that which Acis did sweetly tune in praise of his Galatea, but one of true delft manufacture, and furnished with a charge of fragrant tobacco. With this would he resolutely set himself down before the fortress, and rarely failed, in the process of time, to smoke the fair enemy into a surrender, upon honourable terms.

Such was the happy reign of Wouter Van Twiller, celebrated in many a long-forgotten song as the real golden age, the rest being nothing but counterfeit copper-washed coin. In that delightful period, a sweet and holy calm reigned over the whole province. The burgomaster smoked his pipe in peace—the substantial solace of his domestic cares, after her daily toils were done, sat soberly at the door, with her arms crossed over her apron of snowy white, without being insulted by ribald street-walkers, or vagabond boys—those unlucky urchins, who do so infest our streets, displaying under the roses of youth the thorns and briars of iniquity. Then it was that the lover with ten breeches, and the damsel with petticoats of half a score, indulged in all the innocent endearments of virtuous love, without fear and without reproach; for what had that virtue to fear, which was defended by a shield of good linsey-woolseys, equal at least to the seven bull-hides of the invincible Ajax?

Ah! blissful, and never to be forgotten age! when every thing was better than it has ever been since, or ever will be again—when Buttermilk Channel was quite dry at low water—when the shad in the Hudson were all salmon, and when the moon shone with a pure and resplendent whiteness, instead of that melancholy yellow light which is the consequence of her sickening at the abominations she every night witnesses in this degenerate city!

Happy would it have been for New-Amsterdam, could it always have existed in this state of blissful ignorance and lowly simplicity—but, alas! the days of childhood are too sweet to last! Cities, like men, grow out of them in time, and are doomed alike to grow into the bustle, the cares, and miseries of the world. Let no man congratulate himself, when he beholds the child of his bosom or the city of his birth increasing in magnitude and importance—let the history of his own life teach him the dangers of the one, and this excellent little history of Manna-hata convince him of the calamities of the other.

CHAPTER V.

*In which the reader is beguiled into a delectable walk
which ends very differently from what it com
menced.*

IN the year of our Lord one thousand eight hun
dred and four, on a fine afternoon, in the glowing
month of September, I took my customary walk
upon the Battery, which is at once the pride and bul-
wark of this ancient and impregnable city of New-
York. The ground on which I trod was hallowed
by recollections of the past, and as I slowly wandered through the long alley of poplars, which, like so
many birch-brooms standing on end, diffused a
melancholy and lugubrious shade, my imagination
drew a contrast between the surrounding scenery,
and what it was in the classic days of our forefathers.
Where the government-house by name, but the custom-house by occupation, proudly reared its brick
walls and wooden pillars, there whilome stood the
low but substantial, red-tiled mansion of the renowned Wouter Van Twiller. Around it the mighty
bulwarks of Fort Amsterdam frowned defiance to
every absent foe; but, like many a whiskered warrior and gallant militia captain, confined their martial deeds to frowns alone. The mud breastworks
had long been levelled with the earth, and their site

VOL. I.   Q

converted into the green lawns and leafy alleys of the Battery; where the gay apprentice sported his Sunday coat, and the laborious mechanic, relieved from the dirt and drudgery of the week, poured his weekly tale of love into the half-averted ear of the sentimental chambermaid. The capacious bay still presented the same expansive sheet of water, studded with islands, sprinkled with fishing-boats, and bounded with shores of picturesque beauty. But the dark forests which once clothed these shores had been violated by the savage hand of cultivation; and their tangled mazes, and impenetrable thickets, had degenerated into teeming orchards and waving fields of grain. Even Governor's Island, once a smiling garden, appertaining to the sovereigns of the province, was now covered with fortifications, inclosing a tremendous blockhouse—so that this once peaceful island resembled a fierce little warrior in a big cocked hat, breathing gunpowder and defiance to the world!

For some time did I indulge in this pensive train of thought; contrasting, in sober sadness, the present day with the hallowed years behind the mountains; lamenting the melancholy progress of improvement, and praising the zeal with which our worthy burghers endeavour to preserve the wrecks of venerable customs, prejudices, and errors, from the overwhelming tide of modern innovation—when by degrees my deas took a different turn, and I insensibly awakened to an enjoyment of the beauties around me.

It was one of those rich autumnal days, which Heaven particularly bestows upon the beauteous island of Manna-hata and its vicinity—not a floating cloud obscured the azure firmament—the sun, rolling in glorious splendour through his ethereal course, seemed to expand his honest Dutch countenance into an unusual expression of benevolence, as he smiled his evening salutation upon a city, which he delights to visit with his most bounteous beams—the very winds seemed to hold in their breaths in mute attention, lest they should ruffle the tranquillity of the hour—and the waveless bosom of the bay presented a polished mirror, in which Nature beheld herself and smiled. The standard of our city, reserved, like a choice handkerchief, for days of gala, hung motionless on the flag-staff, which forms the handle to a gigantic churn; and even the tremulous leaves of the poplar and the aspen ceased to vibrate to the breath of heaven. Every thing seemed to acquiesce in the profound repose of nature. The formidable eighteen-pounders slept in the embrasures of the wooden batteries, seemingly gathering fresh strength to fight the battles of their country on the next fourth of July—the solitary drum on Governor's Island forgot to call the garrison to their *shovels*—the evening gun had not yet sounded its signal, for all the regular, well-meaning poultry throughout the country, to go to roost; and the fleet of canoes, at anchor between Gibbet Island and Communipaw, slumbered on their rakes, and suffered the innocent oysters to lie for a while unmolested in the soft mud of their native banks !—My own feelings sympathized with the contagious tranquillity, and I should infallibly have dozed upon one of those fragments of benches, which our benevolent magistrates have provided for the benefit of convalescent loungers, had not the extraordinary inconvenience of the couch set all repose at defiance.

In the midst of this slumber of the soul, my attention was attracted to a black speck, peering above the western horizon, just in the rear of Bergen steeple—gradually it augments, and overhangs the would-be cities of Jersey, Harsimus, and Hoboken, which, like three jockies, are starting on the course of existence, and jostling each other at the commencement of the race. Now it skirts the long shore of ancient Pavonia, spreading its wide shadows from the high settlements at Weehawk quite to the lazaretto and quarantine, erected by the sagacity of our police for the embarrassment of commerce—now it climbs the serene vault of heaven, cloud rolling‧ over cloud, shrouding the orb of day, darkening the vast expanse, and bearing thunder and hail and tempest in its bosom. The earth seems agitated at the confusion of the heavens—the late waveless mirror is lashed into furious waves, that roll in hollow murmurs to the shore—the oyster-boats that erst sported in the placid vicinity of Gibbet Island, now hurry affrighted to the land—the poplar writhes and twists and whistles in the blast--torrents of drenching rain and sounding hail deluge the Battery-walks -the gates are thronged by apprentices, servant-

maids, and little Frenchmen, with pocket handker-
chiefs over their hats, scampering from the storm—
the late beauteous prospect presents one scene of
anarchy and wild uproar, as though old Chaos had
resumed his reign, and was hurling back into one
vast turmoil the conflicting elements of nature.

Whether I fled from the fury of the storm, or remained boldly at my post, as our gallant train-band
captains, who march their soldiers through the rain
without flinching, are points which I leave to the
conjecture of the reader. It is possible he may be
a little perplexed also to know the reason why I introduced this tremendous tempest to disturb the
serenity of my work. On this latter point I will
gratuitously instruct his ignorance. The panorama
view of the Battery was given merely to gratify the
reader with a correct description of that celebrated
place, and the parts adjacent—secondly, the storm
was played off partly to give a little bustle and life
to this tranquil part of my work, and to keep my
drowsy readers from falling asleep—and partly to
serve as an overture to the tempestuous times that
are about to assail the pacific province of Nieuw-
Nederlandts—and that overhang the slumberous administration of the renowned Wouter Van Twiller.
It is thus the experienced playwright puts all the
fiddles, the French horns, the kettledrums, and trum-
pets of his orchestra in requisition, to usher in one
of those horrible and brimstone uproars called
melodrames—and it is thus he discharges his thunder, his lightning, his rosin, and saltpetre, preparatory

Q 2

to the rising of a ghost, or the murdering of a hero.
—We will now proceed with our history.

Whatever may be advanced by philosophers to
the contrary, I am of opinion, that, as to nations, the
old maxim, that "honesty is the best policy," is a
sheer and ruinous mistake. It might have answered
well enough in the honest times when it was made
but in these degenerate days, if a nation pretends to
rely merely upon the justice of its dealings, it will
fare something like an honest man among thieves,
who, unless he have something more than his honesty to depend upon, stands but a poor chance of
profiting by his company. Such at least was the case
with the guileless government of the New-Netherlands; which, like a worthy unsuspicious old burgher,
quietly settled itself down into the city of New-Amsterdam, as into a snug elbow-chair—and fell into a
comfortable nap—while in the mean-time, its cunning neighbours stepped in and picked its pockets.
Thus may we ascribe the commencement of all the
woes of this great province, and its magnificent metropolis, to the tranquil security, or to speak more
accurately, to the unfortunate honesty, of its government. But as I dislike to begin an important part
of my history towards the end of a chapter; and as
my readers, like myself, must doubtless be exceedingly fatigued with the long walk we have taken,
and the tempest we have sustained—I hold it meet
we shut up the book, smoke a pipe, and having thus
refreshed our spirits, take a fair start in the next
chapter.

CHAPTER VI.

*Faithfully describing the ingenious people of Connec-
ticut and thereabouts—Showing, moreover, the true
meaning of liberty of conscience, and a curious
device among these sturdy barbarians, to keep
up a harmony of intercourse, and promote population.*

THAT my readers may the more fully comprehend
the extent of the calamity, at this very moment impending over the honest, unsuspecting province of
Nieuw Nederlandts, and its dubious governor, it is
necessary that I should give some account of a horde
of strange barbarians, bordering upon the eastern
frontier.

Now so it came to pass, that many years previous
to the time of which we are treating, the sage cabinet of England had adopted a certain national creed,
a kind of public walk of faith, or rather a religious
turnpike, in which every loyal subject was directed
to travel to Zion—taking care to pay the *toll-gather-
ers* by the way.

Albeit, a certain shrewd race of men, being very
much given to indulge their own opinions, on all
manner of subjects, (a propensity exceedingly offensive to your free governments of Europe,) did most
presumptuously dare to think for themselves in matters of religion, exercising what they considered a

natural and unextinguishable right—the liberty of conscience.

As, however, they possessed that ingenuous habit of mind which always thinks aloud; which rides cock-a-hoop on the tongue, and is for ever galloping into other people's ears, it naturally followed that their liberty of conscience likewise implied *liberty of speech*, which being freely indulged, soon put the country in a hubbub, and aroused the pious indignation of the vigilant fathers of the church.

The usual methods were adopted to reclaim them, that in those days were considered so efficacious in bringing back stray sheep to the fold; that is to say, they were coaxed, they were admonished, they were menaced, they were buffeted—line upon line, precept upon precept, lash upon lash, here a little and there a great deal, were exhausted without mercy, and without success; until at length the worthy pastors of the church, wearied out by their unparalleled stubbornness, were driven, in the excess of their tender mercy, to adopt the scripture text, and literally "heaped live embers on their heads."

Nothing, however, could subdue that invincible spirit of independence which has ever distinguished this singular race of people, so that rather than submit to such horrible tyranny, they one and all embarked for the wilderness of America, where they might enjoy, unmolested, the inestimable luxury of talking. No sooner did they land on this loquacious soil, than, as if they had caught the disease from the climate, they all lifted up their voices at once, and for the space of one whole year did keep up such a joyful clamour, that we are told they frightened every bird and beast out of the neighbourhood, and so completely dumbfounded certain fish, which abound on their coast, that they have been called *dumb-fish* ever since.

From this simple circumstance, unimportant as it may seem, did first originate that renowned privilege so loudly boasted of throughout this country—which is so eloquently exercised in newspapers, pamphlets, ward meetings, pot-house committees and congressional deliberations—which established the right of talking without ideas and without information—of misrepresenting public affairs—of decrying public measures—of aspersing great characters, and destroying little ones ; in short, that grand palladium of our country, the *liberty of speech.*

The simple aborigines of the land for a while contemplated these strange folk in utter astonishment, but discovering that they wielded harmless though noisy weapons, and were a lively, ingenious, good-humoured race of men, they became very friendly and sociable, and gave them the name of *Yanokies,* which in the Mais-Tchusaeg (or Massachusett) language signifies *silent men*—a waggish appellation, since shortened into the familiar epithet of YANKEES, which they retain unto the present day.

True it is, and my fidelity as a historian will no allow me to pass it over in silence, that the zeal of these good people, to maintain their rights and privileges unimpaired, did for a while betray them into

errors, which it is easier to pardon than defend.
Having served a regular apprenticeship in the school
of persecution, it behoved them to show, that they
had become proficients in the art. They accordingly
employed their leisure hours in banishing, scourging,
or hanging, divers heretical Papists, Quakers, and
Anabaptists, for daring to abuse the *liberty of conscience;* which they now clearly proved to imply
nothing more than that every man should think as he
pleased in matters of religion—*provided* he thought
right ; for otherwise it would be giving a latitude to
damnable heresies. Now as they (the majority)
were perfectly convinced, that *they alone* thought
right, it consequently followed, that whoever thought
different from them thought wrong—and whoever
thought wrong, and obstinately persisted in not being
convinced and converted, was a flagrant violator of
the inestimable liberty of conscience, and a corrupt
and infectious member of the body politic, and deserved to be lopped off and cast into the fire.

Now I'll warrant there are hosts of my readers,
ready at once to lift up their hands and eyes, with
that virtuous indignation with which we always contemplate the faults and errors of our neighbours, an
to exclaim at these well-meaning but mistaken people,
for inflicting on others the injuries they had suffered
themselves—for indulging the preposterous idea of
convincing the mind by tormenting the body, and
establishing the doctrine of charity and forbearance
by intolerant persecution. But, in simple truth, what
are we doing at this very day, and in this very en-

lightened nation, but acting upon the very same principle, in our political controversies? Have we not, within but a few years, released ourselves from the shackles of a government which cruelly denied us the privilege of governing ourselves, and using in full latitude that invaluable member, the tongue? and are we not at this very moment striving our best to tyrannize over the opinions, tie up the tongues, or ruin the fortunes of one another? What are our great political societies, but mere political inquisitions—our pot-house committees, but little tribunals of denunciation—our newspapers, but mere whipping-posts and pillories, where unfortunate individuals are pelted with rotten eggs—and our council of appointment, but a grand *auto de fe*, where culprits are annually sacrificed for their political heresies?

Where then is the difference in principle between our measures and those you are so ready to condemn among the people I am treating of? There is none; the difference is merely circumstantial.—Thus we *denounce*, instead of banishing—we *libel*, instead of scourging—we *turn out of office*, instead of hanging—and where they burnt an offender in *propria persona*, we either tar and feather or *burn him in effigy*—this political persecution being, somehow or other, the grand palladium of our liberties, and an incontrovertible proof that this is *a free country!*

But notwithstanding the fervent zeal with which this holy war was prosecuted against the whole race of unbelievers, we do not find that the population of this new colony was in any wise hindered thereby;

on the contrary, they multiplied to a degree which would be incredible to any man unacquainted with the marvellous fecundity of this growing country.

This amazing increase may, indeed, be partly ascribed to a singular custom prevalent among them, commonly known by the name of *bundling*—a superstitious rite observed by the young people of both sexes, with which they usually terminated their festivities; and which was kept up with religious strictness by the more bigoted and vulgar part of the community. This ceremony was likewise, in those primitive times, considered as an indispensable preliminary to matrimony; their courtships commencing where ours usually finish—by which means they acquired that intimate acquaintance with each other's good qualities before marriage, which has been pronounced by philosophers the sure basis of a happy union. Thus early did this cunning and ingenious people display a shrewdness at making a bargain, which has ever since distinguished them—and a strict adherence to the good old vulgar maxim about "buying a pig in a poke."

To this sagacious custom, therefore, do I chiefly attribute the unparalleled increase of the Yanokie or Yankee tribe; for it is a certain fact, well authenticated by court records and parish registers, that wherever the practice of bundling prevailed, there was an amazing number of sturdy brats annually born unto the State, without the license of the law, or the benefit of clergy. Neither did the irregularity of their birth operate in the least to their disparagement. On the contrary, they grew up a long-sided, raw-boned, hardy race of whoreson whalers, wood-cutters, fishermen, and pedlers, and strapping corn-fed wenches; who by their united efforts tended marvellously towards populating those notable tracts of country called Nantucket, Piscataway, and Cape Cod.

VOL. I.   R

CHAPTER VII.

*How these singular barbarians turned out to be noto-
rious squatters—how they built air castles, and attempted to initiate the Nederlanders in the mystery
of bundling.*

IN the last chapter I have given a faithful and unprejudiced account of the origin of that singular race
of people, inhabiting the country eastward of the
Nieuw Nederlandts; but I have yet to mention certain peculiar habits which rendered them exceedingly
obnoxious to our ever-honoured Dutch ancestors.

The most prominent of these was a certain rambling propensity, with which, like the sons of Ishmael,
they seem to have been gifted by Heaven, and which
continually goads them on, to shift their residence
from place to place, so that a Yankee farmer is in a
constant state of migration; *tarrying* occasionally
here and there; clearing lands for other people to
enjoy, building houses for others to inhabit, and in a
manner may be considered the wandering Arab of
America.

His first thought, on coming to the years of man-
hood, is to *settle* himself in the world—which means
nothing more nor less than to begin his rambles. To
this end he takes unto himself for a wife some buxom
country heiress, passing rich in red ribands, glass
beads, and mock tortoise-shell combs, with a white

gown and morocco shoes for Sunday, and deeply
skilled in the mystery of making apple sweetmeats,
long sauce, and pumpkin pie.

Having thus provided himself, like a pedler, with
a heavy knapsack, wherewith to regale his shoulders
through the journey of life, he literally sets out on
the peregrination. His whole family, household furniture, and farming utensils, are hoisted into a covered cart; his own and his wife's wardrobe packed
up in a firkin—which done, he shoulders his axe,
takes staff in hand, whistles " yankee doodle," and
trudges off to the woods, as confident of the protection of Providence, and relying as cheerfully upon his
own resources, as did ever a patriarch of yore, when
he journeyed into a strange country of the Gen-
tiles. Having buried himself in the wilderness, he
builds himself a log hut, clears away a corn-field and
potatoe-patch, and Providence smiling upon his labours, is soon surrounded by a snug farm and some
half a score of flaxen-headed urchins, who, by their
size, seem to have sprung all at once out of the
earth, like a crop of toad-stools.

But it is not the nature of this most indefatigable
of speculators to rest contented with any state of
sublunary enjoyment—*improvement* is his darling
passion, and having thus improved his lands, the next
care is to provide a mansion worthy the residence of
a landholder. A huge palace of pine boards immediately springs up in the midst of the wilderness,
large enough for a parish church, and furnished with

windows of all dimensions, but so rickety and flimsy withal, that every blast gives it a fit of the ague.

By the time the outside of this mighty air castle is completed, either the funds or the zeal of our adventurer are exhausted, so that he barely manages to half finish one room within, where the whole family burrow together—while the rest of the house is devoted to the curing of pumpkins, or storing of carrots and potatoes, and is decorated with fanciful festoons of dried apples and peaches. The outside remaining unpainted, grows venerably black with time; the family wardrobe is laid under contribution for old hats, petticoats, and breeches, to stuff into the broken windows, while the four winds of heaven keep up a whistling and howling about this aerial palace, and play as many unruly gambols, as they did of yore in the cave of old Æolus.

The humble log hut, which whilome nestled this *improving* family snugly within its narrow but comfortable walls, stands hard by, in ignominious contrast, degraded into a cow-house or pig-sty; and the whole scene reminds one forcibly of a fable, which I am surprised has never been recorded, of an aspiring snail, who abandoned his humble habitation, which he had long filled with great respectability, to crawl into the empty shell of a lobster—where he would no doubt have resided with great style and splendour, the envy and hate of all the pains-taking snails in his neighbourhood, had he not accidentally perished with cold, in one corner of his stupendous mansion.

Being thus completely settled, and, to use his own words, " to rights," one would imagine that he would begin to enjoy the comforts of his situation, to read newspapers, talk politics, neglect his own business, and attend to the affairs of the nation, like a useful and patriotic citizen; but now it is that his wayward disposition begins again to operate. He soon grows tired of a spot where there is no longer any room for improvement—sells his farm, air castle, petticoat windows and all, reloads his cart, shoulders his axe, puts himself at the head of his family, and wanders away in search of new lands—again to fell trees—again to clear corn-fields—again to build a shingle palace, and again to sell off and wander.

Such were the people of Connecticut, who bordered upon the eastern frontier of Nieuw Nederlandts; and my readers may easily imagine what obnoxious neighbours this light-hearted but restless tribe must have been to our tranquil progenitors. If they cannot, I would ask them, if they have ever known one of our regular, well-organized Dutch families, whom it hath pleased Heaven to afflict with the neighbourhood of a French boarding-house? The honest old burgher cannot take his afternoon's pipe on the bench before his door, but he is persecuted with the scraping of fiddles, the chattering of women, and the squalling of children—he cannot sleep at night for the horrible melodies of some amateur, who chooses to serenade the moon, and display his terrible proficiency in *execution*, on the clarionet, the hautboy, or some other soft-toned instrument—nor

R 2

can he leave the street door open, but his house is defiled by the unsavoury visits of a troop of pug dogs, who even sometimes carry their loathsome ravages into the sanctum sanctorum, the parlour !

If my readers have ever witnessed the sufferings of such a family, so situated, they may form some idea how our worthy ancestors were distressed by their mercurial neighbours of Connecticut.

Gangs of these marauders, we are told, penetrated into the New-Netherland settlements, and threw whole villages into consternation by their unparalleled volubility, and their intolerable inquisitiveness—two evil habits hitherto unknown in those parts, or only known to be abhorred; for our ancestors were noted as being men of truly Spartan taciturnity, and who neither knew nor cared aught about any body's concerns but their own. Many enormities were committed on the highways, where several unoffending burghers were brought to a stand, and tortured with questions and guesses, which outrages occasioned as much vexation and heartburning as does the modern right of search on the high seas.

Great jealousy did they likewise stir up, by their intermeddling and successes among the divine sex; for being a race of brisk, likely, pleasant-tongued varlets, they soon seduced the light affections of the simple damsels from their ponderous Dutch gallants. Among other hideous customs, they attempted to introduce among them that of *bundling*, which the Dutch lasses of the Nederlandts, with that eager passion for novelty and foreign fashions natural to their sex, seemed very well inclined to follow, but that their mothers, being more experienced in the world, and better acquainted with men and things, strenuously discountenanced all such outlandish innovations.

But what chiefly operated to embroil our ancestors with these strange folk, was an unwarrantable liberty which they occasionally took of entering in hordes into the territories of the New-Netherlands, and settling themselves down, without leave or license, to *improve* the land, in the manner I have before noticed. This unceremonious mode of taking possession of *new land* was technically termed *squatting*, and hence is derived the appellation of *squatters*; a name odious in the ears of all great landholders, and which is given to those enterprising worthies who seize upon land first, and take their chance to make good their title to it afterwards.

All these grievances, and many others which were constantly accumulating, tended to form that dark and portentous cloud, which, as I observed in a former chapter, was slowly gathering over the tranquil province of New-Netherlands. The pacific cabinet of Van Twiller, however, as will be perceived in the sequel, bore them all with a magnanimity that redounds to their immortal credit—becoming by passive endurance inured to this increasing mass of wrongs; like that mighty man of old, who by dint of carrying about a calf from the time it was born, continued to carry it without difficulty when it had grown to be an ox.

CHAPTER VIII.

How the Fort Goed Hoop was fearfully beleaguered
—how the renowned Wouter fell into a profoun
doubt, and how he finally evaporated.

By this time, my readers must fully perceive what
an arduous task I have undertaken—collecting and
collating, with painful minuteness, the chronicles of
past times, whose events almost defy the powers of
research—exploring a little kind of Herculaneum of
history, which had lain nearly for ages buried under
the rubbish of years, and almost totally forgotten—
raking up the limbs and fragments of disjointed facts,
and endeavouring to put them scrupulously together,
so as to restore them to their original form and connexion—now lugging forth the character of an almost forgotten hero, like a mutilated statue—now
deciphering a half-defaced inscription, and now
lighting upon a mouldering manuscript, which, after
painful study, scarce repays the trouble of perusal.

In such case, how much has the reader to depend
upon the honour and probity of his author, lest, like
a cunning antiquarian, he either impose upon him
some spurious fabrication of his own, for a precious
relic from antiquity—or else dress up the dismem-
bered fragment with such false trappings, that it is
scarcely possible to distinguish the truth from the
fiction with which it is enveloped! This is a grievance which I have more than once had to lament,

ın the course of my wearisome researches among the
works of my fellow-historians, who have strangely
disguised and distorted the facts respecting this country; and particularly respecting the great province
of New-Netherlands; as will be perceived by any
who will take the trouble to compare their romantic
effusions, tricked out in the meretricious gauds of
fable, with this authentic history.

I have had more vexations of this kind to encounter, in those parts of my history which treat of the
transactions on the eastern border, than in any other,
in consequence of the troops of historians who have
infested those quarters, and have shown the honest
people of Nieuw-Nederlandts no mercy in their
works. Among the rest, Mr. Benjamin Trumbull
arrogantly declares, that "the Dutch were always
mere intruders." Now to this I shall make no other
reply than to proceed in the steady narration of my
history, which will contain not only proofs that the
Dutch had clear title and possession in the fair valleys
of the Connecticut, and that they were wrongfully
dispossessed thereof—but likewise, that they have
been scandalously maltreated ever since, by the mis-
representations of the crafty historians of New-England. And in this I shall be guided by a spirit of
truth and impartiality, and a regard to immortal
fame—for I would not wittingly dishonour my work
by a single falsehood, misrepresentation, or preju
dice, though it should gain our forefathers the whole
country of New-England.

It was at an early period of the province, and pre-

vious to the arrival of the renowned Wouter, that
the cabinet of Nieuw-Nederlandts purchased the
lands about the Connecticut, and established, for
their superintendence and protection, a fortified post
on the banks of the river, which was called Fort
Goed Hoop, and was situated hard by the present
fair city of Hartford. The command of this important post, together with the rank, title, and appointment of commissary, were given in charge to
the gallant Jacobus Van Curlet, or, as some historians will have it, Van Curlis—a most doughty sol-
dier, of that stomachful class of which we have such
numbers on parade days—who are famous for eating
all they kill. He was of a very soldierlike appearance, and would have been an exceeding tall man
had his legs been in proportion to his body; but the
latter being long, and the former uncommonly short,
it gave him the uncouth appearance of a tall man's
body mounted upon a little man's legs. He made
up for this turnspit construction of body by throwing
his legs to such an extent when he marched, that you
would have sworn he had on the identical seven-
league boots of the far-famed Jack the giant-killer;
and so astonishingly high did he tread, on any grea
military occasion, that his soldiers were oft times
alarmed, lest he should trample himself under foot.

But notwithstanding the erection of this fort, and
the appointment of this ugly little man of war as a
commander, the intrepid Yankees continued those
daring interlopings, which I have hinted at in my last
chapter; and taking advantage of the character

which the cabinet of Wouter Van Twiller soon acquired, for profound and phlegmatic tranquillity—did
audaciously invade the territories of the Nieuw-
Nederlandts, and *squat* themselves down within the
very jurisdiction of Fort Goed Hoop.

On beholding this outrage, the long-bodied Van
Curlet proceeded as became a prompt and valiant
officer. He immediately protested against these unwarrantable encroachments, in Low Dutch, by way
of inspiring more terror, and forthwith despatched a
copy of the protest to the governor at New-Amsterdam, together with a long and bitter account of the
aggressions of the enemy. This done, he ordered his
men, one and all, to be of good cheer—shut the gate
of the fort, smoked three pipes, went to bed, and
awaited the result with a resolute and intrepid tranquillity, that greatly animated his adherents, and no
doubt struck sore dismay and affright into the hearts
of the enemy.

Now it came to pass, that about this time, the renowned Wouter Van Twiller, full of years and honours, and council dinners, had reached that period of
life and faculty which, according to the great Gulli-
ver, entitles a man to admission into the ancient
order of Struldbruggs. He employed his time in
smoking his Turkish pipe, amid an assembly of sages,
equally enlightened, and nearly as venerable as himself, and who, for their silence. their gravity, their
wisdom, and their cautious averseness to coming to
any conclusion in business, are only to be equalled
by certain profound corporations which I have

known in my time. Upon reading the protest of
the gallant Jacobus Van Curlet, therefore, his excellency fell straightway into one of the deepest doubts
that ever he was known to encounter; his capacious
head gradually drooped on his chest, he closed his
eyes, and inclined his ear to one side, as if listening
with great attention to the discussion that was going
on in his belly ; which all who knew him declared
to be the huge court-house, or council chamber of
his thoughts ; forming to his head what the House
of Representatives do to the Senate. An inarticulate
sound, very much resembling a snore, occasionally
escaped him—but the nature of this internal cogita-
tion was never known, as he never opened his lips
on the subject to man, woman, or child. In the
mean time, the protest of Van Curlet laid quietly on
the table, where it served to light the pipes of the
venerable sages assembled in council ; and in the
great smoke which they raised, the gallant Jacobus,
his protest, and his mighty Fort Goed Hoop, were
soon as completely beclouded and forgotten, as is a
question of emergency swallowed up in the speeches
and resolutions of a modern session of Congress.

There are certain emergencies when your profound legislators and sage deliberative councils are
mightily in the way of a nation; and when an ounce
of hairbrained decision is worth a pound of sage
doubt and cautious discussion. Such, at least, was
the case at present; for while the renowned Wouter
Van Twiller was daily battling with his doubts, and
his resolution growing weaker and weaker in the

contest, the enemy pushed farther and farther into his territories, and assumed a most formidable apearance in the neighbourhood of Fort Goed Hoop. Here they founded the mighty town of *Piquag*, or, as it has since been called, *Weathersfield*, a place which, if we may credit the assertion of that worthy historian, John Josselyn, Gent., " hath been infamous by reason of the witches therein."—And so daring did these men of Piquag become, that they extended those plantations of onions, for which their town is illustrious, under the very noses of the garrison of Fort Goed Hoop—insomuch that the honest Dutchmen could not look toward that quarter without tears in their eyes.

This crying injustice was regarded with proper indignation by the gallant Jacobus Van Curlet. He absolutely trembled with the amazing violence of his choler, and the exacerbations of his valour; which seemed to be the more turbulent in their workings, from the length of the body in which they were agitated. He forthwith proceeded to strengthen his redoubts, heighten his breastworks, deepen his fosse, and fortify his position with a double row of abattis ; after which valiant precautions, he despatched a fresh courier with tremendous accounts of his perilous situation.

The courier chosen to bear these alarming despatches was a fat oily little man, as being least liable to be worn out, or to lose leather on the journey; and to insure his speed, he was mounted on the fleetest wagon-horse in the garrison, remarkable for his length of limb, largeness of bone, and hardness of trot; and so tall, that the little messenger was obliged to climb on his back by means of his tail and crupper. Such extraordinary speed did he make, that he arrived at Fort Amsterdam in little less than a month, though the distance was full two hundred pipes, or about a hundred and twenty miles.

The extraordinary appearance of this portentous stranger would have thrown the whole town of New-Amsterdam into a quandary, had the good people troubled themselves about any thing more than their domestic affairs. With an appearance of great hurry and business, and smoking a short travelling pipe, he proceeded on a long swing trot through the muddy lanes of the metropolis, demolishing whole batches of dirt pies, which the little Dutch children were making in the road; and for which kind of pastry the children of this city have ever been famous. On arriving at the governor's house, he climbed down from his steed in great trepidation; roused the gray-headed door-keeper, old Skaats, who, like his lineal descendant and faithful representative, the venerable crier of our court, was nodding at his post—rattled at the door of the council chamber, and startled the members as they were dozing over a plan for establishing a public market.

At that very moment a gentle grunt, or rather a deep-drawn snore, was heard from the chair of the governor; a whiff of smoke was at the same instant observed to escape from his lips, and a light cloud to ascend from the bowl of his pipe. The council of course supposed him engaged in deep sleep for the good of the community, and, according to custom in all such cases established, every man bawled out silence, in order to maintain tranquillity; when, of a sudden, the door flew open, and the little courier straddled into the apartment, cased to the middle in a pair of Hessian boots, which he had got into for the sake of expedition. In his right hand he held forth the ominous despatches, and with his left he grasped firmly the waistband of his galligaskins, which had unfortunately given way, in the exertion of descending from his horse. He stumped resolutely up to the governor, and with more hurry than perspicuity, delivered his message. But fortunately his ill tidings came too late to ruffle the tranquillity of this most tranquil of rulers. His venerable excellency had just breathed and smoked his last—his lungs and his pipe having been exhausted together, and his peaceful soul having escaped in the last whiff that curled from his tobacco-pipe. In a word, the renowned Walter the Doubter, who had so often slumbered with his contemporaries, now slept with his fathers, and Wilhelmus Kieft governed in his stead.

BOOK IV.

CHAPTER I.

*Showing the nature of history in general; containing
farthermore the universal acquirements of William
the Testy, and how a man may learn so much as to
render himself good for nothing.*

WHEN the lofty Thucydides is about to enter upon
his description of the plague that desolated Athens,
one of his modern commentators assures the reader,
that the history is now going to be exceeding solemn,
serious, and pathetic; and hints, with that air of
chuckling gratulation with which a good dame draws
forth a choice morsel from a cupboard to regale a
favourite, that this plague will give his history a most
agreeable variety.

In like manner did my heart leap within me, when
I came to the dolorous dilemma of Fort Good Hope,
which I at once perceived to be the forerunner of a
series of great events and entertaining disasters.
Such are the true subjects for the historic pen. For
what is history, in fact, but a kind of Newgate calen-
der, a register of the crimes and miseries that man
has inflicted on his fellow-man? It is a huge libel on

S 2

human nature, to which we industriously add page after page, volume after volume, as if we were building up a monument to the honour, rather than the infamy of our species. If we turn over the pages of these chronicles that man has written of himself, what are the characters dignified by the appellation of great, and held up to the admiration of posterity? Tyrants, robbers, conquerors, renowned only for the magnitude of their misdeeds, and the stupendous wrongs and miseries they have inflicted on mankind —warriors, who have hired themselves to the trade of blood, not from motives of virtuous patriotism, or to protect the injured and defenceless, but merely to gain the vaunted glory of being adroit and successful in massacreing their fellow-beings! What are the great events that constitute a glorious era?—The fall of empires—the desolation of happy countries— splendid cities smoking in their ruins—the proudest works of art tumbled in the dust—the shrieks and groans of whole nations ascending unto heaven!

It is thus that historians may be said to thrive on the miseries of mankind, like birds of prey that hover over the field of battle, to fatten on the mighty dead. It was observed by a great projector of inland lock-navigation, that rivers, lakes, and oceans, were only formed to feed canals. In like manner I am tempted to believe, that plots, conspiracies, wars, victories, and massacres, are ordained by Providence only as food for the historian.

It is a source of great delight to the philosopher, in studying the wonderful economy of nature, to trace the mutual dependencies of things, how they are created reciprocally for each other, and how the most noxious and apparently unnecessary animal has its uses. Thus those swarms of flies, which are so often execrated as useless vermin, are created for the sustenance of spiders—and spiders, on the other hand, are evidently made to devour flies. So those heroes who have been such scourges to the world, were bounteously provided as themes for the poet and the historian, while the poet and the historian were destined to record the achievements of heroes!

These, and many similar reflections, naturally arose in my mind, as I took up my pen to commence the reign of William Kieft: for now the stream of our history, which hitherto has rolled in a tranquil current, is about to depart for ever from its peaceful haunts, and brawl through many a turbulent and rugged scene. Like some sleek ox, which, having fed and fattened in a rich clover field, lies sunk in luxurious repose, and will bear repeated taunts and blows, before it heaves its unwieldy limbs and clumsily arouses from its slumbers; so the province of the Nieuw-Nederlandts, having long thrived and grown corpulent, under the prosperous reign of the Doubter, was reluctantly awakened to a melancholy conviction, that, by patient sufferance, its grievances had become so numerous and aggravating, that it was preferable to repel than endure them. The reader will now witness the manner in which a peaceful community advances towards a state of war; which it is too apt to approach, as a horse does a drum, with much prancing and parade, but with little progress—and too often with the wrong end foremost.

WILHELMUS KIEFT, who in 1634 ascended the *gubernatorial* chair (to borrow a favourite, though clumsy appellation of modern phraseologists,) was in form, feature, and character, the very reverse of Wouter Van Twiller, his renowned predecessor. He was of very respectable descent, his father being Inspector of Windmills in the ancient town of Saardam; and our hero, we are told, made very curious investigations into the nature and operations of those machines when a boy, which is one reason why he afterwards came to be so ingenious a governor. His name, according to the most ingenious etymologists, was a corruption of *Kyver*, that is to say, *wrangler* or *scolder*, and expressed the hereditary disposition of his family; which for nearly two centuries had kept the windy town of Saardam in hot water, and produced more tartars and brimstones than any ten families in the place—and so truly did Wilhelmus Kieft inherit this family endowment, that he had scarcely been a year in the discharge of his government, before he was universally known by the appellation of WILLIAM THE TESTY.

He was a brisk, waspish, little old gentleman, who had dried and withered away, partly through the natural process of years, and partly from being parched and burnt up by his fiery soul; which blazed like a vehement rushlight in his bosom, constantly inciting him to most valorous broils, altercations, and misadventures. I have heard it observed by a profound and philosophical judge of human nature, that if a woman waxes fat as she grows old, the tenure of her life is very precarious, but if haply she withers, she lives for ever—such likewise was the case with William the Testy, who grew tougher in proportion as he dried. He was some such a little Dutchman as we may now and then see stumping briskly about the streets of our city, in a broad-skirted coat, with huge buttons, an old-fashioned cocked hat stuck on the back of his head, and a cane as high as his chin. His visage was broad, and his features sharp, his nose turned up with the most petulant curl; his cheeks were scorched into a dusky red—doubtless in consequence of the neighbourhood of two fierce little gray eyes, through which his torrid soul beamed with tropical fervour. The corners of his mouth were curiously modelled into a kind of fretwork, not a little resembling the wrinkled proboscis of an irritable pug dog—in a word, he was one of the most positive, restless, ugly, little men, that ever put himself in a passion about nothing.

Such were the personal endowments of William the Testy; but it was the sterling riches of his mind that raised him to dignity and power. In his youth he had passed with great credit through a celebrated academy at the Hague, noted for producing finished scholars with a despatch unequalled, except by certain of our American colleges. Here he skirmished very smartly on the frontiers of several of the sciences, and made so gallant an inroad in the dead languages,

as to bring off captive a host of Greek nouns and
Latin verbs, together with divers pithy saws and
apophthegms, all which he constantly paraded in
conversation and writing, with as much vain glory as
would a triumphant general of yore display the spoils
of the countries he had ravaged. He had, moreover,
puzzled himself considerably with logic, in which he
had advanced so far as to attain a very familiar acquaintance, by name at least, with the whole family
of syllogisms and dilemmas; but what he chiefly
valued himself on, was his knowledge of metaphysics,
in which, having once upon a time ventured too
deeply, he came well nigh being smothered in a
slough of unintelligible learning—a fearful peril, from
the effects of which he never perfectly recovered.
This, I must confess, was in some measure a misfortune; for he never engaged in argument, of which
he was exceeding fond, but what, between logical
deductions and metaphysical jargon, he soon involved himself and his subject in a fog of contradic-
tions and perplexities, and then would get into a
mighty passion with his adversary for not being convinced gratis.

It is in knowledge as in swimming; he who osten-
tatiously sports and flounders on the surface, makes
more noise and splashing, and attracts more attention,
than the industrious pearl-diver, who plunges in
search of treasures to the bottom. The "universal
acquirements" of William Kieft were the subject of
great marvel and admiration among his countrymen
—he figured about at the Hague with as much vain

glory as does a profound Bonze at Pekin, who has mastered half the letters of the Chinese alphabet; and, in a word, was unanimously pronounced an *universal genius!*—I have known many universal geniuses in my time, though, to speak my mind freely, I never knew one, who, for the ordinary purposes of life, was worth his weight in straw—but, for the purposes of government, a little sound judgment, and plain common sense, is worth all the sparkling genius that ever wrote poetry, or invented theories.

Strange as it may sound, therefore, the *universal acquirements* of the illustrious Wilhelmus were very much in his way; and had he been a less learned man, it is possible he would have been a much greater governor. He was exceedingly fond of trying philosophical and political experiments; and having stuffed his head full of scraps and remnants of ancient republics, and oligarchies, and aristocracies, and monarchies, and the laws of Solon, and Lycurgus, and Charondas, and the imaginary commonwealth of Plato, and the Pandects of Justinian, and a thousand other fragments of venerable antiquity, he was for ever bent upon introducing some one or other of them into use; so that between one contradictory measure and another, he entangled the government of the little province of Nieuw-Nederlandts'in more knots, during his administration, than half-a-dozen successors could have untied.

No sooner had this bustling little man been blown by a whiff of fortune into the seat of government, than he called together his council, and delivered a very animated speech on the affairs of the province. As every body knows what a glorious opportunity a governor, a president, or even an emperor, has, of drubbing his enemies in his speeches, messages, and bulletins, where he has the talk all on his own side, they may be sure the high-mettled William Kieft did not suffer so favourable an occasion to escape him, of evincing that gallantry of tongue, common to all able legislators. Before he commenced, it is recorded that he took out his pocket-handkerchief, and gave a very sonorous blast of the nose, according to the usual custom of great orators. This, in general, I believe, is intended as a signal trumpet, to call the attention of the auditors, but with William the Testy it boasted a more classic cause, for he had read of the singular expedient of that famous demagogue, Caius Gracchus, who, when he harangued the Roman populace, modulated his tones by an oratorical flute or pitchpipe.

This preparatory symphony being performed, he commenced by expressing an humble sense of his own want of talents—his utter unworthiness of the honour conferred upon him, and his humiliating incapacity to discharge the important duties of his new station—in short, he expressed so contemptible an opinion of himself, that many simple country members present, ignorant that these were mere words of course, always used on such occasions, were very uneasy, and even felt wroth that he should accept an office, for which he was consciously so inadequate.

He then proceeded in a manner highly classic and profoundly erudite, though nothing at all to the purpose, being nothing more than a pompous account of all the governments of ancient Greece, and the wars of Rome and Carthage, together with the rise and fall of sundry outlandish empires, about which the assembly knew no more than their great-grandchildren yet unborn. Thus having, after the manner of your learned orators, convinced the audience that he was a man of many words and great erudition, he at length came to the less important part of his speech, the situation of the province—and here he soon worked himself into a fearful rage against the Yankees, whom he compared to the Gauls who desolated Rome, and the Goths and Vandals who overran the fairest plains of Europe—nor did he forget to mention, in terms of adequate opprobrium, the insolence with which they had encroached upon the territories of New-Netherlands, and the unparalleled audacity with which they had commenced the town of New-Plymouth, and planted the onion-patches of Weathersfield, under the very walls of Fort Goed Hoop.

Having thus artfully wrought up his tale of terror to a climax, he assumed a self-satisfied look, and declared, with a nod of knowing import, that he had taken measures to put a final stop to these encroachments—that he had been obliged to have recourse to a dreadful engine of warfare, lately invented, awful in its effects, but authorized by direful necessity. In a word, he was resolved to conquer the Yankees—by proclamation!

For this purpose he had prepared a tremendous instrument of the kind, ordering, commanding, and enjoining the intruders aforesaid, forthwith to re move, depart, and withdraw from the districts, regions and territories aforesaid, under pain of suffering all the penalties, forfeitures, and punishments in such case made and provided. This proclamation, he assured them, would at once exterminate the enemy from the face of the country, and he pledged his valour as a governor, that within two months after it was published, not one stone should remain on an-other in any of the towns which they had built.

The council remained for some time silent after he had finished ; whether struck dumb with admira-tion at the brilliancy of his project, or put to sleep by the length of his harangue, the history of the times does not mention. Suffice it to say, they at length gave a universal grunt of acquiescence—the procla-mation was immediately despatched with due cere-mony, having the great seal of the province, which was about the size of a buckwheat pancake, attached to it by a broad red riband. Governor Kieft having thus vented his indignation, felt greatly relieved—adjourned the council—put on his cocked hat an corduroy small-clothes, and mounting a tall raw boned charger, trotted out to his country-seat, which was situated in a sweet, sequestered swamp, now called Dutch-street, but more commonly known by the name of Dog's Misery.

Here, like the good Numa, he reposed from the toils of legislation, taking lessons in government, not from the nymph Egeria, but from the honoured wife of his bosom; who was one of that peculiar kind of females, sent upon earth a little after the flood, as a punishment for the sins of mankind, and commonly known by the appellation of *knowing women.* In fact, my duty as a historian obliges me to make known a circumstance which was a great secret at the time, and consequently was not a subject of scandal at more than half the tea-tables in New-Amsterdam, but which, like many other great secrets, has leaked out in the lapse of years—and this was, that the great Wilhelmus the Testy, though one of the most potent little men that ever breathed, yet submitted at home to a species of government, neither laid down in Aristotle nor Plato; in short, it partook of the nature of a pure, unmixed tyranny, and is familiarly denominated *petticoat government.*—An absolute sway, which, though exceedingly common in these modern days, was very rare among the ancients, if we may judge from the rout made about the domestic economy of honest Socrates; which is the only ancient case on record.

The great Kieft, however, warded off all the sneers and sarcasms of his particular friends, who are ever ready to joke with a man on sore points of the kind, by alleging that it was a government of his own election, to which he submitted through choice; adding at the same time a profound maxim which he had found in an ancient author, that "he who would aspire to *govern,* should first learn to *obey.*"

CHAPTER II.

In which are recorded the sage projects of a ruler of universal genius—the art of fighting by proclamation—and how that the valiant Jacobus Van Curlet came to be foully dishonoured at Fort Goed Hoop.

NEVER was a more comprehensive, a more expeditious, or, what is still better, a more economical measure devised, than this of defeating the Yankees by proclamation—an expedient, likewise, so humane, so gentle and pacific, there were ten chances to one in favour of its succeeding,—but then there was one chance to ten that it would not succeed—as the ill-natured fates would have it, that single chance carried the day! The proclamation was perfect in all its parts, well constructed, well written, well sealed, and well published—all that was wanting to insure its effect was that the Yankees should stand in awe of it; but, provoking to relate, they treated it with the most absolute contempt, applied it to an unseemly purpose, and thus did the first warlike proclamation come to a shameful end—a fate which I am credibly informed has befallen but too many of its successors.

It was a long time before Wilhelmus Kieft could be persuaded, by the united efforts of all his counsellors, that his war measures had failed in producing any effect. On the contrary, he flew in a passion whenever any one dared to question its efficacy; and swore that, though it was slow in operating, yet when once it began to work, it would soon purge the land of these rapacious intruders. Time, however that test of all experiments, both in philosophy and politics, at length convinced the great Kieft, that his proclamation was abortive; and that notwithstanding he had waited nearly four years in a state of constant irritation, yet he was still farther off than ever from the object of his wishes. His implacable adversaries in the east became more and more troublesome in their encroachments, and founded the thriving colony of Hartford close upon the skirts of Fort Goed Hoop. They, moreover, commenced the fair settlement of New-Haven (otherwise called the Red Hills,) within the domains of their High Mightinesses—while the onion-patches of Piquag were a continual eye-sore to the garrison of Van Curlet. Upon beholding, therefore, the inefficacy of his measure, the sage Kieft, like many a worthy practitioner of physic, laid the blame, not to the medicine, but to the quantity administered, and resolutely resolved to double the dose.

In the year 1638, therefore, that being the fourth year of his reign, he fulminated against them a second proclamation, of heavier metal than the former; written in thundering long sentences, not one word of which was under five syllables. This, in fact, was a kind of non-intercourse bill, forbidding and prohibiting all commerce and connexion between any and every of the said Yankee intruders, and the said fortified post of Fort Goed Hoop, and ordering, commanding, and advising, all his trusty, loyal, and well-beloved subjects, to furnish them with no supplies of gin, gingerbread, or sour-crout; to buy none of their pacing horses, measly pork, apple-brandy, Yankee rum, cider-water, apple sweetmeats, Weathersfield onions, tin-ware, or wooden bowls, but to starve and exterminate them from the face of the land.

Another pause of a twelvemonth ensued, during which this proclamation received the same attention and experienced the same fate as the first. In truth, it was rendered of no avail by the heroic spirit of the Nederlanders themselves. No sooner were they prohibited the use of Yankee merchandise, than it immediately became indispensable to their very existence. The men, who all their lives had been content to drink gin and ride Esopus switch-tails, now swore that it was sheer tyranny to deprive them of apple-brandy and Narraghanset pacers; and as to the women, they declared there was no comfort in life without Weathersfield onions, tin kettles, and wooden bowls. So they all set to work, with might and main, to carry on a smuggling trade over the borders; and the province was as full as ever of Yankee wares,—with this difference, that those who used them had to pay double price, for the trouble and risk incurred in breaking the laws.

A signal benefit arose from these measures of William the Testy. The efforts to evade them had a marvellous effect in sharpening the intellects of the people. They were no longer to be governed without

.aws, as in the time of Oloffe the Dreamer; nor would the jack-knife and tobacco-box of Walter the Doubter have any more served as a judicial process. The old Nederlandt maxim, that "honesty is the best policy," was scouted as the bane of all ingenious enterprise To use a modern phrase, "a great impulse had beer given to the public mind;" and from the time of this first experience in smuggling, we may perceive a vast increase in the number, intricacy, and severity of laws and statutes—a sure proof of the increasing keenness of public intellect.

A twelvemonth having elapsed since the issuing of the proclamation, the gallant Jacobus Van Curlet despatched his annual messenger, with his customary budget of complaints and entreaties. Whether the regular interval of a year, intervening between the arrival of Van Curlet's couriers, was occasioned by the systematic regularity of his movements, or by the immense distance at which he was stationed from the seat of government, is a matter of uncertainty. Some have ascribed it to the slowness of his messengers, who, as I have before noticed, were chosen from the shortest and fattest of his garrison, as least likely to be worn out on the road; and who, being pursy, short-winded little men, generally travelled fifteen miles a day, and then laid by a whole week to rest. All these, however, are matters of conjecture; and I rather think it may be ascribed to the immemorial maxim of this worthy country—and which has ever influenced all its public transactions—not to do things in a hurry.

The gallant Jacobus Van Curlet, in his despatches,

respectfully represented, that several years had now
elapsed since his first application to his late excellency, Wouter Van Twiller; during which interval
his garrison had been reduced nearly one-eighth, by
the death of two of his most valiant and corpulen
soldiers, who had accidentally over-eaten themselve
on some fat salmon, caught in the Varsche river.
He further stated, that the enemy persisted in their
inroads, taking no notice of the fort or its inhabitants;
but squatting themselves down, and forming settlements all around it; so that, in a little while, he
should find himself inclosed and blockaded by the
enemy, and totally at their mercy.

But among the most atrocious of his grievances, I
find the following still on record, which may serve
to show the bloody-minded outrages of these savage
intruders. "In the mean time, they of Hartford
have not onely usurped and taken in the lands of
Connecticott, although unrighteously and against the
lawes of nations, but have hindred our nation in
sowing theire own purchased broken up lands, but
have also sowed them with corne in the night, which
the Netherlanders had broken up and intended to
sowe: and have beaten the servants of the high and
mighty the honored companie, which were labour-
ing upon theire master's lands, from theire lands, with
sticks and plow staves in hostile manner laming, and
among the rest, struck Ever Duckings* a hole in his

---

* This name is no doubt mispelt. In some old Dutch MSS.
of the time, we find the name of Evert Duyckingh, who is unquestionably the unfortunate hero above alluded to.

head, with a stick, so that the blood ran downe very strongly downe upon his body."

But what is still more atrocious—

" Those of Hartford sold a hogg, that belonged to the honored companie, under pretence that it had eaten of theire grounde grass, when they had not any foot of inheritance. They proffered the hogg for 5s. if the commissioners would have given 5s. for damage; which the commissioners denied, because noe man's own hogg (as men used to say) can trespass upon his owne master's grounde."*

The receipt of this melancholy intelligence incensed the whole community—there was something in it that spoke to the dull comprehension, and touched the obtuse feelings, even of the puissant vulgar, who generally require a kick in the rear to awaken their slumbering dignity. I have known my profound fellow-citizens bear, without murmur, a thousand essential infringements of their rights, merely because they were not immediately obvious to their senses—but the moment the unlucky Pearce was shot upon our coasts, the whole body politic was in a ferment—so the enlightened Nederlanders, though they had treated the encroachments of their eastern neighbours with but little regard, and left their quill-valiant governor to bear the whole brunt of war with his single pen—yet now every individual felt his head broken in the broken head of Duckings—and the unhappy fate of their fellow-citizen the hog

---

* Haz. Col. State Papers.

being impressed, carried and sold into captivity, awakened a grunt of sympathy from every bosom.

The governor and council, goaded by the clamours of the multitude, now set themselves earnestly to deliberate upon what was to be done.—Proclamations had at length fallen into temporary disrepute: some were for sending the Yankees a tribute, as we make peace-offering to the petty Barbary powers, or as the Indians sacrifice to the devil; others were for buying them out, but this was opposed, as it would be acknowledging their title to the land they had seized. A variety of measures were, as usual in such cases, produced, discussed, and abandoned; and the council had at last to adopt the means, which being the most common and obvious, had been knowingly overlooked—for your amazing acute politicians are for ever looking through telescopes, which only enable them to see such objects as are far off, and unattainable, but which incapacitate them to see such things as are in their reach, and obvious to all simple folks, who are content to look with the naked eyes Heaven has given them. The profound council, as I have said, in the pursuit after Jack-o'-lanterns, accidentally stumbled on the very measure they were in need of; which was to raise a body of troops, and despatch them to the relief and reenforcement of the garrison. This measure was carried into such prompt operation, that in less than twelve months, the whole expedition, consisting of a sergeant and twelve men, was ready to march; and was reviewed for that purpose, in the public square, now known by the name of the Bowling-Green. Just at this juncture, the whole community was thrown into consternation, by the sudden arrival of the gallant Jacobus Van Curlet; who came straggling into town at the head of his crew of tatterdemalions, and bringing the melancholy tidings of his own defeat, and the capture of the redoubtable post of Fort Goed Hoop, by the ferocious Yankees.

The fate of this important fortress is an impressive warning to all military commanders. It was neither carried by storm nor famine; no practicable breach was effected by cannon or mines; no magazines were blown up by red-hot shot, nor were the barracks demolished, or the garrison destroyed, by the bursting of bombshells. In fact, the place was taken by a stratagem no less singular than effectual; and one that can never fail of success, whenever an opportunity occurs of putting it in practice. Happy am I to add, for the credit of our illustrious ancestors, that it was a stratagem, which though it impeached the vigilance, yet left the bravery of the intrepid Van Curlet and his garrison perfectly free from reproach.

It apppears that the crafty Yankees, having heard of the regular habits of the garrison, watched a favourable opportunity, and silently introduced themselves into the fort, about the middle of a sultry day; when its vigilant defenders, having gorged themselves with a hearty dinner, and smoked out their pipes were one and all snoring most obstreperously at their posts, little dreaming of so disastrous an occurrence.

The enemy most inhumanly seized Jacobus Van Curlet and his sturdy myrmidons by the nape of the neck, gallanted them to the gate of the fort, and dismissed them severally, with a kick on the crupper, as Charles the Twelfth dismissed the heavy-bottomed Russians, after the battle of Narva—only taking care to give two kicks to Van Curlet, as a signal mark of distinction.

A strong garrison was immediately established in the fort, consisting of twenty long-sided, hard-fisted Yankees, with Weathersfield onions stuck in their hats by way of cockades and feathers—long rusty fowling-pieces for muskets—hasty-pudding, dumb-fish, pork and molasses, for stores; and a huge pumpkin was hoisted on the end of a pole, as a standard—liberty caps not having as yet come into fashion.

CHAPTER III.

Containing the fearful wrath of William the Testy, and the great dolour of the New-Amsterdammers, because of the affair of Fort Goed Hoop—and, moreover, how William the Testy did strongly fortify the city—together with the exploits of Stoffel Brinkerhoff.

LANGUAGE cannot express the prodigious fury into which the testy Wilhelmus Kieft was thrown by this provoking intelligence. For three good hours the rage of the little man was too great for words, or rather the words were too great for him; and he was nearly choked by some dozen huge, misshapen, nine-cornered Dutch oaths, that crowded all at once into his gullet. Having blazed off the first broadside, he kept up a constant firing for three whole days—anathematizing the Yankees, man, woman, and child, body and soul, for a set of dieven, schobbejaken, deugenieten, twist-zoekeren, loozen-schalken, blaes-kaken, kakken-bedden, and a thousand other names, of which, unfortunately for posterity, history does not make mention. Finally, he swore that he would have nothing more to do with such a squatting, bundling, guessing, questioning, swapping, pumpkin-eating, molasses-daubing, shingle-splitting, cider-watering, horse-jockeying, notion-peddling crew—that they might stay at Fort Goed Hoop and rot, before he would dirty his hands by attempting to drive them away; in proof of which, he ordered the new-raised troops to be marched forthwith into winter quarters, although it was not as yet quite mid-summer. Governor Kieft faithfully kept his word, and his adversaries as faithfully kept their post; and thus the glorious river Connecticut, and all the gay valleys through which it rolls, together with the salmon, shad, and other fish within its waters, fell into the hands of the victorious Yankees, by whom they are held at this very day.

Great despondency seized upon the city of New-Amsterdam, in consequence of these melancholy events. The name of Yankee became as terrible among our good ancestors as was that of Gaul among the ancient Romans; and all the sage old women of the province used it as a bugbear, wherewith to frighten their unruly children into obedience.

The eyes of all the province were now turned upon their governor, to know what he would do for the protection of the common weal, in these days of darkness and peril. Great apprehensions prevailed among the reflecting part of the community, especially the old women, that these terrible warriors of Connecticut, not content with the conquest of Fort Goed Hoop, would incontinently march on to New-Amsterdam and take it by storm—and as these old ladies, through means of the governor's spouse, who, as has been already hinted, was "the better horse," had obtained considerable influence in public affairs, keeping the province under a kind of petticoat govcrnment, it was determined that measures should be taken for the effective fortification of the city.

Now it happened, that at this time there sojourned in New-Amsterdam one Anthony Van Corlear,* a jolly fat Dutch trumpeter, of a pleasant burly visage, famous for his long wind and his huge whiskers, and who, as the story goes, could twang so potently upon his instrument, as to produce an effect upon all within hearing, as though ten thousand bag-pipes were singing right lustily i' the nose. Him did the illustrious Kieft pick out as the man of all the world most fitted to be the champion of New-Amsterdam, and to garrison its fort; making little doubt but that his instrument would be as effectual and offensive in war as was that of the Paladin Astolpho, or the more classic horn of Alecto. It would have done one's heart good to have seen the governor snapping his fingers and fidgeting with delight, while his sturdy trumpeter strutted up and down the ramparts, fearlessly twanging his trumpet in the face of the whole world, like a thrice-valorous editor daringly insulting all the principalities and powers—on the other side of the Atlantic.

Nor was he content with thus strongly garrisoning the fort, but he likewise added exceedingly to its strength, by furnishing it with a formidable battery

---

* David Pietrez *De Vries*, in his " Reyze naer Nieuw-Nederlant onder het year 1640," makes mention of one *Corlear*, a trumpeter in Fort Amsterdam, who gave name to Corlear's Hook, and who was doubtless this same champion described by Mr. Knickerbocker.—EDITOR.

of quaker guns—rearing a stupendous flag-staff in the centre, which overtopped the whole city—and, moreover, by building a great windmill on one of the bastions.* This last, to be sure, was somewhat of a novelty in the art of fortification, but, as I have already observed, William Kieft was notorious for innovations and experiments; and traditions do affirm, that he was much given to mechanical inventions—constructing patent smoke-jacks—carts that went before the horses, and especially erecting windmills, for which machines he had acquired a singular predilection in his native town of Saardam.

All these scientific vagaries of the little governor were cried up with ecstasy by his adherents, as proofs of his universal genius—but there were not wanting ill-natured grumblers, who railed at him as employing his mind in frivolous pursuits, and devoting that time to smoke-jacks and windmills which should have been occupied in the more important concerns of the province. Nay, they even went so far as to hint, once or twice, that his head was turned by his experiments, and that he really thought to manage his government as he did his mills—by mere wind!—such are the illiberality and slander to which enlightened rulers are ever subject.

Notwithstanding all the measures, therefore, of William the Testy, to place the city in a posture of defence, the inhabitants continued in great alarm and

* De Vries mentions that this windmill stood on the southeast bastion; and it is likewise to be seen, together with the flag-staff, in Justus Danker's View of New-Amsterdam.

despondency. But fortune, who seems always careful, in the very nick of time, to throw a bone for hope to gnaw upon, that the starveling elf may be kept alive, did about this time crown the arms of the province with success in another quarter, and thus cheered the drooping hearts of the forlorn Nederlanders; otherwise, there is no knowing to what lengths they might have gone in the excess of their sorrowing—"for grief," says the profound historian of the seven champions of Christendom, " is companion with despair, and despair a procurer of infamous death!"

Among the numerous inroads of the mosstroopers of Connecticut, which for some time past, had occasioned such great tribulation, I should particularly have mentioned a settlement made on the eastern part of Long Island, at a place which, from the peculiar excellence of its shell-fish, was called Oyster Bay. This was attacking the province in the most sensible part, and occasioned great agitation at New-Amsterdam.

It is an incontrovertible fact, well known to skilful physiologists, that the high road to the affections is through the throat; and this may be accounted for on the same principles which I have already quoted in my strictures on fat aldermen. Nor is the fact unknown to the world at large; and hence do we observe, that the surest way to gain the hearts of the million, is to feed them well—and that a man is never so disposed to flatter, to please and serve another, as when he is feeding at his expense; which

U 2

is one reason why your rich men, who give frequent dinners, have such abundance of sincere and faithful friends. It is on this principle that our knowing leaders of parties secure the affections of their partisans, by rewarding them bountifully with loaves and fishes; and entrap the suffrages of the greasy mob, by treating them with bull feasts and roasted oxen. I have known many a man, in this same city, acquire considerable importance in society, and usurp a large share of the good-will of his enlightened fellow-citizens, when the only thing that could be said in his eulogium was, that "he gave a good dinner, and kept excellent wine."

Since, then, the heart and the stomach are so nearly allied, it follows conclusively that what affects the one, must sympathetically affect the other. Now, it is an equally incontrovertible fact, that of all offerings to the stomach, there is none more grateful than the testaceous marine animal, known commonly by the vulgar name of Oyster. And in such great reverence has it ever been held, by my gormandizing fellow-citizens, that temples have been dedicated to it, time out of mind, in every street, lane, and alley, throughout this well-fed city. It is not to be expected, therefore, that the seizing of Oyster Bay, a place abounding with their favourite delicacy, would be tolerated by the inhabitants of New-Amsterdam. An attack upon their honour they might have pardoned; even the massacre of a few citizens might nave been passed over in silence; but an outrage tnat affected the larders of the great city of New-

Amsterdam, and threatened the stomachs of its corpulent burgomasters, was too serious to pass unre-
venged.—The whole council was unanimous in opinion, that the intruders should be immediately driven
by force of arms from Oyster Bay and its vicinity
and a detachment was accordingly despatched for
the purpose, under the command of one Stoffel
Brinkerhoff, or Brinkerhoofd, (*i. e.* Stoffel, the head-
breaker,) so called because he was a man of mighty
deeds, famous throughout the whole extent of Nieuw-
Nederlandts for his skill at quarter-staff; and for
size, he would have been a match for Colbrand, the
Danish champion, slain by Guy of Warwick.

Stoffel Brinkerhoff was a man of few words, but
prompt actions—one of your straight-going officers,
who march directly forward, and do their orders
without making any parade. He used no extraordinary speed in his movements, but trudged steadily on,
through Nineveh and Babylon, and Jericho and Pat-
chog, and the mighty town of Quag, and various
other renowned cities of yore, which, by some unac-
countable witchcraft of the Yankees, have been
strangely transplanted to Long Island, until he arrived
in the neighbourhood of Oyster Bay.

Here was he encountered by a tumultuous host of
valiant warriors, headed by Preserved Fish, and Hab-
bakuk Nutter, and Return Strong, and Zerubbabel
Fisk, and Jonathan Doolittle, and Determined Cock!
—at the sound of whose names the courageous
Stoffel verily believed that the whole parliament of
Praise-God-Barebones had been let loose to discomfit

him. Finding, however, that this formidable body was composed merely of the "select men" of the settlement, armed with no other weapon but their tongues, and that they had issued forth with no other intent than to meet him on the field of argument—he succeeded in putting them to the rout with little difficulty, and completely broke up their settlement. Without waiting to write an account of his victory on the spot, and thus letting the enemy slip through his fingers, while he was securing his own laurels, as a more experienced general would have done, the brave Stoffel thought of nothing but completing his enterprise, and utterly driving the Yankees from the island. This hardy enterprise he performed in much the same manner as he had been accustomed to drive his oxen; for as the Yankees fled before him, he pulled up his breeches and trudged steadily after them, and would infallibly have driven them into the sea, had they not begged for quarter, and agreed to pay tribute.

The news of this achievement was a seasonable restorative to the spirits of the citizens of New-Amsterdam. To gratify them still more, the governor resolved to astonish them with one of those gorgeous spectacles, known in the days of classic antiquity, a full account of which had been flogged into his memory, when a school-boy at the Hague. A grand triumph, therefore, was decreed to Stoffel Brinkerhoff, who made his triumphant entrance into town riding on a Naraganset pacer; five pumpkins, which, like Roman eagles, had served the enemy for standards, were carried before him—fifty cart-loads of oysters, five hundred bushels of Weathersfield onions, a hundred quintals of codfish, two hogsheads of molasses, and various other treasures, were exhibited as the spoils and tribute of the Yankees ; while three notorious counterfeiters of Manhattan notes * were led captive, to grace the hero's triumph. The procession was enlivened by martial music from the trumpet of Anthony Van Corlear the champion, accompanied by a select band of boys and negroes performing on the national instruments of rattle-bones and clam-shells. The citizens devoured the spoils in sheer gladness of heart—every man did honour to the conquerer, by getting devoutly drunk on New-England rum—and the learned Wilhelmus Kieft, calling to mind, in a momentary fit of enthusiasm and generosity, that it was customary among the ancients to honour their victorious generals with public statues, passed a gracious decree, by which every tavern-keeper was permitted to paint the head of the intrepid Stoffel on his sign !

* This is one of those trivial anachronisms, that now and then occur in the course of this otherwise authentic history. How could Manhattan notes be counterfeited, when as yet Banks were unknown in this country?—and our simple progenitors had not even dreamt of those inexhaustible mines of *paper opulence.*—PRINT. DEV.

CHAPTER IV.

Philosophical reflections on the folly of being happy in times of prosperity—Sundry troubles on the Southern Frontiers—How William the Testy had well nigh ruined the province through a cabalistic word—as also the secret expedition of Jan Jansen Alpendam, and his astonishing reward.

If we could but get a peep at the tally of dame Fortune, where, like a notable landlady, she regularly chalks up the debtor and creditor accounts of mankind, we should find that, upon the whole, good and evil are pretty near balanced in this world; and that though we may for a long while revel in the very lap of prosperity, the time will at length come when we must ruefully pay off the reckoning. Fortune, in fact, is a pestilent shrew, and withal a most inexorable creditor; for though she may indulge her favourites in long credits, and overwhelm them with her favours, yet sooner or later she brings up her arrears with the rigour of an experienced publican, and washes out her scores with their tears. "Since," says good old Boetius, "no man can retain her at his pleasure, and since her flight is so deeply lamented, what are her favours but sure prognostications of approaching trouble and calamity?"

There is nothing that more moves my contempt at the stupidity and want of reflection of my fellow-men, than to behold them rejoicing, and indulging in security and self-confidence, in times of prosperity. To a wise man, who is blessed with the light of reason, those are the very moments of anxiety and apprehension; well knowing that according to the system of things, happiness is at best but transient— and that the higher he is elevated by the capricious breath of fortune, the lower must be his proportionate depression. Whereas, he who is overwhelmed by calamity, has the less chance of encountering fresh disasters, as a man at the bottom of a ladder runs very little risk of breaking his neck by tumbling to the top.

This is the very essence of true wisdom, which consists in knowing when we ought to be miserable; and was discovered much about the same time with that invaluable secret, that " every thing is vanity and vexation of spirit;" in consequence of which maxim, your wise men have ever been the unhappiest of the human race; esteeming it as an infallible mark of genius to be distressed without reason—since any man may be miserable in time of misfortune, but it is the philosopher alone who can discover cause for grief in the very hour of prosperity.

According to the principle I have just advanced, we find that the colony of New-Netherlands, which under the reign of the renowned Van Twiller, had flourished in such alarming and fatal serenity, is now paying for its former welfare, and discharging the enormous debt of comfort which it contracted. Foes harass it from different quarters; the city of

New-Amsterdam, while yet in its infancy, is kept in constant alarm; and its valiant commander, William the Testy, answers the vulgar, but expressive idea, of "a man in a peck of troubles."

While busily engaged repelling his bitter enemies the Yankees on one side, we find him suddenly molested in another quarter, and by other assailants. A vagrant colony of Swedes, under the conduct of Peter Minnewits, and professing allegiance to that redoubtable virago, Christina, queen of Sweden, had settled themselves and erected a fort on South (or Delaware) River—within the boundaries claimed by the government of the New-Netherlands. History is mute as to the particulars of their first landing, and their real pretensions to the soil; and this is the more to be lamented, as this same colony of Swedes will hereafter be found most materially to affect not only the interests of the Nederlanders, but of the world at large!

In whatever manner, therefore, this vagabond colony of Swedes first took possession of the country, it is certain that in 1638 they established a fort, and Minnewits, according to the off-hand usage of his contemporaries, declared himself governor of all the adjacent country, under the name of the province of NEW-SWEDEN. No sooner did this reach the ears of the choleric Wilhelmus, than, like a true spirited chieftain, he immediately broke into a violent rage, and calling together his council, belaboured the Swedes most lustily in the longest speech that had ever been heard in the colony, since the memorable dispute of Ten Breeches and Tough Breeches. Having thus given vent to the first ebullitions of his indignation, he had resort to his favourite measure of proclamation, and despatched one, piping hot, in the first year of his reign, informing Peter Minnewits that the whole territory, bordering on the South river, had, time out of mind, been in possession of the Dutch colonists, having been " beset with forts, and sealed with their blood."

The latter sanguinary sentence would convey an idea of direful war and bloodshed, were we not relieved by the information that it merely related to a fray, in which some half-a-dozen Dutchmen had been killed by the Indians, in their benevolent attempts to establish a colony and promote civilization. By this it will be seen, that William Kieft, though a very small man, delighted in big expressions, and was much given to a praiseworthy figure of rhetoric, generally cultivated by your little great men, called hyperbole—a figure which has been found of infinite service among many of his class, and which has helped to swell the grandeur of many a mighty, self-important, but windy chief magistrate. Nor can I refrain in this place from observing how much my beloved country is indebted to this same figure of hyperbole, for supporting certain of her greatest characters—statesmen, orators, civilians, and divines; who, by dint of big words, inflated periods, and windy doctrines, are kept afloat on the surface of society, as ignorant swimmers are buoyed up by blown bladders.

VOL. I.   X

The proclamation against Minnewits concluded by ordering the self-dubbed governor, and his gang of Swedish adventurers, immediately to leave the country, under penalty of the high displeasure and inevitable vengeance of the puissant government of the Nieuw-Nederlandts. This " strong measure,' however, does not seem to have had a whit more effect than its predecessors which had been thundered against the Yankees—the Swedes resolutely held on to the territory they had taken possession of—whereupon matters for the present remained in statu quo.

That Wilhelmus Kieft should put up with this insolent obstinacy in the Swedes, would appear incompatible with his valorous temperament ; but we find that about this time the little man had his hands full, and, what with one annoyance and another, was kept continually on the bounce.

There is a certain description of active legislators, who, by shrewd management, contrive always to have a hundred irons on the anvil, every one of which must be immediately attended to ; who consequently are ever full of temporary shifts and expedients, patching up the public welfare, and cobbling the national affairs, so as to make nine holes where they mend one—stopping chinks and flaws with whatever comes first to hand, like the Yankees I have mentioned, stuffing old clothes in broken windows. Of this class of statesmen was William the Testy—and had he only been blessed with powers equal to his zeal, or his zeal been disciplined by a little discretion, there is very little doubt that he would have made the greatest governor of his size on record—the renowned governor of the island of Barataria alone excepted.

The great defect of Wilhelmus Kieft's policy was, that though no man could be more ready to stand forth in an hour of emergency, yet he was so intent upon guarding the national pocket, that he suffered the enemy to break its head—in other words, whatever precaution for public safety he adopted, he was so intent upon rendering it cheap, that he invariably rendered it ineffectual. All this was a remote consequence of his profound education at the Hague—where, having acquired a smattering of knowledge, he was ever after a great conner of indexes, continually dipping into books, without ever studying to the bottom of any subject; so that he had the scum of all kinds of authors fermenting in his pericranium. In some of these title-page researches, he unluckily stumbled over a grand political *cabalistic word*, which, with his customary facility, he immediately incorporated into his great scheme of government, to the irretrievable injury and delusion of the honest province of Nieuw-Nederlandts, and the eternal misleading of all experimental rulers.

In vain have I pored over the theurgia of the Chaldeans, the cabala of the Jews, the necromancy of the Arabians, the magic of the Persians, the hocus-pocus of the English, the witchcraft of the Yankees, or the powwowing of the Indians, to discover where the little man first laid eyes on this terrible word.

Neither the Sephir Jetzirah, that famous cabalistic volume, ascribed to the patriarch Abraham; nor the pages of Zohar, containing the mysteries of the cabala, recorded by the learned rabbi Simon Sochaides, yield any light to my inquiries—nor am I in the least benefited by my painful researches in the Shem-hamphorah of Benjamin, the wandering Jew, though it enabled Davidus Elm to make a ten days' journey in twenty-four hours. Neither can I perceive the slightest affinity in the Tetragrammaton, or sacred name of four letters, the profoundest word of the Hebrew cabala; a mystery sublime, ineffable, and incommunicable—and the letters of which, Jod-He-Vau-He, having been stolen by the pagans, constituted their great name Jao or Jove. In short, in all my cabalistic, theurgic, necromantic, magical, and astrological researches, from the Tetractys of Pythagoras to the recondite works of Breslaw and Mother Bunch, I have not discovered the least vestige of an origin of this word, nor have I discovered any word of sufficient potency to counteract it.

Not to keep my reader in any suspense, the word which had so wonderfully arrested the attention of William the Testy, and which in German characters had a particularly black and ominous aspect, on being fairly translated into the English, is no other than ECONOMY—a talismanic term, which, by constant use and frequent mention, has ceased to be formidable in our eyes, but which has as terrible potency as any in the arcana of necromancy.

When pronounced in a national assembly, it has

an immediate effect in closing the hearts, beclouding the intellects, drawing the purse-strings, and buttoning the breeches-pockets of all philosophic legislators. Nor are its effects on the eyes less wonderful. It produces a contraction of the retina, an obscurity of the crystalline lens, a viscidity of the vitreous, and an inspissation of the aqueous humours, an induration of the tunica sclerotica, and a convexity of the cornea ; insomuch that the organ of vision loses its strength and perspicuity, and the unfortunate patient becomes *myopes*, or in plain English, purblind ; perceiving only the amount of immediate expense, without being able to look farther, and regard it in connexion with the ultimate object to be effected—" So that," to quote the words of the eloquent Burke, " a briar at his nose is of greater magnitude than an oak at five hundred yards' distance." Such are its instantaneous operations, and the results are still more astonishing. By its magic influence, seventy-fours shrink into frigates—frigates into sloops, and sloops into gun-boats.

This all-potent word, which served as his touchstone in politics, at once explains the whole system of proclamations, protests, empty threats, windmills, trumpeters, and paper war, carried on by Wilhelmus the Testy—and we may trace its operations in an armament which he fitted out in 1642 in a moment of great wrath, consisting of two sloops and thirty men, under the command of Mynher Jan Jansen Alpendam, as admiral of the fleet, and commander-in-chief of the forces. This formidable expedition,

X 2

which can only be paralleled by some of the daring
cruisers of our infant navy about the bay and up the
sound, was intended to drive the Marylanders from
the Schuylkill, of which they had recently taken possession—and which was claimed as part of the province of New-Nederlandts—for it appears that at this
time our infant colony was in that enviable state, so
much coveted by ambitious nations, that is to say,
the government had a vast extent of territory, part
of which it enjoyed, and the greater part of which it
had continually to quarrel about.

Admiral Jan Jansen Alpendam was a man of great
mettle and prowess, and no way dismayed at the
character of the enemy, who were represented as a
gigantic, gunpowder race of men, who lived on hoe-
cakes and bacon, drank mint-juleps and apple-toddy,
and were exceedingly expert at boxing, biting, goug-
ing, tar and feathering, and a variety of other athletic
accomplishments, which they had borrowed from
their cousins-german and prototypes the Virginians,
to whom they have ever borne considerable resemblance.   Notwithstanding all these alarming representations, the admiral entered the Schuylkill most
undauntedly with his fleet, and arrived without disaster or opposition at the place of destination.

Here he attacked the enemy in a vigorous speech
in Low Dutch, which the wary Kieft had previously
put in his pocket; wherein he courteously commenced by calling them a pack of lazy, louting, dram-
drinking, cock-fighting, horse-racing, slave-driving,
tavern-haunting, sabbath-breaking, mulatto-breeding

upstarts—and concluded by ordering them to evacu-
ate the country immediately—to which they most
laconically replied in plain English, "they'd see him
d——d first."

Now this was a reply for which neither Jan Jansen Alpendam nor Wilhelmus Kieft had made any
calculation—and finding himself totally unprepared
to answer so terrible a rebuff with suitable hostility,
he concluded that his wisest course was to return
home and report progress. He accordingly sailed
back to New-Amsterdam, where he was received
with great honours, and considered as a pattern for
all commanders ; having achieved a most hazardous
enterprise, at a trifling expense of treasure, and without losing a single man to the state !—He was unanimously called the deliverer of his country, (an appellation liberally bestowed on all great men ;) his
two sloops, having done their duty, were laid up (or
dry-docked) in a cove now called the Albany basin,
where they quietly rotted in the mud ; and to immor-
talize his name, they erected, by subscription, a magnificent shingle monument on the top of Flatten-bar-
rack hill, which lasted three whole years ; when it
fell to pieces, and was burnt for firewood.

CHAPTER V.

*How William the Testy enriched the province by a
multitude of laws, and came to be the patron of
lawyers and bum-bailiffs—and how the people became exceedingly enlightened and unhappy under
his instructions.*

AMONG the many wrecks and fragments of ex-
alted wisdom, which have floated down the stream
of time, from venerable antiquity, and have been
carefully picked up by those humble, but industrious
wights, who ply along the shores of literature, we
find the following sage ordinance of Charondas, the
Locrian legislator. Anxious to preserve the ancient
laws of the state from the additions and improvements of profound " country members," or officious
candidates for popularity, he ordained, that whoever
proposed a new law, should do it with a halter about
his neck ; so that in case his proposition was reject-
ed, they just hung him up—and there the matter
ended.

This salutary institution had such an effect, that for
more than two hundred years there was only one
trifling alteration in the criminal code—and the
whole race of lawyers starved to death for want of
employment. The consequence of this was, that the
Locrians, being unprotected by an overwhelming
load of excellent laws, and undefended by a stand-

ing army of pettifoggers and sheriff's officers, lived very lovingly together, and were such a happy people, that they scarce make any figure throughout the whole Grecian history—for it is well known that none but your unlucky, quarrelsome, rantipole nations make any noise in the world.

Well would it have been for William the Testy, had he haply, in the course of his "universal acquirements," stumbled upon this precaution of the good Charondas. On the contrary, he conceived that the true policy of a legislator was to multiply laws, and thus secure the property, the persons, and the morals of the people, by surrounding them in a manner with men-traps and spring-guns, and besetting even the sweet sequestered walks of private life with quickset hedges, so that a man could scarcely turn, without the risk of encountering some of these pestiferous protectors. Thus was he continually coining petty laws for every petty offence that occurred, until in time they became too numerous to be remembered, and remained like those of certain modern legislators, mere dead letters—revived occasionally for the purpose of individual oppression, or to entrap ignorant offenders.

Petty courts consequently began to appear, where the law was administered with nearly as much wisdom and impartiality as in those august tribunals, the alderman's and justice's courts of the present day. The plaintiff was generally favoured, as being a customer and bringing business to the shop; the offences of the rich were discreetly winked at—for fear of hurting the feelings of their friends ;—but it could never be laid to the charge of the vigilant burgomasters, that they suffered vice to skulk unpunished, under the disgraceful rags of poverty.

About this time may we date the first introduction of capital punishments—a goodly gallows being erected on the water-side, about where Whitehall stairs are at present, a little to the east of the Battery. Hard by also was erected another gibbet of a very strange, uncouth, and unmatchable description, but on which the ingenious William Kieft valued himself not a little, being a punishment entirely of his own invention.

It was for loftiness of altitude not a whit inferior to that of Haman, so renowned in bible history ; but the marvel of the contrivance was, that the culprit, instead of being suspended by the neck, according to venerable custom, was hoisted by the waistband, and was kept for an hour together, dangling and sprawling between heaven and earth—to the infinite entertainment and doubtless great edification of the multitude of respectable citizens, who usually attend upon exhibitions of the kind.

It is incredible how the little governor chuckle at beholding caitiff vagrants and sturdy beggars thus swinging by the crupper, and cutting antic gambols in the air. He had a thousand pleasantries and mirthful conceits to utter upon these occasions. He called them his dandle-lions—his wild-fowl—his high-flyers—his spread eagles—his goshawks—his scarecrows, and finally his *gallows-birds*, which ingenious appellation, though originally confined to worthies who had taken the air in this strange manner, has since grown to be a cant name given to all candidates for legal elevation. This punishment, moreover, if we may credit the assertions of certain grave etymologists, gave the first hint for a kind of harnessing, or strapping, by which our forefathers braced up their multifarious breeches, and which has of late years been revived, and continues to be worn at the present day.

Such were the admirable improvements of William Kieft in criminal law—nor was his civil code less a matter of wonderment; and much does it grieve me that the limits of my work will not suffer me to expatiate on both, with the prolixity they deserve. Let it suffice then to say, that in a little while the blessings of innumerable laws became notoriously apparent. It was soon found necessary to have a certain class of men to expound and confound them—divers pettifoggers accordingly made their appearance, under whose protecting care the community was soon set together by the ears.

I would not here be thought to insinuate any thing derogatory to the profession of the law, or to its dignified members. Well am I aware, that we have in this ancient city innumerable worthy gentlemen who have embraced that honourable order, not for the sordid love of filthy lucre, nor the selfish cravings of renown, but through no other motives, but a fervent zeal for the correct administration of justice, and a generous and disinterested devotion to the in-

terests of their fellow-citizens!—Sooner would I
throw this trusty pen into the flames, and cork up
my ink-bottle for ever, than infringe even for a nail's
breadth upon the dignity of this truly benevolent
class of citizens—on the contrary, I allude solely to
that crew of caitiff scouts, who, in these latter days
of evil, have become so numerous—who infest the
skirts of the profession, as did the recreant Cornish
knights the honourable order of chivalry—who,
under its auspices, commit their depredations on society—who thrive by quibbles, quirks, and chicanery,
and, like vermin, swarm most where there is most
corruption.

Nothing so soon awakens the malevolent passions,
as the facility of gratification. The courts of law
would never be so constantly crowded with petty,
vexatious, and disgraceful suits, were it not for the
herds of pettifogging lawyers that infest them. These
tamper with the passions of the lower and more ignorant classes; who, as if poverty were not a sufficient misery in itself, are always ready to heighten
it by the bitterness of litigation. They are in law
what quacks are in medicine—exciting the malady
for the purpose of profiting by the cure, and re
tarding the cure for the purpose of augmenting the
fees. Where one destroys the constitution, the other
impoverishes the purse; and it may likewise be observed, that a patient, who has once been under the
hands of a quack, is ever after dabbling in drugs, and
poisoning himself with infallible remedies; and an

ignorant man, who has once meddled with the law under the auspices of one of these empirics, is for ever after embroiling himself with his neighbours, and impoverishing himself with successful law-suits.—My readers will excuse this digression, into which I have been unwarily betrayed; but I could not avoid giving a cool, unprejudiced account of an abomination too prevalent in this excellent city, and with the effects of which I am unluckily acquainted to my cost; having been nearly ruined by a law-suit, which was unjustly decided against me—and my ruin having been completed by another, which was decided in my favour.

It has been remarked by the observant writer of the Stuyvesant manuscript, that under the administration of Wilhelmus Kieft the disposition of the inhabitants of New-Amsterdam experienced an essential change, so that they became very meddlesome and factious. The constant exacerbations of temper into which the little governor was thrown, by the maraudings on his frontiers, and his unfortunate propensity to experiment and innovation, occasioned him to keep his council in a continual worry—and the council being to the people at large, what yest or leaven is to a batch, they threw the whole community into a ferment—and the people at large being to the city what the mind is to the body, the unhappy commotions they underwent operated most disastrously upon New-Amsterdam—insomuch, that in certain of their paroxysms of consternation and per-

plexity, they begat several of the most crooked, distorted, and abominable streets, lanes, and alleys, with
which this metropolis is disfigured.

But the worst of the matter was, that just about
this time the mob, since called the sovereign people,
like Balaam's ass, began to grow more enlightened
than its rider, and exhibited a strange desire of governing itself. This was another effect of the "universal acquirements" of William the Testy. In some
of his pestilent researches among the rubbish of antiquity, he was struck with admiration at the institution of public tables among the Lacedæmonians,
where they discussed topics of a general and interesting nature—at the schools of the philosophers, where
they engaged in profound disputes upon politics and
morals—where gray-beards were taught the rudi-
ments of wisdom, and youths learned to become little
men before they were boys. "There is nothing,"
said the ingenious Kieft, shutting up the book, "there
is nothing more essential to the well management of
a country, than education among the people; the
basis of a good government should be laid in the
public mind."—Now this was true enough, but it
was ever the wayward fate, of William the Testy,
that when he thought right, he was sure to go to
work wrong. In the present instance, he could
scarcely eat or sleep until he had set on foot brawling debating societies among the simple citizens of
New-Amsterdam. This was the one thing wanting
to complete his confusion. The honest Dutch burgh-

ers, though in truth but little given to argument or
wordy altercation, yet by dint of meeting often together, fuddling themselves with strong drink, beclouding their brains with tobacco-smoke, and listening to
the harangues of some half-a-dozen oracles, soon became exceedingly wise, and—as is always the case
where the mob is politically enlightened—exceedingly discontented. They found out, with wonderful quickness of discernment, the fearful error in
which they had indulged, in fancying themselves the
happiest people in creation—and were fortunately
convinced, that, all circumstances to the contrary
notwithstanding, they were a very unhappy, deluded,
and consequently, ruined people.

In a short time, the quidnuncs of New-Amsterdam
formed themselves into sage juntos of political croak-
ers, who daily met together to groan over political
affairs, and make themselves miserable ; thronging to
these unhappy assemblages, with the same eagerness
that zealots have in all ages abandoned the milder
and more peaceful paths of religion, to crowd to the
howling convocations of fanaticism. We are naturally prone to discontent, and avaricious after imaginary causes of lamentation—like lubberly monks,
we belabour our own shoulders, and seem to take a
vast satisfaction in the music of our own groans.
Nor is this said for the sake of paradox ; daily experience shows the truth of these observations. It is
almost impossible to elevate the spirits of a man
groaning under ideal calamities; but nothing is more
easy than to render him wretched, though on the

pinnacle of felicity; as it is a Herculean task to
hoist a man to the top of a steeple, though the merest
child can topple him off thence.

In the sage assemblages I have noticed, the reader
will at once perceive the faint germs of those sapient
convocations called popular meetings, prevalent at
our day. Thither resorted all those idlers and
" squires of low degree," who, like rags, hang loose
upon the back of society, and are ready to be blown
away by every wind of doctrine. Cobblers abandoned their stalls, and hastened thither to give lessons
on political economy—blacksmiths left their handicraft and suffered their own fires to go out, while
they blew the bellows and stirred up the fire of faction; and even tailors, though but the shreds and
patches, the ninth parts of humanity, neglected their
own measures, to attend to the measures of government.—Nothing was wanting but half-a-dozen newspapers and patriotic editors, to have completed this
public illumination, and to have thrown the whole
province in an uproar!

I should not forget to mention, that these popular
meetings were held at a noted tavern; for houses of
that description have always been found the most
fostering nurseries of politics; abounding with those
genial streams which give strength and sustenance to
faction. We are told that the ancient Germans had
an admirable mode of treating any question of importance; they first deliberated upon it when drunk,
and afterwards reconsidered it when sober. The

shrewder mobs of America, who dislike having two minds upón a subject, both determine and act upon it drunk ; by which means a world of cold and tedious speculation is dispensed with—and as it is universally allowed, that when a man is drunk he sees double, it follows most conclusively that he sees twice as well as his sober neighbours.

CHAPTER VI.

Of the great pipe plot—and of the dolorous perplex-
ities into which William the Testy was thrown, by
reason of his having enlightened the multitude.

WILHELMUS KIEFT, as has already been made
manifest, was a great legislator upon a small scale.
He was of an active, or rather a busy mind ; that is
to say, his was one of those small, but brisk minds,
which make up by bustle and constant motion for
the want of great scope and power. He had, when
quite a youngling, been impressed with the advice of
Solomon, "go to the ant thou sluggard, consider her
ways and be wise ;" in conformity to which, he had
ever been of a restless ant-like turn, worrying hither
and thither, busying himself about little matters, with
an air of great importance and anxiety—laying up
wisdom by the morsel, and often toiling and puffing
at a grain of mustard-seed, under the full conviction
that he was moving a mountain.

Thus we are told, that once upon a time, in one
of his fits of mental bustle, which he termed deliberation, he framed an unlucky law, to prohibit the universal practice of smoking. This he proved, by
mathematical demonstration, to be, not merely a
heavy tax on the public pocket, but an incredible
consumer of time, a great encourager of idleness, and,

of course, a deadly bane to the prosperity and morals of the people. Ill-fated Kieft! had he lived in this enlightened and libel-loving age, and attempted to subvert the inestimable liberty of the press, he could not have struck more closely on the sensibilities of the million.

The populace were in as violent a turmoil as the constitutional gravity of their deportment would permit—a mob of factious citizens had even the hardihood to assemble before the governor's house, where, setting themselves resolutely down, like a besieging army before a fortress, they one and all fell to smoking with a determined perseverance, that seemed as though it were their intention to smoke him into terms. The testy William issued out of his mansion like a wrathful spider, and demanded to know the cause of this seditious assemblage, and this lawless fumigation; to which these sturdy rioters made no other reply, than to loll back phlegmatically in their seats, and puff away with redoubled fury; whereby they raised such a murky cloud, that the governor was fain to take refuge in the interior of his castle.

The governor immediately perceived the object of this unusual tumult, and that it would be impossible to suppress a practice, which, by long indulgence, had become a second nature. And here I would observe, partly to explain why I have so often made mention of this practice in my history, that it was inseparably connected with all the affairs, both public and private, of our revered ancestors. The pipe, in fact, was never from the mouth of the true-born Nederlander. It was his companion in solitude, the relaxation of his gayer hours, his counsellor, his consoler, his joy, his pride; in a word, he seemed to think and breathe through his pipe.

When William the Testy bethought himself of al these matters, which he certainly did, although a little too late, he came to a compromise with the besieging multitude. The result was, that though he continued to permit the custom of smoking, yet did he abolish the fair long pipes which were used in the days of Wouter Van Twiller, denoting ease, tranquillity, and sobriety of deportment; and, in place thereof, did introduce little, captious, short pipes, two inches in length; which, he observed, could be stuck in one corner of the mouth, or twisted in the hatband, and would not be in the way of business. By this the multitude seemed somewhat appeased, and dispersed to their habitations. Thus ended this alarming insurrection, which was long known by the name of the *pipe plot*, and which, it has been somewhat quaintly observed, did end, like most other plots, seditions, and conspiracies, in mere smoke.

But mark, oh reader! the deplorable consequences that did afterwards result. The smoke of these villanous little pipes, continually ascending in a cloud about the nose, penetrated into, and befogged the cerebellum, dried up all the kindly moisture of the brain, and rendered the people that used them as vapourish and testy as their renowned little governor —nay, what is more, from a goodly, burly race of folk, they became, like our worthy Dutch farmers, who smoke short pipes, a lantern-jawed, smoke-dried, leathern-hided race of men.

Nor was this all, for from hence may we date the rise of parties in this province. Certain of the more wealthy and important burghers adhering to the ancient fashion, formed a kind of aristocracy, which went by the appellation of the *Long Pipes*—while the lower orders, submitting to the innovation, which they found to be more convenient in their handicraft employments, and to leave them more liberty of action, were branded with the plebeian name of *Short Pipes*. A third party likewise sprang up, differing from both the other, headed by the descendants of the famous Robert Chewit, the companion of the great Hudson. These entirely discarded the use of pipes, and took to chewing tobacco, and hence they were called *Quids*. It is worthy of notice, that this last appellation has since come to be invariably applied to those mongrel or third parties, that will sometimes spring up between two great contending parties, as a mule is produced between a horse and an ass.

And here I would remark the great benefit of these party distinctions, by which the people at large are saved the vast trouble of thinking. Hesiod divides mankind into three classes, those who think for themselves, those who let others think for them, and those who will neither do one nor the other. The second class, however, comprises the great mass of society ; and hence is the origin of *party*, by which is meant a large body of people, some few of whom

think, and all the rest talk. The former, who are
called the leaders, marshal out and discipline the
latter, teaching them what they must approve—what
they must hoot at—what they must say—whom they
must support—but, above all, whom they must hate
—for no man can be a right good partisan, unless he
be a determined and thorough-going hater.

But when the sovereign people are thus properly
broken to the harness, yoked, curbed, and reined, it
is delectable to see with what docility and harmony
they jog onward, through mud and mire, at the will
of their drivers, dragging the dirt-carts of faction at
their heels. How many a patriotic member of Congress have I seen, who would never have known how
to make up his mind on any question, and might
have run a great risk of voting right by mere accident, had he not had others to think for him, and a
file-leader to vote after!

Thus then the enlightened inhabitants of the Manhattoes, being divided into parties, were enabled to
organize dissension, and to oppose and hate one
another more accurately. And now the great business of politics went bravely on—the parties as-
sembling in separate beer-houses, and smoking a
each other with implacable animosity, to the great
support of the state, and emolument of the tavern-
keepers. Some, indeed, who were more zealous
than the rest, went farther, and began to bespatter
one another with numerous very hard names and
scandalous little words, to be found in the Dutch
language; every partisan believing religiously that

he was serving his country, when he traduced the character, or impoverished the pocket of a political adversary. But, however they might differ between themselves, all parties agreed on one point, to cavil at and condemn every measure of government, whether right or wrong; for as the governor was by his station independent of their power, and was not elected by their choice, and as he had not decided in favour of either faction, neither of them was interested in his success, or in the prosperity of the country, while under his administration.

"Unhappy William Kieft!" exclaims the sage writer of the Stuyvesant manuscript—"doomed to contend with enemies too knowing to be entrapped, and to reign over a people too wise to be governed!" All his expeditions against his enemies were baffled and set at nought, and all his measures for the public safety were cavilled at by the people. Did he propose levying an efficient body of troops for internal defence—the mob, that is to say those vagabond members of the community who have nothing to lose, immediately took the alarm, vociferated that their interests were in danger—that a standing army was a legion of moths, preying on the pockets of society; a rod of iron in the hands of government; and that a government with a military force at its command would inevitably swell into a despotism. Did he, as was but too commonly the case, defer preparation until the moment of emergency, and then hastily collect a handfull of undisciplined vagrants— the measure was hooted at as feeble and inadequate, as trifling with the public dignity and safety, and as lavishing the public funds on impotent enterprises. Did he resort to the economic measure of proclamation—he was laughed at by the Yankees; did he back it by non-intercourse—it was evaded and counteracted by his own subjects. Whichever way he turned himself, he was beleaguered and distracted by petitions of "numerous and respectable meetings," consisting of some half-a-dozen brawling pot-house politicians—all of which he read, and, what is worse, all of which he attended to. The consequence was, that by incessantly changing his measures, he gave none of them a fair trial; and by listening to the clamours of the mob, and endeavouring to do every thing, he, in sober truth, did nothing.

I would not have it supposed, however, that he took all these memorials and interferences goodnaturedly, for such an idea would do injustice to his valiant spirit; on the contrary, he never received a piece of advice in the whole course of his life, without first getting into a passion with the giver. But I have ever observed that your passionate little men, like small boats with large sails, are the easiest upset or blown out of their course; and this is demonstrated by Governor Kieft, who, though in temperament as hot as an old radish, and with a mind, the territory of which was subjected to perpetual whirlwinds and tornadoes, yet never failed to be carried away by the last piece of advice that was blown into his ear. Lucky was it for him that his power was not dependent upon the greasy multitude, and that as yet the populace did not possess the important privilege of nominating their chief magistrate! They, however, did their best to help along public affairs; pestering their governor incessantly, by goading him on with harangues and petitions, and then thwarting his fiery spirit with reproaches and memorials, like Sunday jockies managing an unlucky devil of a hackhorse—so that Wilhelmus Kieft may be said to have been kept either on a worry or a hand-gallop throughout the whole of his administration.

CHAPTER VII.

*Containing divers fearful accounts of Border Wars,
and the flagrant outrages of the Mosstroopers of
Connecticut—with the rise of the great Amphyctionic Council of the east, and the decline of William the Testy.*

It was asserted by the wise men of ancient times,
who were intimately acquainted with these matters,
that at the gate of Jupiter's palace lay two huge
tuns, the one filled with blessings, the other with
misfortunes—and it verily seems as if the latter had
been completely overturned, and left to deluge the
unlucky province of Nieuw-Nederlandts. Among
the many internal and external causes of irritation,
the incessant irruptions of the Yankees upon his
frontiers were continually adding fuel to the inflam-
mable temper of William the Testy. Numerous accounts of these molestations may still be found
among the records of the times; for the commanders
on the frontiers were especially careful to evince
their vigilance and zeal, by striving who should send
home the most frequent and voluminous budgets of
complaints—as your faithful servant is eternally running with complaints to the parlour, of the petty
squabbles and misdemeanours of the kitchen.

Far be it from me to insinuate, however, that our
worthy ancestors indulged in groundless alarms; on

the contrary, they were daily suffering a repetition of cruel wrongs,* not one of which but was a sufficient reason, according to the maxims of national dignity and honour, for throwing the whole universe into hostility and confusion.

Oh ye powers! into what indignation did every one of these outrages throw the philosophic William! letter after letter, protest after protest, proclamation after proclamation, bad Latin, worse English, and hideous Low Dutch, were exhausted in vain upon the inexorable Yankees; and the four-and-twenty letters of the alphabet, which, excepting his champion the sturdy trumpeter Van Corlear, composed

---

* From among a multitude of bitter grievances still on record, I select a few of the most atrocious, and leave my readers to judge if our ancestors were not justifiable in getting into a very valiant passion on the occasion.

"24 June, 1641. Some of Hartford have taken a hogg out of the vlact or common, and shut it up out of meer hate or other prejudice, causing it to starve for hunger in the stye!"

"26 July. The foremencioned English did again drive the Companie's hoggs out of the vlact of Sicojoke into Hartford; contending daily with reproaches, blows, beating the people with all disgrace that they could imagine."

"May 20, 1642. The English of Hartford have violently cut loose a horse of the honoured Companie's, that stood bound upon the common or vlact."

"May 9, 1643. The Companie's horses pastured upon the Companie's ground, were driven away by them of Connecticott or Hartford, and the herdsmen lustily beaten with hatchets and sticks."

"16. Again they sold a young hogg belonging to the Companie, which piggs had pastured on the Companie's land."

Haz. Col. State Papers.

the only standing army he had at his command, were never off duty throughout the whole of his administration. Nor was Antony, the trumpeter, a whit behind his patron in fiery zeal; but like a faithful champion of the public safety, on the arrival of every fresh article of news, he was sure to sound his trumpet from the ramparts, with most disastrous notes, throwing the people into violent alarms, and disturbing their rest at all times and seasons—which caused him to be held in very great regard, the public pampering and rewarding him, as we do brawling editors, for similar services.

I am well aware of the perils that environ me in this part of my history.   While raking with curious hands but pious heart, among the mouldering remains of former days, anxious to draw therefrom the honey of wisdom, I may fare somewhat like that valiant worthy, Samson, who in meddling with the carcass of a dead lion, drew a swarm of bees about his ears. Thus, while narrating the many misdeeds of the Yanokie, or Yankee tribe, it is ten chances to one but I offend the morbid sensibilities of certain of their unreasonable descendants, who may fly out and raise such a buzzing about this unlucky head of mine, that I shall need the tough hide of an Achilles, or an Orlando Furioso, to protect me from their stings.

Should such be the case, I should deeply and sincerely lament—not my misfortune in giving offence —but the wrong-headed perverseness of an ill-natured generation, in taking offence at any thing I say. That their ancestors did use my ancestors ill, is true, and I am very sorry for it. I would, with all my heart, the fact were otherwise; but as I am recording the sacred events of history, I'd not bate one nail's breadth of the honest truth, though I were sure the whole edition of my work should be bought up and burnt by the common hangman of Connecticut. And in sooth, now that these testy gentlemen have drawn me out, I will make bold to go farther and observe, that this is one of the grand purposes for which we impartial historians are sent into the world—to redress wrongs, and render justice on the heads of the guilty. So that, though a powerful nation may wrong its neighbours with temporary impunity, yet sooner or later a historian springs up, who wreaks ample chastisement on it in return.

Thus these mosstroopers of the east, little thought, I'll warrant it, while they were harassing the inoffensive province of Nieuw-Nederlandts, and driving its unhappy governor to his wit's end, that a historian should ever arise and give them their own with interest. Since then I am but performing my bounden duty as a historian, in avenging the wrongs of our revered ancestors, I shall make no further apology; and indeed, when it is considered that I have all these ancient borderers of the east in my power, and at the mercy of my pen, I trust that it will be admitted I conduct myself with great humanity and moderation.

To resume then the course of my history.—Appearances to the eastward began now to assume a more formidable aspect than ever—for I would have you note that hitherto the province had been chiefly

Z 2

molested by its immediate neighbours, the people of Connecticut, particularly of Hartford; which, if we may judge from ancient chronicles, was the strong-hold of these sturdy mosstroopers, from whence they sallied forth, on their daring incursions, carrying ter-ror and devastation into the barns, the hen-roosts, and pig-styes of our revered ancestors.

Albeit, about the year 1643, the people of the east country, inhabiting the colonies of Massachusetts, Connecticut, New-Plymouth, and New-Haven, gath-ered together into a mighty conclave, and after buz-zing and debating for many days, like a political hive of bees in swarming time, at length settled them-selves into a formidable confederation, under the title of the United Colonies of New-England. By this union, they pledged themselves to stand by one another in all perils and assaults, and to co-operate in all measures, offensive and defensive, against the surrounding savages, among which were doubtlessly included our honoured ancestors of the Manhattoes; and to give more strength and system to this confed-eration, a general assembly or grand council was to be annually held, composed of representatives from each of the provinces.

On receiving accounts of this combination, Wilhel-mus Kieft was struck with consternation, and, for the first time in his whole life, forgot to bounce, at hearing an unwelcome piece of intelligence—which a venerable historian of the times observes, was espe-cially noticed among the politicians of New-Amster-dam. The truth was, on turning over in his mind all that he had read at the Hague, about leagues and combinations, he found that this was an exact imitation of the Amphyctionic council, by which the states of Greece were enabled to attain to such power and supremacy, and the very idea made his heart to quake for the safety of his empire at the Manhattoes.

He strenuously insisted, that the whole object of this confederation was to drive the Nederlanders out of their fair domains; and always flew into a great rage if any one presumed to doubt the probability of his conjecture. Nor was he wholly unwarranted in such a suspicion; for at the very first annual meeting of the grand council, held at Boston, (which governor Kieft denominated the Delphos of this truly classic league,) strong representations were made against the Nederlanders, forasmuch as that in their dealings with the Indians, they carried on a traffic in "guns, powther, and shott—a trade damnable and injurious to the colonists."* Not but what certain of the Connecticut traders did likewise dabble a little in this "damnable traffic"—but then they always sold the Indians such scurvy guns, that they burst at the first discharge—and consequently hurt no one but these pagan savages.

The rise of this potent confederacy was a death-blow to the glory of William the Testy, for from that day forward, it was remarked by many, he never held up his head, but appeared quite crestfallen. His subsequent reign, therefore, affords but scanty

* Haz. Col. State Papers.

food for the historic pen—we find the grand council continually augmenting in power, and threatening to overwhelm the province of Nieuw-Nederlandts; while Wilhelmus Kieft kept constantly fulminating proclamations and protests, like a shrewd sea-captain firing off carronades and swivels, in order to break and disperse a waterspout—but alas! they had no more effect than if they had been so many blank cartridges.

The last document on record of this learned, philosophic, but unfortunate little man, is a long letter to the council of the Amphyctions, wherein, in the bitterness of his heart, he rails at the people of New-Haven, or Red Hills, for their uncourteous contempt of his protest, levelled at them for squatting within the province of their High Mightinesses. From this letter, which is a model of epistolary writing, abounding with pithy apophthegms and classic figures, my limits will barely allow me to extract the following recondite passage:—"Certainly when we heare the Inhabitants of New-Hartford complayninge of us, we seem to heare Esop's wolfe complayninge of the lamb, or the admonition of the younge man, who cryed out to his mother, chideing with her neighboures, 'Oh Mother revile her, lest she first take up that practice against you.' But being taught by precedent passages, we received such an answer to our protest from the inhabitants of New-Haven as we expected; *the Eagle always despiseth the Beetle Fly;* yet notwithstanding we do undauntedly continue on our purpose of pursuing our own right, by just arms and

righteous means, and doe hope without scruple to execute the express commands of our superiors."*
To show that this last sentence was not a mere empty menace, he concluded his letter, by intrepidly protesting against the whole council, as a horde of *squatters* and interlopers, inasmuch as they held their meeting at New-Haven, or the Red Hills, which he claimed as being within the province of the New-Netherlands.

Thus end the authenticated chronicles of the reign of William the Testy—for henceforth, in the troubles, the perplexities and the confusion of the times, he seems to have been totally overlooked, and to have slipped for ever through the fingers of scrupulous history. Indeed, for some cause or other which I cannot divine, there appears to have been a combination among historians to sink his very name into oblivion, in consequence of which they have one and all forborne even to speak of his exploits. This shows how important it is for great men to cultivate the favour of the learned, if they are ambitious of honour and renown. "Insult not the dervise," said a wise caliph to his son, "lest thou offend thine historian;" and many a mighty man of the olden time, had he observed so obvious a maxim, might have escaped divers cruel wipes of the pen, which have been drawn across his character.

It has been a matter of deep concern to me, that such darkness and obscurity should hang over the

* Vide Haz. Col. State Papers.

latter days of the illustrious Kieft—for he was a mighty and great little man, worthy of being utterly renowned, seeing that he was the first potentate that introduced into this land the art of fighting by proclamation, and defending a country by trumpeters and windmills—an economic and humane mode of warfare, since revived with great applause, and which promises, if it can ever be carried into full effect, to save great trouble and treasure, and spare infinitely more bloodshed than either the discovery of gunpowder, or the invention of torpedoes.

It is true, that certain of the early provincial poets, of whom there were great numbers in the Nieuw-Nederlandts, taking advantage of the mysterious exit of William the Testy, have fabled, that like Romulus, he was translated to the skies, and forms a very fiery little star, somewhere on the left claw of the crab; while others, equally fanciful, declare that he had experienced a fate similar to that of the good King Arthur; who, we are assured by ancient bards, was carried away to the delicious abodes of fairy land, where he still exists, in pristine worth and vigour, and will one day or another return to restore the gallantry, the honour, and the immaculate probity, which prevailed in the glorious days of the Round Table.*

---

* The old Welch bards believed that king Arthur was not dead, but carried awaie by the faries into some pleasant place, where he shold remaine for a time, and then returne againe and reigne in as great authority as ever.—*Hollingshed*.

All these, however, are but pleasing fantasies, the cobweb visions of those dreaming varlets, the poets, to which I would not have my judicious reader attach any credibility. Neither am I disposed to yield any credit to the assertion of an ancient and rather apocryphal historian, who alleges that the ngenious Wilhelmus was annihilated by the blowing down of one of his windmills—nor to that of a writer of later times, who affirms that he fell a victim to a philosophical experiment, which he had for many years been vainly striving to accomplish; having the misfortune to break his neck from the garret-window of the stadt-house, in an ineffectual attempt to catch swallows, by sprinkling fresh salt upon their tails.

The most probable account, and to which I am inclined to give my implicit faith, is contained in a very obscure tradition, which declares, that what with the constant troubles on his frontiers—the incessant schemings and projects going on in his own pericranium—the memorials, petitions, remonstrances, and sage pieces of advice from divers respectable meetings of the sovereign people—together with the refractory disposition of his council, who were sure to differ from him on every point, and uniformly to be in the wrong—all these, I say, did eternally

The Britons suppose that he shall come yet and conquere all Britaigne, for certes, this is the prophicye of Merlyn—He say'd that his deth shall be doubteous; and said soth, for men thereof yet have doubte and shullen for ever more—for men wyt not whether that he lyveth or is dede.—*De Leew. Chron.*

operate to keep his mind in a kind of furnace heat, until he at length became as completely burnt out as a Dutch family pipe which has passed through three generations of hard smokers. In this manner did the choleric but magnanimous William the Testy undergo a kind of animal combustion, consuming away like a farthing rush-light—so that, when grim Death finally snuffed him out, there was scarce left enough of him to bury!

END OF **VOL. I.**

Printed in the United States
26185LVS00001B/1-51